SIMONE VAN DER VLUGT was born in .... 1966, and has been internationally acclaimed for her psychological thrillers. In Holland, *The Reunion* has sold over 250,000 copies. She lives with her husband and two children in Alkmaar.

MICHELE HUTCHISON has worked in the publishing industry for ten years. She was born in the United Kingdom, and now lives in Amsterdam with her Dutch husband and two children.

SIMONE VAN DER VLUGT

The Reunion

Translated from the Dutch
by Michele Hutchison

Harper
Press

Harper*Press*
An imprint of HarperCollins*Publishers*
77–85 Fulham Palace Road
Hammersmith
London W6 8JB

www.harpercollins.co.uk
Love this book? www.bookarmy.com

This Harper*Press* paperback edition published 2010
1

First published in Great Britain by Harper*Press* in 2009

Original text © Simone van der Vlugt 2004
English language translation © Michele Hutchison 2008
First published in Dutch by Ambo Anthos, The Netherlands
First published in English by Text Publishing Co Melbourne
Literary Corner © HarperCollins*Publishers* 2009 except 'A Modern Intellect'
© Simone van der Vlugt 2009

Simone van der Vlugt asserts the moral right to be identified as the author of this work

A catalogue record for this book is available from the British Library

ISBN 978–0–00–730137–9

Printed and bound in Great Britain by Clays Ltd, St Ives plc

Mixed Sources
Product group from well-managed
forests and other controlled sources
www.fsc.org Cert no. SW-COC-1806
© 1996 Forest Stewardship Council

FSC is a non-profit international organisation established to promote the
responsible management of the world's forests. Products carrying the FSC
label are independently certified to assure consumers that they come
from forests that are managed to meet the social, economic and
ecological needs of present and future generations.

Find out more about HarperCollins and the environment at
www.harpercollins.co.uk/green

THE REUNION

Prologue

She cycles the last part alone. She waves to her girlfriend and then turns to the road ahead. She sings softly to herself, her back straight, a carefree look in her eyes.

School's out. It's Friday afternoon. The weekend can begin.

She's strapped her jacket onto the luggage rack behind her, over her black canvas school bag. She feels the heat of the sun on her bare arms.

It's a glorious day, the beginning of a promising summer. The blue sky extends like a high, radiant dome above her.

At the traffic light, she brakes and dismounts. It's a solitary light, a little outside of the city centre, where the bustle of school children on their bikes, mopeds and car traffic lessens.

She's completely alone. No cars or buses go by. She looks from left to right, frustrated at the pointlessness of waiting.

A delivery van draws up behind her and stops, its engine throbbing.

Green.

The girl gets back on her bike and rides on. The van overtakes her and envelops her in a thick cloud of diesel smoke. She coughs, flaps her hand at the smoke and stops pedalling.

The van tears away, in the direction of the Dark Dunes. The girl thinks about her meeting. She's having second thoughts now – perhaps she should have chosen a less isolated place.

1

I stand at the entrance to the beach, my hands in the pockets of my jacket, and look out to sea. It's 6 May and way too cold for this time of year. Apart from a solitary beachcomber, the beach is deserted. The sea is the colour of lead. Snarling and foaming, it swallows up more and more sand.

A little further up, a young girl sits on a bench. She too looks out to sea, hunched up in her padded jacket. She's wearing sturdy shoes that can withstand the wind and rain. A school bag lies at her feet. Not far from where she's sitting, her bike leans against the barbed wire fence. It's padlocked, even though she's nearby.

I knew I would find her here.

She stares blindly out to sea. Even the wind, which tugs at her clothing, can't get a grip on her. It catches her light brown hair whirling around her head, but not her attention.

Despite the fact that she doesn't feel the cold, there's a vulnerability about this girl that touches me.

I know her, yet I hesitate to speak to her because she doesn't know me. But it's extremely important that she gets to know me, that she listens to me, that I get through to her.

I walk towards the bench, my gaze fixed on the sea as if I've come here to enjoy the angry waves.

The girl looks the other way, her face expressionless. For a moment she seems to want to get up and leave, but then resigns herself to having her solitude invaded.

We sit next to each other on the bench, our hands in our pockets, and watch how air and water merge. I must say something. She'll leave soon and we won't have exchanged a word. But what do you say when every word counts?

As I take a deep breath and turn towards her, she looks over at me. Our eyes are the same colour. We probably have the same expression too.

She's about fifteen. The age Isabel was when she was murdered.

Years ago I went to school in this area. Every day I rode ten kilometres there and back, sometimes with the sea wind behind me, but mostly straight into it.

The wind blew in from the sea, unhindered by anything on the flat polders, the drained fields reclaimed from the sea. It caught up with me on my bike. The daily struggle against it made my body strong. The distance between school and home, that no-man's-land of meadows and salty wind, was like a buffer zone between the two worlds I inhabited.

I look at the sea, its waves casting up memory after memory. I should never have come back.

What brought me here? That short announcement in the newspaper.

Two weeks ago I was standing at the kitchen table with a mug of coffee, leafing through the paper. It was eight o'clock. I was dressed and had eaten breakfast, but I didn't have much time. A quick glance through the headlines was all I could manage.

I turned the page and a small notice in a side column caught my eye: HELDER HIGH SCHOOL REUNION.

3

My old school, which, in the meantime, has amalgamated with some other schools in Den Helder.

I'm twenty-three. My school days are thankfully long over. I'm not even thinking of going.

The girl has left. I let her escape while I was deep in thought. It doesn't matter. I'll see her again.

The wind blows my hair into my face and every so often steals my breath. Yes, this is just how it used to be. I'd pedal into the wind with tears running down my cheeks. I'd put my hair up in a ponytail, otherwise it would get hopelessly knotted. When I washed it in the evening, it would smell of sea salt.

The scent of the beach is the same, of course. Its familiarity takes me by surprise, bringing back old memories and allowing me into the dark corners of my mind.

Why did I come back? What did I hope to achieve?

The only thing that might come of it is more clarity. I don't know if I'm ready for that.

As I stroll back to my car sand flurries around me and the wind pushes at my back, urging me to hurry. I'm not welcome here. I don't belong here anymore.

But I'm not planning to return to Amsterdam yet. Even when it begins to pour, I don't quicken my pace. My car stands alone in the large carpark. Normally it would be packed here, but summer has abandoned us temporarily. I think about the rows of cars parked here on hot days, glistening in the sun. It was good to live on the coast. You could ride right past the sweaty drivers stranded in traffic jams, throw your bike against the fence, pull your towel out from the luggage rack and look for a place to stretch out in the sun. In Zandvoort these days, you can't find a spot anymore if you're not on the beach by nine.

Heating on, radio on, a bag of liquorice on the seat next to me, I drive out of the abandoned carpark, past the woods, the Dark Dunes, towards the town centre.

Den Helder is not a comforting sight in the rain. Neither is Amsterdam, but at least Amsterdam doesn't shut down in the winter. Den Helder looks like a city where the air-raid sirens have just gone off. I haven't been back since my parents moved to Spain five years ago.

I love cities with a soul, with a historic centre. But the only thing old about Den Helder are the people who live there. All the young people go to Alkmaar and Amsterdam when they leave school. The only people left are sailors and tourists taking the boat to Texel.

I drive along the Middenweg towards my old school. When I reach it, the school grounds are almost empty. A small group of students are defying the drizzle to get a fix of nicotine that will help them through the day.

Once around the school and then along the same route I used to ride home, past the military camp towards the Lange Vliet. The cross wind can't touch me now. In the corner of my eye I can see the bike path.

Isabel lived in the same village as me. We didn't ride home together that day, but she must have taken the Lange Vliet route. I saw her ride out of the school grounds. I'd deliberately lingered before leaving. If I'd ridden after her, nothing might have happened.

I accelerate and drive at the speed limit along the Lange Vliet. At Juliana Village I take the first left onto the motorway. As I drive along the canal I change into fifth and turn up the radio.

Out of here. Back to Amsterdam.

I sing along at the top of my voice to the chart hits blaring out of the radio and fish one piece of liquorice after the other out of the bag next to me. Only when Alkmaar is behind me do I return to the present. I think about my work. The Bank. I have to go back on Monday. It's Thursday today, I still have three days to myself. Even though I don't want to go back to work, I think it will be good for me. I've been home alone for too long, watching unexpected and incomprehensible images passing like dreams before my eyes. I'm starting back on a trial basis – mornings only, to see how I feel.

That's what the doctor ordered, after all.

2

There's no cake to celebrate my return, no banners in the office. Not that I was expecting them. Well, maybe a little. As I stand in the doorway, breathing heavily after walking up the stairs, it takes a while for my colleagues to notice me. I take in all of the changes: my impounded desk, the relaxed way in which my replacement sits talking to my colleagues, the many new faces. It feels like I'm coming to be interviewed for my own job.

I could have taken the lift of course, but my doctor says I should take the stairs more often. He doesn't know I work on the ninth floor.

Then I'm spotted and my workmates come over to greet me. I scan their faces, searching for the one person I can't see.

'Sabine! How you doing?'

'Are you sure you're up to it?'

'Brace yourself. It's a mad house here.'

'How are you? You look so well.'

I haven't seen any of them all the time I've been off sick, except for Jeanine.

Renée comes up with a plastic cup of coffee in her hand. 'Hello Sabine,' she says. 'Everything all right?'

I nod, still looking at my desk.

'Let me introduce you to your replacement, Margot.' She

follows my gaze. 'She's been filling in for you all this time. She'll stay on until you're back full-time.'

I walk towards my old desk but Renée stops me. 'There's still a free desk at the back, Sabine. Margot's been working here so long now, it would be silly to make her move.'

I decide that making a scene over something so trivial as a desk is not the best start to my first day back. My new desk is in the furthest corner of the office far away from the others. My eyes remain fixed on the desk I used to face.

'Where's Jeanine?' I ask, but just then the printer begins to rattle.

It's just a desk. Breathe in, breathe out.

Something has changed. The atmosphere is different. Any interest in my return has evaporated. I'd expected some catch up chats, particularly with Jeanine, but there is only empty space around me.

Everyone is busy again and I sit in my corner. I take a pile of letters from the mail tray and say to no one in particular, 'Where is Jeanine? Is she on holiday?'

'Jeanine left last month,' Renée says, without looking up from her computer. 'Zinzy has replaced her. You'll meet her later in the week, she's having a couple of days off.'

'Jeanine's left?' I'm dumbfounded. 'I had no idea.'

'There are other changes you don't know about,' says Renée, her eyes still fixed on her computer.

'Such as?' I ask.

She turns towards me. 'In January, Walter promoted me to head of the department.'

We stare at each other.

'There's no such position.'

'Someone had to pick up the pieces.'

Renée turns back to her screen.

So much is going on in my head that I don't know what to say. The morning stretches out endlessly before me. I resist the impulse to call Jeanine. Why didn't she tell me she'd resigned?

I stare out of the window until I notice that Renée is watching me. She keeps on looking until I'm hunched over the mail.

Welcome back, Sabine.

The first time I came to The Bank's head office, I was impressed. It has an imposing entrance in a beautiful park and, when I walked through the revolving doors into a world of space and marble, I felt myself shrivelling into insignificance.

But I liked it. The stylish suits and jackets around me turned out to be worn by very normal people. Remembering my mother's advice that I would get more out of a few expensive good quality basics than a drawer full of bargains, I bought a new wardrobe. Tailored jackets, knee-length skirts and dark tights became my standard uniform. This was how I entered the imposing lobby every day – disguised.

Working for a multinational is not the sort of work I aspired to. I trained as a Dutch and French teacher, but it was difficult to find a school I wanted to teach at – and I gave up applying for jobs pretty quickly. During placement I'd taught classes full of rebellious teenagers and it had been dreadful.

Jeanine and I joined The Bank at the same time, when they had just set up a new trust fund. The job itself didn't excite me. It had sounded great: administrator/office support, good communication skills and a broad knowledge of languages needed.

But I needn't have taken out a student loan to say, 'Please hold the line', and replenish the supply of glue sticks. That's probably what they meant by 'flexibility' in the job description.

But there was a good atmosphere in the office. Jeanine and I gossiped about the execs we were working for, we reorganised the filing system and picked up each other's telephones when one of us wanted to nip out to the shops for half an hour.

I was independent and I had a job. My new life had begun.

After a while, we were really busy. The wave of business managers hired to work on the trust fund grew and we could barely keep up with the work. We needed more people, and fast.

Jeanine and I presided over the interviews and that's how Renée came to work with us. She was good at her job, but the atmosphere changed almost immediately. She knew how things should be run. Renée felt that our department didn't come up to scratch and nor did Jeanine or I. She had no truck with extended lunch breaks. Of course she was right, but we had no truck with the fact that she had a personal meeting with Walter behind closed doors to air her complaints. Walter was pleased with Renée, she was a worthy addition to the Trust.

'And to think that we hired her ourselves,' said Jeanine.

Walter felt that Renée should be in charge of hiring a fourth staff member. She had a good eye, according to him.

'And we don't?' I said to Jeanine.

'So it seems.'

Renée placed ads in the main newspapers and called the employment agencies. She got so involved with it that the bulk of her workload fell to Jeanine and me. She spent entire afternoons meeting more and less suitable people, but no one was taken on.

'It's so difficult to find good staff,' she said, shaking her head as she came out of the meeting room after yet another interview. 'Before you know it, you're overrun with people who think that office support is nothing more than typing and faxing. Try and build a good, solid team from that.'

And so we struggled on, because the Trust was growing and work was piling up.

We worked overtime every day and often through our lunch breaks. I became exhausted. I could no longer sleep properly. I felt hounded. I lay with a pounding heart staring at the ceiling, and as soon as I closed my eyes, found myself overcome by a dizziness that spun me round in accelerating circles. I struggled on for a few months but a year after I began I collapsed. I can't describe it any other way. A feeling of complete apathy set in, spread through me and made everything look grey.

I pull the pile of mail towards me and open envelopes and remove elastic bands. After half an hour I'm already fed up.

What's the time? Not yet nine o'clock? How am I going to make it through the day?

I glance across the office. Margot is a few metres away; her desk is against Renée's so that they can talk to each other without me overhearing a thing.

The sales force go in and out with rough copies that need to be typed up, mail that needs to be sent by special delivery. Renée delegates like the captain of a ship. She gives the worst jobs to me. And there are quite a few of them. Cardboard boxes to be made up for the archive, coffee to prepare for the meeting room, visitors to collect in the lobby. And it's still only mid-morning. When I pack up at twelve-thirty, I haven't exchanged a friendly word with anybody and I'm shattered.

3

I arrive home exhausted. My face is drained, I have sweat patches under my arms and my two-room apartment is a tip. After the utilitarian neatness of the office, my scruffy furniture seems even more tightly crammed together.

I've never quite managed to turn this flat into a real home, or to put my own stamp on it. As a teenager I dreamed of the moment I'd live alone, and I knew exactly how I'd arrange things. I could picture it entirely.

No one warned me that my entire salary would go on mortgage repayments and the weekly shop. That I wouldn't have enough money left to keep up with the latest trends. When I go into the kitchen I have stop myself from tearing the brown and orange 1970s tiles from the walls. I could invest in new tiles but not without upsetting the harmonious balance of the brown cabinets and the coffee-coloured lino. So I leave it as it is. My burn-out saps me dry. I lie down on the sofa like a squeezed-out lemon.

I lived at home for the first year of my studies. It wasn't so bad. I didn't have to worry about washing and ironing. And in the evenings dinner was always ready on the table, meat and fresh vegetables, instead of the junk the other students were eating. Most of all, it was nice at home. I didn't think about moving out until my parents decided to emigrate. I was nineteen when they told me about their plans, and I completely flipped out. Where on earth had they got the idea that I was a grown-up? That I could stand on my own two feet and didn't need their help anymore? I wouldn't be able to manage without them. Where would I go to at the weekend? Where would I belong? I sat next to my parents on the sofa, covered my face with my hands and burst into tears.

Afterwards I felt a bit ashamed that I'd made it so difficult for Mum and Dad. Robin told me later that they'd considered calling the whole thing off but that he'd convinced them not to let me rule their lives so much.

They gave me the money to buy a flat in Amsterdam and they left. They came back to visit me at the drop of a hat, but only at the beginning.

My answering machine is flashing. A message?

I press the play button, curious. The engaged tone – whoever called didn't bother to leave a message. I press delete. If there's one thing I hate, it's people who hang up after the beep. I can spend the rest of the day wondering who called.

It can't have been my mother because when she calls she talks until the whole tape is full. She spends most of the year with my father in their house in Spain. I hardly see them.

It was probably Robin, my brother. He rarely calls, only when it is absolutely necessary. If he gets the answering machine he seldom leaves a message.

In the kitchen, I flip down the breadboard, get the strawberries from the fridge, pull a couple of slices of brown bread from the bag and make my usual lunch. There's nothing more delicious than fresh strawberries on bread. I'm addicted. I think they've even helped my depression. Strawberries in yoghurt, strawberries with cream, strawberries on rusk. Each year as the strawberries in the supermarket become more and more taste-less, I begin to worry. The season is over, and that means going cold turkey. Perhaps there are addictive substances in strawberries, like in chocolate. That's something else I'm hooked on. In the winter I always eat a thick layer of Nutella on bread, and put on weight.

While I'm halving my strawberries, my thoughts turn to that missed call. Maybe it wasn't Robin but Jeanine. But why would she call me? We haven't been in contact for such a long time.

I stuff an enormous strawberry into my mouth, and gaze out of the kitchen window. Jeanine and I hit it off immediately but the bond didn't stretch further than the office until just before I went off sick. She came by a couple of times in the beginning, but someone who lies listlessly on the sofa, staring into midair, is hardly good company. We drifted out of touch. Still, I was looking forward to seeing her again, and I didn't blame her for not going to more trouble. I was hard work.

Jeanine opens the door and her head is covered in foil. 'Sabine!'

We look at each other a little ill at ease. Just as I'm about to mumble an apology for my unexpected appearance, she opens the door wide. 'I thought you were Mark. Come in!'

We kiss each other on the cheek.

'Suits you,' I say, looking at the foil in her hair.

'I'm in the middle of dyeing it, that's why I'm wearing this old housecoat. You can still see the stains from last time. I almost jumped out of my skin when the bell went.'

'Then you shouldn't have opened the door.'

'I always want to know who's standing at my door. Luckily it was you.'

I decide to take that as a compliment. 'Who's Mark?' I ask as we make our way along the narrow hall to the living room.

'A sexy thing I've been seeing for a couple of weeks. He's seen me without make-up, he's seen my dirty knickers in the laundry basket and he knows that I slurp when I eat, but I'd still rather he didn't know I dyed my hair.' Jeanine chuckles and drops down onto the sofa. Her housecoat falls open a little and reveals a faded pink T-shirt with holes in it.

If Mark's not welcome tonight, perhaps I'm not either. I sink into a wicker chair with a white cushion; it's more comfortable than I'd expected. We look at each other and smile uncertainly.

'Do you want some coffee? Or is it time for something stronger?' She glances at the clock. 'Half-eight. Wine?'

'I'll start with a coffee,' I say but as she's walking to the kitchen I call after her, 'and bring the wine out with it.'

I hear laughter from the kitchen. It was a good idea to visit Jeanine. A bit of a gossip and a bottle of wine, much better than an evening in my flat. This is the kind of life I'd imagined when I moved out of home.

'Are you back at work?' Jeanine is carrying two mugs of coffee. She puts them down, fetches two wine glasses from the cupboard and places them alongside.

'Today was my first day back.'

'And? How did it go?'

I take my coffee from the table and peer into the mug. 'It was...' I search for the right word. 'I was happy when it was twelve-thirty.'

'Awful then.'

'You could say that.'

We drink our coffee in silence.

'That's why I left,' Jeanine says after a while. 'Renée was only taking on people she could manipulate. The atmosphere had changed so much. I told Walter that when I resigned. But you know what he's like – crazy about our dictator. How did she act towards you?'

'We hardly spoke to each other. Or to be exact, I hardly spoke to anybody. Most of the people were completely new to me and only about half of them took the trouble to introduce themselves. I had a lovely time opening the post and making cardboard boxes.'

'You have to leave, as soon as possible.'

'And then what?'

'You'll find something else. Just register with a temping agency.'

'So I can be sent to Timbuktu to sort out files and spend whole days making lists. No thank you, those days are over! I'll see how it goes. The first day is always the worst. I'll keep an eye out for something else. By the way, I've no idea what you're doing now!'

'I'm working in a small solicitor's office,' says Jeanine. 'The work is the same, but the atmosphere is great. I'll keep an eye out for a job for you. I talk to so many people there.' I look at her gratefully. 'If you'd do that…'

'Of course!' She smiles. 'Does Olaf still work at The Bank?'

'Olaf? Olaf who?'

'He came to work in IT. He's completely hot. The computers were working fine, it was the department that crashed.' Jeanine laughs.

'I haven't met him yet,' I say.

'Then you'll have to drop into IT,' Jeanine advises. 'Pull the plug out of your computer and call Olaf.'

'Don't be silly.'

'Renée is crazy about him. Keep an eye on her when he comes in. You won't be able to stop laughing!' She jumps up and does an impression of Renée flirting, and it's true, it's very funny. 'Have you finished your coffee? Let's move on to the wine. You pour, I'm going to rinse my hair. Otherwise it will be orange tomorrow.'

While Jeanine is splashing around in the bathroom, I fill the wine glasses. I haven't felt this happy for a long time. It was good to take the initiative. I should do that more often, not stand back and wait. Maybe Renée feels like going on a little cinema outing with me. The thought makes me smile.

Jeanine returns with wet, dark red hair. She's changed into jeans and a white T-shirt and looks cheerful and lively. She's back to her old self, apart from the hair colour.

'Nice colour,' I say. 'Quite striking, after brown. I can't believe you dare!'

'It looks a bit darker because it's wet. When my hair's dry it should have a kind of a coppery shine. My own colour is so boring.'

Every day I spend ages blow-drying my hair, but I'm never happy with it. I once thought about getting it cut off, not too short, just a shoulder-length cut. A bit of colour and the metamorphosis would have been complete. But I've never got round to it.

Jeanine gives me the lowdown on all the new people. Her conclusion is that they're alright, but that no one has realised just how manipulative Renée is.

'She complained about you to the others,' warns Jeanine. 'Don't wait until they come to you because they won't. Go to them yourself and prove that you're the opposite of what Renée has said.'

'Has she really painted me so black?' I say, dubious.

'As far as she's concerned, you're only sick if you're lying in Intensive Care or you're in plaster,' Jeanine says. 'One time she said that you're only as sick as you want to be, and that she always gets on with her work, however miserable she feels. And that's true. She uses up a box of tissues in half an hour and the next day the whole department is sniffing and coughing. She thinks depression is something you just have to get over.' Jeanine gets up.

I've slipped off my shoes. I sit with my legs curled to one side and pull my cold feet under my thighs.

While she is rummaging around in the kitchen cupboards, she carries on talking, a bit more loudly so that I can hear her. 'I know so many people who've had a burn-out. My uncle had one, my father too and I've seen enough at work. That's what it was, a burn-out, wasn't it?' She returns with a bowl of chips.

I nod. Burn-outs, depression and break-downs are pretty much the same kind of thing.

Jeanine fills her glass again and tucks her feet under her folded legs. 'Once when I had flu and called in sick she sent a doctor round to check up on me. Usually they don't come to visit you until the next day, or two days later, but a couple of hours after my phone call there was the knock at the door. A special request from my boss, that's what the bloke said. I'll give you one guess who lit a fire under Walter's arse.'

'What bastards,' I say wholeheartedly and take a handful of chips. Somehow a chip catches in my windpipe and lodges there. I burst into a rally of coughs that bring tears to my eyes, but the chip stays wedged.

'Have a sip of wine,' Jeanine hands me my glass. I push her hand away – I'm still coughing so hard that I think I'm going to throw up.

'Just have a sip!' shouts Jeanine.

I gesture that I can't.

It might not be a bad idea for her to hit me on the back, and to convey that to her, I hit myself on the back. It's much too low but I can't reach between my shoulderblades.

Jeanine gets up and whacks me on the spine, much too hard and much too low.

I raise my hand to tell her to stop but she thinks I'm encouraging her and hits me even harder. 'Should I do the Heimlich manoeuvre? Get up!' But then the chip dislodges and I begin to breathe again. I lie back against the sofa cushions panting, wipe the tears from my eyes and drink some wine.

'Idiot,' I say. 'You nearly put me in a wheelchair.'

'I saved you!'

'You have to hit between the shoulderblades! God knows what

would have happened if you'd tried the Heimlich manoeuvre!' I shout back.

Jeanine stares at me speechless, I return the look and we both burst out laughing.

'Where did I hit you?' asks Jeanine, gasping with laughter. 'There? And where should it have been? Oh, then it wasn't far off?' And we fall about laughing again.

'What do you think? Have we drunk too much?' I lisp.

'No-oh,' says Jeanine. 'I can only see two of you, usually I see four.'

She giggles and I giggle back.

'You'd better stay over,' Jeanine says. 'I can't let you go out into the street like that. What time is it in fact? Oh my God, 2 a.m.'

'You've got to be joking!' I jump up. 'I've got to work tomorrow!'

'Call in sick,' Jeanine laughs again. 'Renée will totally understand.'

We pull bedding from the loft space and make a bed up for me on the sofa.

'Good night,' she says sleepily.

'Good night,' I mumble back, crawling under the covers. I lay my head on one of the sofa cushions and sink into an overwhelming softness.

4

People are talking about me. I can tell from the silence that descends when I enter the department with the letters book, from the quick glances people give me, and the guilty faces. I pull a requisitions form towards me and fill in scissors, hole punches and paperclips. I keep an eye on the clock. Do the hands sometimes stop?

A deep voice breaks the silence of the office. 'Has somebody here got a problem?'

I swivel my chair and see a body that's six feet four, a handsome face crowned with thick, blond hair, a broad smile.

'If it isn't Sabine!' He perches on the edge of my desk. 'I thought it was you yesterday. You don't recognise me do you?'

'Oh, yes, aren't you…I mean…'

My colleagues are looking at me with a mixture of amazement and envy.

'Olaf,' he says. 'Olaf van Oirschot, you know, Robin's friend.'

The haze in my brain begins to clear. I take a deep breath of relief. Lanky Olaf, a friend of my brother's. When we were both at secondary school, Robin hung out with a group of idiots who were more interested in practical jokes than their exam results.

'Now you remember,' he says, pleased.

I lean towards him to get a better look.

'Weren't you the one who pretended to be blind in that café?'

Olaf laughs, looks embarrassed. 'What can I say? We were young. We've made up for it now.'

Close by, Renée has discovered something urgent in the overflowing in-tray, which she usually ignores. She turns to Olaf as if she's only just noticed that he's here, and says, 'Oh, Olaf, I've got a bit of a problem with my computer. When I save something, I get all these strange messages. Would you mind taking a look?' As she speaks she guides Olaf towards her desk.

Olaf turns back towards me, 'See you later, Sabine.'

I try to concentrate on the order forms. It doesn't work. The unexpected confrontation with a period of my past I'd long since put behind me has left me reeling. And apart from that, I can't get over the fact that Olaf has become so good-looking.

When I finally leave at half-past twelve, we bump into each other in the lift.

'Are you off to lunch too?' Olaf asks.

'No, I'm going home.'

'Even better!'

'I only work half days.' I find myself compelled to explain.

'So do I mainly, even though I'm here for the whole day,' Olaf says.

Arms folded, he leans against the side with the mirrors and checks me out without any sign of embarrassment. The lift feels smaller by the second.

I lean against my side of the lift, my arms also folded but I can't keep my eyes still. I laugh at Olaf's joke, but my laugh sounds nervous to me. Don't act like a teenager Sabine, I tell myself. This is Olaf, you know him.

But it doesn't feel like that. Not now that he's looking at me in that way. I try to think of something natural to say. 'You haven't worked here for that long have you? I mean, I haven't seen you here before.'

'A few months.' His eyes wander shamelessly from my legs to my breasts. The appreciation in his expression flusters me.

'I've been off sick for quite a while. A burn-out.' I explain. Depression suddenly sounds so neurotic.

Olaf makes a clicking sound with his tongue. 'Were you out of circulation for long?'

'Quite a while.'

'And now you're easing back into it.'

I nod. Then there's a silence while we look at each other. *Why* do I find him so attractive? His features are too angular and irregular to really be called handsome. His blue eyes are too pale to contrast with his blonde eyelashes and eyebrows. His hair is thick but messy, the sort that never looks neat. He's changed. And he seems just as surprised by my appearance, even though I don't think I've changed much. I've still got my straight, light brown hair, I barely use any make-up, just a bit of kohl and mascara, and my taste in clothes isn't really any different. But Olaf's looking at me like I'm gorgeous, which is nonsense, of course. He's probably winding me up.

'What a coincidence, meeting again like this,' Olaf says. 'On the other hand, everyone seems to have moved to Amsterdam. Sooner or later you bump into everyone. Tell you what, do you really want to go home or shall we have lunch together?'

I look at him alarmed. Have lunch together? His eyes glued to my face while I lift my fork to my lips with trembling hands?

'Sorry, I have to head off. Another time perhaps.'

The lift stops and the doors open. Renée and some other colleagues are getting out of the other lift.

'Don't be silly,' Olaf says. 'You have to eat, don't you? We can do that just as easily together.'

Renée looks from me to Olaf with a glimmer of disbelief.

'Why not then. I'd like to catch up,' I say.

We walk into the canteen together as if we'd remained in touch all those years.

'I'm going to go for the bread roll with a meat croquette,' Olaf says. 'You too?'

'Alright.' Over the past year I've put on five kilos from the Prozac and from comfort-eating chocolate. One croquette isn't going to make a difference.

We pick a table near to where Renée and her cronies have set up. They arrange themselves so that they can keep an eye on me.

I try to relax and smile at Olaf.

'Did you read about the school reunion?' He spreads a layer of mustard onto his croquette.

I nod and cut my roll into smaller pieces. There's no way I'm going to try to eat this whole thing with my hands.

'Are you going to go?' Olaf asks.

I think about the school grounds during the breaks, the little groups dotted around it, the wall I used to lean against, on my own.

'No way.' I take a bite.

Olaf laughs. 'I don't really feel like it either.' He mashes his croquette onto his bread. 'If I'd wanted to stay in touch with somebody I would have. But still, we haven't seen each other for years and it is good to see you again.'

I still don't quite feel comfortable with him. Each time he looks at me, I become even more conscious of my limp hair, my tired, pale face and the sweat patches on my jumper.

Just then Olaf attacks his sandwich like a buzzard after prey. He eats with perceptible and audible pleasure. I don't usually like men who let you see exactly how they chew their food. But in this case I'm filled with relief and renewed confidence. Sweat patches might be nasty but lumps of croquette falling out of your mouth are worse.

Olaf doesn't seem in the least bit bothered by it. He picks up the pieces again with his fork and puts them back into his mouth. He hasn't yet swallowed them when he begins to talk again. 'If you change your mind, tell me. We could drive together. By the way, how is Robin these days?'

'Good. He's living in England.' I'm relieved that we've dropped the subject of school.

'What's he doing there?'

'He also works in IT,' I say.

'In what sort of company?' Olaf asks.

'Clothing,' I say. 'Men's fashion.'

'And he's going to stay there? Or is it just temporary?'

'I hope it's only temporary,' I say. 'If he emigrates as well… My parents already live in Spain, you know. Robin and I both lived and worked in Amsterdam but then his company decided to set up a new branch. Once it's off the ground he'll come back, I hope.'

'The two of you were always close, I remember that.' Olaf takes such a huge bite of his roll that I look away as a precaution. I only look at him again when it's obvious that the mouthful has been safely disposed of. He wipes the remains from around his mouth and rinses the rest away with a gulp of coffee.

'I'd better get back to the grind. That was really nice, let's do it again soon.'

'We'll do that,' I say, and I mean it, despite the croquette.

We carry our trays to the rack, shove them in, plate, cutlery and all, and walk to the lift together.

'You're going home now, right?' Olaf says. 'I'll come down with you.'

He doesn't have to do that; he could just take a different lift. There is a churning in my stomach. When we reach the bottom and the doors open, Olaf gets out with me.

I look at him a little uneasily. I know what's coming, that

testing the waters phase. Wanting to ask someone out, dodging around the subject, angling to see if the other person is interested. I need to smile and flirt a little to urge him to take that step, and I'm not very good at that.

'See you tomorrow then. Enjoy your work!' I pull my bag up higher onto my shoulder, raise my hand and walk into the lobby. I don't look back but I'm almost certain that Olaf is looking at me, dumbfounded.

5

The May sunlight accompanies me to my bike. I have a car, a little Ford Ka, which I only use when it's raining. In Amsterdam you can get around faster by bike, especially during the morning rush hour.

I'm glad I'm not driving. I need a dose of fresh air. My temples are throbbing.

I ride through the Rembrandt park where the trees are blooming a fresh spring green. People are walking their dogs, a couple of school kids with a bag of chips sit smoking on one of the benches and the ducks are noisy in the pond. I'm going so slowly that joggers overtake me.

I feel like a prisoner who's just been released from her cell. A dog runs alongside me barking for a while but I'm not bothered, I love dogs. I wouldn't mind having one myself. You give them food, a roof, a pat and they're your friend for life. They carry on loving you, grateful for every friendly word, even if you hit them or tell them off.

I've heard that dog owners choose the breeds that most resemble themselves and this seems right to me. If reincarnation exists and I have to come back in the next life as a dog, I think I'd be a golden retriever. My brother Robin has something of a pit bull in him.

Inside and out, we're not very much alike, my brother and me. He's two heads taller, has builder's arms, and darker, close-cropped hair. Add an extroverted, dominant personality and you've got someone you'd better not mess with. At least other people shouldn't – he's the kind of brother every girl dreams of and I miss him even more than my parents.

One sunny day in April when I was fourteen, I was riding home from school along the bulb fields, rows of daffodils nodding their yellow heads at me in the wind. I thought how happy mum would be if I surprised her with flowers, and before I knew it, I'd laid my bike down on the side of the road, glanced towards the little house next to the bulb field and jumped over the small ditch which separated the bike path from the field.

Doing something like that wasn't really me. I was scared that a farmer would come charging after me, but I couldn't see anyone around and I went deeper into the field. By the time I saw the owner walking towards me, it was too late – he'd gone round me and was blocking my escape route. I froze among the daffodils, stammered something about paying, but he grabbed me by the arm, dragged me towards the ditch and threw me in. Literally. I couldn't sit down for days for the bruises. I climbed up the bank, crying, and rode home. My mother and Robin were in the garden when I arrived. It took them a while to get to the bottom of what had happened.

'Well, dear, you shouldn't go into farmers' fields,' my mother said. 'Imagine if everyone decided to pick a bunch of daffodils.'

That was typical of my mother. Of course she was right, but the daffodils had been meant for her and I'd reckoned on some sympathy. My mother has always been quite rational. A row with a teacher? Then you'd probably done something you shouldn't have. Knocked off your bike in the shopping centre? Well, dear, you shouldn't have been riding in the shopping centre.

But Robin listened to my sobbed-out story with growing indignation. 'But the bastard didn't have to throw her in the ditch did he? Throw, mind you. What a hero, fighting a four-teen-year-old girl. Look at her; she can barely sit down. Where did it happen, Sabine?'

I told him and Robin stood up and put on his leather jacket.

'What are you going to do?' asked my mother.

'I'm going to make it very clear that he should keep his hands to himself,' Robin answered.

'No, you're not,' my mother said.

But Robin was sixteen by then, and tall and strong for his age, as well as stubborn. We heard the splutter of his moped and he was off. That evening during dinner he told us what had happened. He'd gone to the farmyard and had seen a man in blue overalls with a wheelbarrow. He'd stopped him and asked whether he was the wanker who'd thrown his sister into the ditch that afternoon. The farmer had confirmed it and before he could finish his sentence, Robin had hit him and pushed him into the ditch.

The farmer didn't make an official complaint, something my mother was afraid of for a long time, and I worshipped my brother even more than before.

I leave the park and ride along the tramway towards home. My neighbourhood isn't particularly chic but I like it, the Turkish bakery on the corner and the greengrocers with its crates of cooking bananas in front of the door. They give colour to the neighbourhood, much more than the dirty windows and china knick-knacks of other inhabitants. Or maybe it is precisely this combination that makes the Amsterdam suburbs so special. I'll never go back to Den Helder to live.

I've got the whole afternoon ahead of me, protected inside

the walls of my nest. Or should I go out? A walk in the park? I could clean the windows, they look like they're made of frosted glass now that the sun is shining. But then I'd first have to clear the window seat, go through the piles of paper that have built up there and dust the lamps and ornaments. And then fetch a bucket of hot water and window cleaner, clean away the dust and the muck with big sweeps and then have it all dry without leaving any streaks. After that there'd be the outside and that's always a real nightmare, using a chamois leather on a stick to reach them and it never quite works. I once hired a window cleaner, he came four times and then disappeared without any decent explanation.

I take a deep breath, already tired from the thought of all that hassle. I could buy plants for inside the apartment. I have a balcony garden, but I always forget to water inside plants and they always die. A couple of fake ones might be a solution. These days you can get ones that look quite real. Should I go out and buy a couple?

The sun is shining on the dirty windows. A feeling of exhaustion overcomes me. I sit back down on the sofa and switch on the TV. There's nothing much on until *As the World Turns* begins. It's my favourite soap. I can count on my telly friends. They help me get through each day. It's a comforting thought that there are others worse off than you. At least I'm not accidentally pregnant and I don't have a life-threatening illness. In fact I don't really have anything to complain about, that is if it's a good thing not to have anyone to make you pregnant or to stand by you through your life-threatening illness.

Bart comes into my thoughts. What has triggered that? I haven't thought about Bart for years. Maybe it's because of running into Olaf today. Meeting someone from back then reminds me too much of before, the memories are unleashing.

I try to concentrate on *As the World Turns*, but Bart looks back at me from the screen and Isabel has taken over the role of Rose.

I zap to another station but it's useless. The memories won't let up. I'm getting flashbacks of things I'd long since forgotten.

I switch off the TV, pull on a jacket, get my red handbag.

Plastic plants. Where can you find them?

Inside the Bijenkorf department store I melt into the masses of shoppers. Why do the shops get so full as soon as the sun comes out? Why are people inside when the weather is so nice? I guess they must all be fed up with their sofas, chairs, clothes, shoes, jumpers and trousers, because every floor is jam-packed. The escalator takes me up and I see what I'm looking for right away: white gypsophila that looks real, pink and white sweet peas in lovely stone pots. I pick up a basket from next to the checkout and fill it with unusual greed. Tomorrow I'm going to clean the windows, clear out the cupboards and chuck out all my useless junk.

The checkout girl rings up the plants with impossibly long fingernails and says tonelessly, 'That'll be fifty-five euros and ten cents, please.

'How much?' I ask, shocked.

'Fifty-five euros, ten cents,' she repeats.

'So much?'

'Yeah,' she says.

Fifty-five euros for a few fake branches and a couple of pots.

'Forget it.' I put the sweet peas back into the basket. 'I'll put them back myself.'

I go downstairs and glance at a rack of skirts. A saleswoman comes towards me. She has short black hair, dark-blue eyes and for a heart-stopping moment I think it is Isabel come back from the dead.

I'm rushing towards the escalator. Get downstairs, down, away from here. Outside, fast. Back on the bike, around all the shoppers. Home, back to my nest. I ride as fast as I can and arrive home in a complete sweat. Bike back in the corridor, lock, upstairs. The door closes behind me with a reassuring click.

No messages on the answering machine.

No flowers.

Only memories.

6

Isabel Hartman went missing on a hot day in May, nine years ago. She was riding home from school but never got there. We were fifteen. I'd already lost her before that; when we were both in Year 7 our paths began to diverge. But she was a determining factor in my life. She still is – she's beginning to dominate my thoughts again.

From the beginning of primary school Isabel was my best friend and we were inseparable. We spent hours in her bedroom. Isabel had a really cool table and chairs where we'd install ourselves with coke, nachos and dipping sauce. We'd listen to music and chat about everything we were interested in: friendship, love, her first bra, who in class had had her first period and who hadn't.

I can still remember how it felt when we began to grow apart.

Isabel and I were both twelve and starting secondary school. We'd ride there together, and enter separate worlds. I would fade into the background and Isabel would blossom. The moment she rode in to the school grounds there was a clear change in her posture. She sat up straighter, stopped giggling, and would look around her with an almost queenly arrogance. Even the older boys looked at her.

Isabel began to dress differently. She was already a B cup when my hormones were still asleep and I still had a helmet brace. She had her long, dark hair cut off and started wearing a leather jacket and ripped jeans; she had her nose and navel pierced.

One day she rode away from me the second we got into the school grounds, she locked her bike quite far from mine, and walked towards the others with a self-confidence which won her attention and respect.

I didn't dare go after her. I could only look on at Isabel and the other girls from my class. They were all tall and slim and dressed alike in tight tops which showed off their bellies. Long hair, dyed blonde or red, floated around their heads or was casually tied up, with refined wisps, which framed their sun-tanned faces. They all smoked, and chatted in a language I didn't speak.

I realised that I'd been missing something they'd all been aware of and that it was too late to change.

Isabel had epilepsy, but very few people knew. Her really bad fits were controlled by medicine, but sometimes she'd have blackouts or light fits. I could usually tell if one was coming. If she had time, she'd give me a sign, but mostly I'd see it in her blank expression or in the twitches in her hands.

When we were still riding to school and back together, sometimes we'd have to stop because a black-out was coming. I'd lay our bikes on the roadside and we'd sit down on the grass, if necessary in the pouring rain, in our waterproof jackets. After a bad attack, Isabel would be really tired and I'd push her home on her bike.

It was like this for a long time but our friendship would always end the moment we entered the school grounds.

On the day she disappeared we hadn't been friends for two years. That's why I was riding quite a way behind her when we left the school. She was with Miriam Visser who she was hanging out with a lot at the time, and I didn't feel like latching on. They wouldn't have appreciated it either. I needed to go the same way and slowed down so that I wouldn't catch up with them. Isabel and Miriam were riding slowly, hands on each other's arms. I can still see their straight backs and hear their carefree voices. It was nice weather; summer was in the air.

At a certain point, Miriam had to turn right and Isabel and I would usually carry straight on. Miriam did indeed turn right but so did Isabel. I followed them, I don't know why because it wasn't my usual route. I was probably thinking of going home through the dunes, something my parents had forbidden because the dunes were so isolated. But I did go that way quite often even so.

We rode behind each other to the Jan Verfailleweg which led to the dunes. Miriam lived in one of the side streets. She turned off and held up her hand to Isabel who continued alone. This surprised me. I'd been expecting Isabel to go to Miriam's house.

I carried on behind Isabel, keeping a safe distance. She dismounted for a red light at an intersection. I stopped pedalling, hoping that the light would quickly turn green. It would be embarrassing to find ourselves next to each other and to have to find something to say. Then a small van stopped behind her shielding me as I drew closer. The light turned green and the van set off in a cloud of exhaust fumes. Isabel got back on her bike and went on her way. If I'd also gone straight I would have ended up right behind her and I didn't want that. I turned right and took a slight detour to the dunes.

That was the last time I saw Isabel.

My memories of the time are a little foggy. It is strange how unimportant details remain razor sharp in your mind, while everything of significance is lost. For example, I can't remember anything else special about that day, just that I rode behind Isabel and Miriam and how trustingly they rested their hands on each other's arm. I can't even remember the moment I learned that Isabel was missing. I only know what my mother told me about it later. Our parents had known each other earlier when we were still best friends, but that had petered out too, with our friendship. That evening, Isabel's mother had telephoned mine when Isabel didn't come home. My mother came upstairs to my room where I was busy doing my homework and asked me if I knew where Isabel was. I said I didn't. That didn't surprise her – Isabel hadn't been round for ages.

Isabel's parents had called the police right away. A fifteen-year-old girl who had stayed out all night? She was probably at a friend's house, the duty officer had said. Isabel's father spent the whole night combing the village and neighbouring areas while her mother called everyone who knew her daughter.

When she hadn't turned up after two days, the police got involved. The officers interviewed everyone within her circle of friends, but because I wasn't part of that anymore they didn't ask me anything. I couldn't really have told them that much, only that I was the last person to have seen her, not Miriam Visser. But what difference did it make? Since I'd turned off early, I couldn't be sure that she'd ridden home through the dunes.

With the help of the army, helicopters, tracker dogs and infrared scanners, the whole area was searched. Isabel's mother and her neighbours stuck up missing posters in bus shelters, public places and in house windows.

They found no trace of Isabel.

At school it was obviously *the* subject of conversation. Everyone had something to say about it, but I can't remember much. Robin once reminded me about the wild rumours that were being spread: she had been kidnapped, raped, murdered, perhaps all three. And if it could happen to her it could happen to anybody. Nobody thought that Isabel might have run away. She had nothing to run away from, after all. She was the most popular girl in the school.

Teachers who Isabel had recently had problems with were treated with suspicion. As were boys she'd dumped. The depths of the North Holland canals were searched and an aeroplane combed the beach. Police motorbike officers drove along all of the walking paths in the dune area from Huisduinen to Callantsoog.

Isabel's parents were filmed for programs like *Missing* and *The Five O'Clock Show*. After each broadcast, the tip-offs would come pouring in and people from all over the country volunteered for a large scale search because the police were not prepared to provide the necessary manpower. The search took place. Part of the army joined in. Psychics tried to help. But Isabel was not found.

I must have really retreated into my own world since I can remember so little. Finally the excitement died down. Worries about forthcoming reports, having to retake classes, the next school year and all those other cares gained the upper hand. Life went on. That's to say, it should have gone on, but I still wonder what happened to Isabel.

Not long ago, her case was reopened in *Missing*. I was surfing the channels and got a shock when Isabel's smiling face and short dark hair appeared on the screen. Spell-bound, I watched the reconstruction of the day she disappeared. All possible gruesome scenarios were played out while Isabel's face smiled down at me from a box in the top right of the screen.

'There must be people who know something more about the disappearance of Isabel Hartman,' the presenter said earnestly.

'If you'd like to come forward, please call our team. The number is about to come up on your screens. If you know something, please don't hesitate. Pick up the phone and get in touch with us. There's a reward of two thousand euros for any tip which leads to the case being solved.'

The reconstruction has triggered something and I'm getting a headache. I try to dredge something from the depths of my memory; something that I'm not entirely sure is there. I don't know what it is, but I do know all of a sudden that Isabel is not alive.

7

That evening, I sit down at my computer with a bottle of wine, go to the chat room and pour my heart out to friends I've never met and probably never will.

The bell makes me jump. It's nine o'clock. I get up, a little woozy from the wine and press the button that opens the door downstairs.

'It's me,' Jeanine shouts.

She comes up and looks around. 'What are you up to?'

'Chatting. I'll just shut down.' I log off.

Jeanine goes through to the kitchen and stops. 'How long has that lot taken you?' she calls out, pointing to the bench top covered in empty bottles.

'Oh, I'm not sure exactly.'

'Not very long, I think.' She studies my face. 'What's the matter?'

'Nothing. I just like a glass of wine.'

'If you drink that much, you don't 'just' like a glass of wine, you need alcohol. And if you need alcohol you've got a problem.'

I'm uneasy under Jeanine's sharp gaze.

'Perhaps you'd be better off finding out why you feel so miserable, instead of kidding yourself that you just like a glass.'

Her expression is so worried that my irritation melts away. It's been a long time since anyone has looked at me in that way, apart from my psychologist, but she was paid for it. We sit down at the kitchen table and I stare at its wooden top.

'This is not just because of Renée, is it? This is still something to do with your depression,' Jeanine says.

I nod.

'But you did see a psychologist, didn't you? Didn't that help?'

'After a while she couldn't see how she could help me any more. Things were going better, but she had the feeling that she couldn't get to the heart of the problem.'

I fiddle with the fruit in the fruit bowl. It is a pretty ceramic bowl that I bought in Spain and paid too much for. I laugh and tell her that.

'Sabine…' Jeanine says.

I keep my eyes fixed on the fruit bowl and try to decide whether to go on. Then I look up and ask, 'Do you ever feel that there's something in your memory that you can no longer get to?'

'Sometimes,' Jeanine says. 'When I've forgotten someone's name. It will be on the tip of my tongue and then just when I want to say it, it will disappear.'

'Yes, exactly.' I take a banana and gesture towards her with it. 'That is exactly what it is like.'

'What's it got to do with then?' Jeanine asks. 'Or have you forgotten that too?'

I snap off the top of the banana and slowly peel it. There it is again, that spark, the memory that surfaces. I sit frozen, stare at a framed print on the wall and then it has gone again. I eat the banana, frustrated.

Jeanine hasn't noticed a thing. 'I've forgotten so much of the past,' she says.

'I have told you about Isabel haven't I?' I say.

'Yes.'

'I get the impression that I might know what happened to her.'

Jeanine stares at me. 'But they never found her, did they? How can you know what happened to her?'

'That's just it,' I sigh. 'That is what I am trying to remember.'

That night I sleep badly again. I wake up with a mind full of confusing dreams, dreams about the past, about school. When I'm fully awake, I can't remember any of the details. The only thing that remains is Bart's smiling face, close to mine, and the deep sound of his voice in my ears. Bart, my first real love, the first and the only boy I've slept with. I haven't seen him since school. I can't remember ever having dreamt about him before. Why is the past pursuing me so relentlessly?

'I've got a suggestion.' Renée comes in to the office, takes off her coat and places a large pink piggy bank on her desk. 'I've discussed it with Walter and he agrees with me. Too much paper is wasted on typos. Often the mistakes would have been found if you'd read over your work again. We all make mistakes occasionally, but recently the paper bin has been getting really full.'

She so deliberately avoids looking in my direction that I know who is being held responsible.

'If we were to put ten cents in the piggy bank for each wasted sheet of paper, we could use the money to pay for our Friday afternoon drinks. What do you all think?' She looks around expectantly.

I can't believe it. I've got a headache and have been keeping an eye out for Olaf. It would be handy if something small could go wrong with my computer, but the PC starts up just fine.

'Hmm, yeah,' Zinzy says.

I met her for the first time this morning and she seemed quite nice. She's small, dark, very delicate, but in one way or another able to stand up to Renée.

'I think it's a good idea,' says Margot, who types the fewest letters. 'A lot of paper is thrown away.'

'Why don't you all have a think about it,' Renée says.

I don't agree, but I don't feel like sticking my neck out. Zinzy doesn't say anything else.

To escape Renée's gaze, I swivel back to the screen and an email from Olaf pops up. *Good morning, Sabine. It seems that your computer is working alright. Pity!*

A smile spreads across my face. I immediately send him a message back: *It is a bit slower than normal.*

It isn't long before I get a reply. *I'll come and have a look. ASAP!*

On my way to get a coffee, I bump into Olaf.

'That was quick,' I say, laughing.

We're standing in the hall, looking at each other.

'So, there is something wrong with your computer,' begins Olaf, at the moment that I say, 'What a bit of luck that you…' I break off my sentence but Olaf gestures for me to continue.

'What's a bit of luck?' he asks.

'That you emailed when I was in the middle of thinking how slow my computer was.' I walk over to the coffee machine. Olaf comes with me and leans against the kitchen unit.

'That's why I'm in IT. I can sense that kind of thing.'

'Coffee?' I ask.

'Black.'

I place an empty cup in the machine. We make no move to go to the admin department.

'Did you do anything good yesterday afternoon?' Olaf asks as he takes his cup from the machine and puts one in for me.

I press 'white coffee'.

'I tried to clean the windows but stopped myself in time. After that I went to buy fake plants in the Bijenkorf, went up to the cash desk with them and took them back again. I was home just in time for *The Bold and the Beautiful*.'

Olaf laughs so hard that he spills coffee onto his shoes. Renée, who is just walking by, turns around. I step to the side so that Olaf blocks out her sour expression.

'And what are your plans for this afternoon?' he asks.

'I'm going to Den Helder.' I pick up the scorching plastic cup and blow into it.

'Den Helder.' He looks at me with interest. 'What do you want to go there for?'

I shrug my shoulders and smile, but don't answer.

'Do your parents still live there?' Olaf asks.

'No, they emigrated to Spain five years ago.'

'Oh yeah, you told me that yesterday. Not a bad move.'

'It depends how you look at it. Robin is in London, my parents are in Spain…'

'Ah, poor thing, so you're left behind all on your own?'

Olaf puts his arm around my shoulders and leaves it there for a while. His arm feels like lead. It would be terrible to shake him off but that is my first impulse. The way he strokes my arm suggests a bond that isn't there at all. Not yet. It could also be the first step towards something unthinkable. Is Olaf interested in me? Is that possible?

'I must get back to work.'

'But wasn't your computer a bit slow?' he says.

'No slower than me, so it will be alright.'

Olaf stays in my thoughts for the rest of the morning. Every time someone comes in, I look up, and I keep thinking I can hear his voice. Every ten minutes I check for new mail. But, no, that was it for today, and now my uncertainty drives away the hopeful butterflies in my stomach.

42

It's been a long time since I felt this way. The first time I fell in love was with Bart at the school disco, and his reciprocal interest brought about the same feeling of amazement I'm now experiencing with Olaf. That nothing came of my other relationships was my own doing.

Renée comes into the office and I get back to my work. She sends a cool glance in my direction, slides behind her desk and from then on checks every other minute to see what I'm doing. With a sense of deep relief, I pick up my bag at twelve-thirty and leave without saying goodbye to anyone.

I spend the whole afternoon lying on the sofa and zapping through all of the television channels, waiting for *As the World Turns*. The sun shines in, revealing the dust on every object in the room.

I'd planned to do some cleaning but energy has deserted me. Even making a cup of tea seems like too much effort.

With my feet, I shift a book on the table towards me. A woman with a challenging look and hands on her hips is on the cover. *The Assertive Woman* is written in menacing letters at the top.

It's one I recently got from the library. It is full of tips and psychological insights that offer solutions to every problem. All you need to do is learn a list of assertive sentences by heart and then use them at the appropriate moment.

It's not my problem./I'm off. Bye!/What difference does it make to me?/I want to be left alone now./I'm not taking that./Do it yourself./I'm not going to do that./I don't want to do it./I'm against it.

They would all be usable against Renée. I memorise them until I hear the theme tune to *As the World Turns*.

8

'Have you all thought about it?' Renée asks the next day once we have all arrived.

I say nothing and carry on calmly typing.

'About what?' Zinzy asks.

'That we pay fines for unnecessarily wasted paper.'

'I'm for it,' Margot says. 'It is a brilliant idea, Renée.'

Renée's eyes wander over to Zinzy and me. 'Sabine?' she asks.

I picture the list of assertive sentences. An 'I' message would be particularly good here. It sounds powerful and commands respect.

'I'm against it,' I say.

There is a moment's silence.

'Given the amount of mistakes in your letters this doesn't surprise me, Sabine,' Renée says.

'I'm against it,' I repeat. 'It's a terrible idea.'

Margot and Zinzy remain silent.

'Zinzy?' asks Renée. 'Do you think that too?'

'Well, I'm not sure…' Zinzy falters. 'If you think it's necessary…'

'We have to all want to do it,' Renée says.

I recognise Walter in her words.

'Listen, Renée,' I say. 'I come here to earn money, not to finance the weekly drinks. I don't think that we deliberately make typos, so if we just agree to check our work more thoroughly before we print it that should be enough.'

They all look at me, gobsmacked. I'm rather good at this.

'Some people make more mistakes than others,' Renée says coolly.

'If it's taken up by the union, we'll implement it, otherwise not,' I say, equally coolly, and turn my back on her.

Renée doesn't speak to me for the rest of the morning and Margot and Zinzy avoid me. The tension in the office is so tangible that anyone who comes in immediately lowers their voice. My in-tray is filled up with drafts covered in yellow post-it notes. If Renée needs to speak to me, it comes through Zinzy and Margot.

'Do you know what the problem is?' Zinzy says. We are hanging around by the vending machine, where I used to stand with Jeanine. 'You don't give the impression that you want to get back to work. You sit at your desk with a stony face and that puts people off. Everyone thinks that you're a grumpy cow who'd rather be at home on sick leave.'

'However would they have come up with that?' I say.

Zinzy seems to be nice. Slim, petite, shiny black hair, big brown eyes. I'd like to look like her. There's something uncertain in her manner that makes her come across as insecure – which she absolutely isn't. She's just told me exactly what people think of me, after all.

The ultimate proof of her independence is this particular risky venture: eating Mars bars with me by the vending machine.

Her words are illuminating. So that's how they see me. Well, they are not really wrong. I don't really want to be back at work, but it wasn't always like this.

'Do you find me grumpy?' I ask.

'Not right now, but when Renée comes over, I see you go all stiff. Why do you have such a problem with her?'

I screw up the Mars bar wrapper and throw it into the bin.

'You'll find out for yourself one day,' I say.

At twelve-thirty I go to the lift. I could take the stairs but just the thought of all those stairs makes me feel dizzy. Lifts are there to provide people with a service. You'd have to be stupid not to take advantage of them.

There's a ping and a moment later the lift arrives and opens. I rebound off a wall of bodies.

'Oh,' I say, 'full.'

'Not quite, Sabine! You can fit in. Breathe in, everyone.' It's Olaf from somewhere at the back.

On the second floor, I almost fall out when the doors open.

I wait until everyone is out to get back into the lift. Olaf hovers outside the lift.

'From now on I'll resort to the stairs,' I hold the door open with my foot so I can talk to him. At the canteen, there is a long queue by the buffet. 'It smells of pancakes.' I enjoy the greasy, sweet waft.

'Do you like them?'

'They're delicious. Especially with a slab of butter and a thick layer of icing sugar…'

His gaze glides over my body. 'I can't tell.'

'Because I never eat them. I've banned them from my diet,' I say.

Olaf shakes his head. 'If there's one thing I hate,' he says, 'it's that women are always denying themselves things.'

'What?'

'I once had a girlfriend who was always dieting. She couldn't talk about anything else. Montignac, juice diets, Slimfast, you name it. I became an expert in the field. Pounds flew off and kilos went back on. If I ever cooked anything, she would have just started a carrot diet. I got sick of it.'

I laugh despite the unexpected pang I felt when Olaf started talking about an ex.

'You're not on a diet are you?' he asks.

'What difference would it make? I'm not your girlfriend am I?'

'That's true.' He looks at me with a mysterious smile. 'What do you like, apart from pancakes?'

'Greek food,' I say, 'I love Greek food.'

He nods. 'Then we'll go out and eat Greek sometime, okay?'

'Okay.'

9

I've only just got home when the doorbell rings. Out of the window, I see Olaf. My heart turns somersaults as if it's been let loose in my rib cage. I press the button in the hall and hear the downstairs door spring open. Olaf's heavy footsteps come upstairs and a moment later he is inside, holding takeaway Greek in a big box.

'I thought you might be hungry,' he says. 'You like Greek food don't you?'

I look at him, slack-jawed. 'I was just making toasted sandwiches.'

'Toasted sandwiches!' Olaf says contemptuously, and comes further into my flat.

He sets out the trays of rice, salad, pita bread and souvlaki on the table and a greasy smell pervades the room. In the kitchen the toasted sandwiches are burning. I rush in and unplug the toaster from the wall.

'Whoever eats Greek for lunch?' I say, laughing.

'Greeks,' Olaf says. 'Go and sit down, it's getting cold.'

We eat together, facing each other at the table, the plastic trays between us.

'I was sure you liked doing things spontaneously,' Olaf says with his mouth full. 'Nice food, eh?'

'It's delicious. Where does it come from?' I take a piece of bread and scoop some tzatziki from the tray onto the edge of my plate.

'Iridion, on the corner. More wine?' Olaf raises the bottle of white wine he has opened and I nod. He fills our glasses and serves himself some more pita bread.

I push my plate away from me and take in his huge appetite with awe.

'God, you eat a lot.'

'Always have done,' Olaf beams. 'My mother messed me up totally. She always made my favourite dishes and then gave me two or three helpings. She was crazy about cooking.'

'Was? Has she died?' I collected the empty trays and put them into the cardboard box.

'No, but she doesn't cook much anymore. I'm an only child and my father died five years ago; she doesn't feel like going to all that effort just for herself. She cooks once a week, freezes everything in portions and eats it every day. When I go home for dinner, she cooks for me, makes too much and freezes that too.' Olaf scrapes his plate clean, gnaws at a bone and chucks it into the cardboard box. He burps loudly and slaps his full stomach.

'Do you have to burp like that?' I can't stop myself saying.

'In many cultures, it's polite behaviour. If you don't burp, they keep on serving you because they're afraid that you haven't had enough.'

'In which cultures is that?'

'In Asian countries, I think.' Olaf pushes back his chair, and clears the table, takes everything into the kitchen. Then he pulls me from my chair. Holding me tightly in his arms he kisses me. Bits of rice and souvlaki get into my mouth and I swallow them. Kissing is actually really dirty, I think as his tongue wraps around mine. You have to really like someone to go through this.

He pulls back a little. 'I have to get back to The Bank, I'll over-run my lunch break. Are you doing anything tonight?'

'I wanted to re-watch old episodes of *As the World Turns*, and I've got my book *The Assertive Woman* to finish,' I say.

He laughs. 'Shall we go out for dinner tonight?'

'Great,' I hear myself say. 'But not too early.'

'Okay, I'll pick you up at eight. See you tonight.' Olaf kisses me again and leaves. I look out of the window to see if he is looking up. We wave at each other and I turn away with a smile.

I've got a date. And I've still got the whole afternoon to play around with my hair and decide what to wear. I go to my wardrobe. In a dark, forgotten corner I find a single dress that approximates evening wear. It's too long, too orange and too small.

I try it on against my better judgment. Orange is really out of fashion, although the bright colour does suit me. It would, if I could get the material over my hips. Did this ever fit me?

I pinch my side and give the bulging seams a disgusted look.

This is a harder blow than discovering that my desk had been nabbed. Much harder. Like watching a film on fast rewind, I see myself lying on the sofa with bags of liquorice and chocolate, chips and pistachios. I'm crazy about pistachios. Put a bag next to me and I'll free them from their shells at the speed of light.

I peel the dress from my body and throw it out of sight. Hands on my hips, I stand in front of the wardrobe mirror.

'Okay,' I say aloud to the fat rolls which are trying to obscure my pants. 'Enough is enough! No excuses!'

I consider this evening's dinner with regret. 'Salad is delicious, too,' I say to my reflection. 'A healthy salad and lean meat, and small amounts of everything. A bit of eating out can suit the dieter.'

But this still doesn't solve the problem of my outfit. I try on everything in my wardrobe and throw it all on the bed with disgust. Too old, too boring, totally out of fashion, too small, too tight, really too tight.

Finally I pick up the telephone and call Jeanine on her mobile.

She's at work but is instantly all ears when I tell her about my date with Olaf van Oirschot.

She squeals. 'You've got to be kidding. How did you swing that one?'

'Tummy in, tits out,' I say, collapsing into uncontrollable giggles.

'Works every time,' laughs Jeanine, and then more seriously: 'What are you going to wear?'

'That's exactly the problem. I don't have anything. I know that's what all women say, but I really don't have anything!'

'I'll come round to yours after work. Then we'll have dinner, you'll cook, and after that we'll pop into town. It's late night shopping so that's perfect.'

'But our date is tonight.'

There's silence at the other end of the line.

'Oh,' she says, 'then I'd better take some time off now.'

I stare in amazement at the receiver. 'I only need some suggestions over the phone.'

'That's never going to work. I need to see your wardrobe, perhaps there is something hidden in there. Otherwise we'll go shopping, that's always fun.' She sounds so determined and delighted that I don't protest.

'You're fab,' I say.

'I know. I'm just going to go and see if I can get the time off. If there's a problem, I'll call you.'

Half an hour later she rings at my door. 'Let's take a look at this wardrobe of yours!' her voice resounds up the stairs.

Jeanine follows me inside, making a beeline for my bedroom. The sight of the mess on my bed stops her in her tracks.

'Oh my God.' She stares at the mountain of faded T-shirts, worn jeans and neat but boring suits. With thumb and forefinger, she lifts up a pair of shapeless leggings I'd bought at the height of my depression because they were so comfortable. Even getting to the shops at that time was an ordeal.

The situation isn't that embarrassing until she pulls open my drawers and peers in at a pile of baggy knickers. Two white bras – or at least they started off white – nestle next to them. In the places where the fabric is worn, the underwire pokes out.

'What's that?' Jeanine asks.

I explain that it's my underwear.

Jeanine wrinkles her nose.

'They,' she exclaims, 'are a disgrace. You were right, you desperately need help. Throw all this rubbish away, we're going to buy you a whole new set of everything.'

'Of everything? Have you any idea how much that will cost?'

'Then you'll be overdrawn for a little while. This can't go on. What kind of nightwear have you got?'

My long T-shirt with The Bank's logo comes to mind, but I daren't mention it.

'Oh, a pair of pyjamas,' I say.

'Pyjamas?'

'Yes. Don't you have any?' I say in a defensive tone. 'Or do you go to bed in a slip in the winter?'

'It isn't winter, it's almost summer and anyway your bed is not outside. Of course I've got some flannel pyjamas, but I've also got a slip. It's part of a woman's basic kit. Come on, I've seen enough. We're going shopping.'

Tingling with excitement, I sit next to Jeanine in the tram and let line 13 take me to the Dam. I have a date, I even have a friend to go clothes shopping with, I fit in.

We get out at the Nieuwezids Voorburgwal and allow ourselves to be drawn into the throng in the Kalverstraat.

I haven't been here for ages. When did I lose interest in my appearance? How could it have happened? You feel so much better when you're looking good. And there's one thing I know for certain, I don't look good in my boring work outfits. Who taught me that you mustn't look good in the office? That you should wear a black skirt and a white blouse?

'First, lingerie.' Jeanine pulls me along.

We go into a lingerie shop, which is a first for me. As long as I can remember I've bought my underwear in Hema. We glide between rails full of sweet pastel-coloured satin on the one side and daring red and black knickers and bras on the other.

Jeanine picks up a hanger, which seems to me to hold only scraps of transparent lace, but on closer inspection they turn out to be a tiny pair of underpants and a matching bra.

'This!' she insists. 'And this too!' In a single move she draws a transparent pink slip from the rack. I look at it hesitantly.

'Isn't that a bit slutty?' I ask.

'Sexy is the word,' Jeanine corrects me. 'Just try it on. This is the kind of thing you have to see on.' She pushes me towards the changing rooms and while I undress and slip the negligee over my head, she throws a couple more matching sets in. A while later she slides into the cubicle. 'So? Does it fit?'

I look at myself in the mirror and see a pastel-coloured sex kitten.

'I'm not sure, Jeanine. It's not really me.'

'You don't have to dress as who you are but as who you want to be. It looks wonderful on you, Sabine. You have to take it.'

I can't do much in the face of such persuasion. I take them to the checkout. As I'm putting in my PIN, I look anxiously at the total, but quickly press the Okay button and put my card away.

'So,' says Jeanine. 'What's next?'

We go from shop to shop and it's a great success. The plastic bags cut into my hand as we hunt for shoes to match the clothes I've bought. If only I was tanned, but I've spent the whole month lying around getting pale in my flat. What possessed me? From now on I'm going to the Amsterdam forest or to the beach at Zandvoort every single afternoon.

Around six o'clock we collapse exhausted into the tram.

'I'm going straight home, I've had it,' says Jeanine as we stand in front of my door. 'Thank God I don't have to go out tonight.'

'I've had it too,' I moan.

'Have a shower and massage your feet. And call me tomorrow, I want to know everything.'

We say goodbye and I climb the stairs to my apartment with a heavy tread. Exhausted from carrying all the bags, I open the door and kick it closed behind me, dropping all of my purchases onto the hall floor. I take off my shoes and collapse onto the sofa. Shop until you drop, the British say. Now I understand why.

I give my feet a strong massage and when I feel that I can walk again, I have a lukewarm shower. I feel much better afterwards. I clip the labels from the underwear sets, skirts and tops, and try everything on once again. It's true; lingerie does make you feel special. Nobody knows that you are wearing it, except you. I strike a pose, hands on hips, toss my hair back and look into the mirror with the arrogant stare of a model.

A *femme fatale*, until I let my hands drop and my fat rolls remind me that one or two things need to happen. But the new skirt disguises them. In the end I'm pleased with the result.

I blow-dry my newly washed, fresh-smelling hair and put it up. I'm still doing my make-up when I hear a loud honking.

10

Olaf is in a black Peugeot, the windows wound down, a cigarette in the corner of his mouth. His fingers drum on the roof of the car, marking time to Robbie Williams' latest single. He hasn't bothered to dress up, he's wearing jeans and a T-shirt.

My own metamorphosis suddenly seems rather over the top. Isn't that pink a bit too sweet? These strappy high-heeled shoes might be great, but my top is tight around my breasts and the straps keep falling down.

I give myself a last once over in the mirror, apply a coat of mascara and put on a pair of crystal earrings. My hair looks good. Nice to have it all out of my face. It's a shame that I'm so pale but the self-tanner I used made one of my legs look like a carrot, so I didn't dare try it on my face. I didn't do the other leg either, so I'm now walking round with one orangey leg. In the restaurant my legs will be under the table though, and in the car I'll cross my white leg over the orange one.

The horn echoes against the walls of the houses. Olaf spots me and sticks his head out of the window. 'Are you ready?' he shouts.

I'm outside in the blink of an eye, but he still finds an opportunity to blow his horn again.

I stalk across the road. Olaf is blocking the narrow street

without bothering to leave any room. I pull open the door and snap, 'Drive.'

'Yes, miss! You look as pretty as a picture.'

I turn away and remain silent.

'What's the matter? Isn't that what you're supposed to say when you take a lady out?' Olaf is genuinely surprised.

'When you take a lady out you shouldn't honk in the street like a crazy person!' I regret my remark instantly. I don't want to give him the impression that he's picked up his granny from the retirement home. And he does have that feeling; I can see it in the way he is looking at me. Worse, he hasn't driven off, but remains blocking the street.

'You could have rung my bell,' I suggest, more gently.

'But then I'd have had to double park,' he defends himself. 'Have you seen those wheel clamps in the street?'

'Then call me on my mobile. Why don't you drive off? There are five cars behind us!' I look over my shoulder. One of the drivers gets out, another begins to toot his horn.

'Oy, don't do that! You should call me on my mobile!' shouts Olaf out of the window. He puts his foot down and the car roars out of the street.

I can't help it, I have to laugh. 'You feel at home in Amsterdam, don't you? No one would think you were actually a beachcomber from Den Helder.'

'In Den Helder, they might call me a beachcomber, here I'm an Amsterdammer. Do you know what they call people from Tilburg by the way?'

'No idea.'

'Pot-pissers. It comes from when Tilburg was the centre of the textile industry. In order to make felt you needed urine, amongst other things. In Tilburg it was collected from the inhabitants, they were paid to fill a pot. Gross, eh?'

'Hilarious,' I say.

This makes him laugh. 'You're a dry one.'

'I'm just happy I'm not from Tilburg. I know exactly what nickname you'd have given me then. That's what you used to do.'

'Me?'

'Don't you remember what you used to call me?'

'Sabine, perhaps?'

'No. Little Miss Shy.'

Olaf slaps his chest. 'That's true! God, you've got the memory of an elephant. You were a real Little Miss Shy.'

We turn onto the Nassaukade and into a traffic jam. Olaf looks in his rear view mirror but there are cars behind us and we can't turn round.

'Shit.' Olaf turns the wheel to the left and mounts the tram lane. A tram behind us complains with a loud tinkling noise. Olaf gestures that he'll get out of the way soon and drives on. The Marriott Hotel comes into view.

I straighten up. I'm not dressed for that place.

But we drive on past the Marriott and turn left onto the Leidseplein. The Amsterdam American Hotel then. Damn, if I'd known that. I pull down the sun visor and inspect my make-up. I'll pass.

Olaf turns into a side street and parks illegally.

'What on earth are you doing? They'll tow you away.'

'No, they won't.' Olaf brings out a card and puts it on the dashboard.

'Since when have you been an invalid?'

'I always get a terrible stitch in my side when I have to walk too far,' Olaf explains. 'A friend of mine couldn't bear it and sorted out this card for me.'

Shaking my head, I throw the card back onto the dashboard and climb out. 'Hasn't the Amsterdam American Hotel got a carpark?'

'Probably.' Olaf locks the car. 'But only for guests.'

I go to cross the tram rails but Olaf turns around and gestures for me to follow him.

I spot a garish pancake stall with a terrace full of plastic chairs.

'Where would you like to sit? There, in the corner? Then we can watch everyone go by.' Olaf springs onto the terrace and pulls out a bright red plastic chair. His eyes question me, the chair dangling awkwardly in his hands.

His eyes are shining and I find myself moved. On second thoughts, the pancake place seems much nicer than the Marriott or the American. You don't have to worry what you are wearing at least.

A waiter takes our order. Two large portions of mini pancakes, extra icing sugar and two beers.

Olaf reclines. The small chair nearly tips backwards. He folds his arms behind his head.

'Good idea of yours.' He looks pleased. 'It's been ages since I had pancakes.'

'I can't remember having suggested it.'

'You did, this afternoon near the canteen. You said you really fancied pancakes.'

'I said that I could smell pancakes.'

He leans forward. 'Would you rather eat somewhere else?'

'No,' I reassure him. 'This is perfect.' I relax into my chair.

And then there's silence. It's the kind of silence that happens when you're both scouring your minds for things to say. What have we got to talk about? Do we even really know each other?

'How do you find it at The Bank?' I ask. Stupid question, Sabine.

'I like the guys I work with,' Olaf says. 'Sometimes the humour is a bit dodgy, but that's what you get in a department full of men.'

'But don't two women work with you?'

Olaf grins. 'They're a bit overwhelmed by all the male jokes. It's exactly the opposite for you, isn't it? Only women.'

'Yep.'

'Is it friendly?'

'You have no idea how friendly.'

He doesn't hear the irony in my voice. 'That Renée strikes me as being a pretty dominating type.'

'Renée? She's a really lovely girl, always so understanding, sociable, warm. Yes, we've struck gold with her.'

Olaf frowns then spots my expression and smiles. 'A bitch.'

'A bitch,' I confirm.

'I thought so. She's always nice when she sees me, but I've heard her telling people off.'

I don't say anything and Olaf doesn't seem to want to talk about Renée. What links us is the past, so it doesn't surprise me when Olaf mentions it. He lights up a cigarette, blows the smoke upwards and looks at the sky. 'Little Miss Shy,' he ponders. 'You can't have enjoyed that.'

'I was used to it with an older brother.'

Olaf laughs. 'How is Robin?'

'Good. Busy. He's working hard. I haven't spoken to him for a while but the last time he called he was pretty enthusiastic about someone called Mandy.'

'Good for him,' Olaf says. 'I'll give him a ring sometime. Do you have his number?'

'Not on me. I'll email it to you tomorrow.'

Olaf nods and gazes at the smoke from his cigarette as he touches on the one subject I've been trying to avoid.

'Tell me,' he says. 'You were a friend of Isabel Hartman's weren't you? Have you ever heard anything more about her?'

I pick up the packet of cigarettes that is lying between us on the table and light one. Silence stretches out.

11

I've forgotten a lot about my time at high school. When I read back through my diaries or listen to Robin's stories, I come across completely unknown events, as if another person was living then in my place. And yet a recollection can suddenly knife its way through my mind, a spark that lights up the grey matter of my memory for an instant. I don't understand how memory works. I don't understand why it lets you down in one instance, then confronts you with something you'd rather forget.

The flashback I get when Olaf mentions Isabel's name isn't pleasant. I see myself standing in the school canteen, looking for somewhere to sit and eat my sandwiches. My classmates have settled not far away. Isabel is sitting on the edge of the table and leading the conversation. I'm twelve and until recently I was part of this group. I take a chair and walk towards them. They don't look up but I see the exchange of glances, as if they were surrounded by a magnetic field which launched an alarm signal as soon as I broached it.

I go to put my chair down with the others, but there's a scrape of dragged chair legs and the circle closes. I sit down at an empty table right by them and watch the minutes tick by on the clock until lunch is over. One time my eyes meet Isabel's. She doesn't look away; it is as if she is looking right through me.

'Wasn't she your friend?' Olaf sips his beer.

'Isabel? At primary school she was.' I inhale deeply on my cigarette.

'They still don't know what happened to her, do they?' Olaf says. It's a statement, not a question, but I still answer.

'No. Her disappearance was just recently on *Missing*.'

'What do you think happened to her?' Olaf asks. 'Didn't she have some kind of illness?'

'Epilepsy.' Images from the past come flooding out. I try to stop them, to break away, but Olaf carries on.

'Yes, epilepsy, that was it. Could she have had an attack?'

'I don't think so. An attack doesn't last long. You feel it coming on and when it's over, you need a while to come round. If it is a light attack, at least. I know all about it, I was so often with her when she had one.'

'So you don't think the epilepsy had anything to do with her disappearance?'

I signal to the waiter for another glass of beer and shake my head. I really don't think so and never have done.

'I can barely remember anything from those days around Isabel's disappearance,' I tell him. 'It's weird, isn't it? I mean, you'd think I would remember the first time I heard she didn't come home. Her parents came around to talk to me the following day, hoping that I might be able to tell them something. It got a lot of attention, at school and in the media, but I only know about it through hearsay.'

Olaf looks sceptical. 'You must remember something.'

'No.'

'The entire school was talking about it!'

'Yes, but I really don't remember much more. I always feel so wretched when I think back to that time. Now, I get the feeling that I've forgotten things. Important things. I think I knew more then than I'm conscious of now, but it's all gone, lost.'

Olaf sprinkles icing sugar over his pancakes.

'Is that why you wanted to go to Den Helder?'

'I was hoping that it would all become clearer if I was there, but it didn't work. It is too long ago.'

Olaf stuffs five mini-pancakes into his mouth at the same time. 'Perhaps you were in shock and got through those early days in a kind of daze. I can understand that. Isabel used to be your best friend. It must have had an effect on you.'

I stab my fork into a clammy, cold pancake.

'Last year, just after I'd gone on sick leave, I asked my mother how I'd reacted to Isabel's disappearance,' I say. 'She couldn't tell me much. When Isabel went missing, my father had just had another heart attack and was in hospital, so she had other things on her mind.'

Olaf's light blue eyes look at me.

'My mother thought that Isabel had run away from home at first,' I continue. 'She'd often had older boyfriends, even some in Amsterdam. God knows where she found them. Who knows, perhaps she did run away.'

'Do you really believe that?'

I think about it and shake my head. 'Why would she? Her parents gave her an enormous amount of freedom. Sometimes even a bit too much, my parents thought. They never said anything but I think they were relieved when Isabel and I didn't get on so well anymore. Isabel could go out as late as she liked, with whoever she wanted. Her parents didn't go on at her about her homework. They'd let her go out with a vague group of friends to Amsterdam. That kind of thing. It didn't surprise my mother that something happened to Isabel, of all people. She's always believed that something happened to her in Amsterdam.'

'That's not likely,' Olaf says. 'She disappeared during the day, after school.'

I look up, surprised that he's so familiar with the facts.

'Yes, that's right. I was riding home behind her. She was with Miriam Visser and when Miriam turned off, Isabel went on alone. I was going the same way, but I rode really slowly because I didn't want to draw attention to myself and then I took a side street to avoid her. I rode back through the dunes, but it wasn't as nice as I'd thought it would be. I was completely out of breath when I got home. It's funny, the kind of thing you remember. But I've no idea what I did for the rest of day. I might have gone to the library or something. Or done my homework.'

'But the next day? Or after that, when it was clear that Isabel really was missing? It was the biggest topic of conversation at school!'

'It is as if there's a hole in my memory. Now and then a bit of it fills in, but then I lose it again.'

'Hmm.' Olaf leans back and lights up another cigarette. He offers me another one too but I shake my head.

There is a long silence. I drink my beer in large gulps. I'm not used to silences, I don't know how to react to them, even though there's nothing uncomfortable about Olaf's silence. He's not waiting for an explanation, expects no further emotional outpouring and I don't make the mistake of babbling inanely. He doesn't say anything and neither do I.

So we just sit there while he smokes his cigarette and I finally cadge another. Smoking a cigarette at the right moment can make you look like you've got purpose.

'Did you know Isabel well?' I let my ash fall into the ashtray.

'Not really. I used to see her walking around at school and I spoke to her occasionally. Robin told me that you used to be friends. But that was before I came to your house, I think, because I didn't ever see her round yours.'

'Our friendship was over by then,' I say.

Olaf's gaze rests on me. He doesn't say anything, just looks me straight in the eye – always a good way of unnerving some- one and keeping them talking.

'The last years of primary school were really great. The first years of secondary were a shock, but later on it was good.' I'm rambling. 'I'd really changed then. I was relaxed, didn't let anyone bully me anymore. I was a completely different Sabine, the other me. You wouldn't think so would you? You never knew me like that. You know, sometimes I have the feeling that I'm several different people, all with different personalities that take over without me having any say in the matter.'

What am I saying? I tap my cigarette against the side of the ashtray and let out a forced laugh. 'I sound like a schizophrenic, don't I?'

'Oh, I don't know,' Olaf says. 'I recognise that myself. Aren't we all made up of different personalities? For each situation you put on a different face, a different manner, a different way of talking. You're constantly adapting. At work I show a whole different Olaf.'

It's quiet again. The waiter comes to collect our plates. He doesn't ask whether we've enjoyed the food but looks at us questioningly.

'Two coffees, please,' Olaf says.

The waiter nods and walks away.

'And it was delicious, thank you,' Olaf adds.

The waiter doesn't react and Olaf rolls his eyes. 'He's thinking, it's only pancakes, man.'

'Which is why they should be delicious.'

'Exactly.'

We wait for the coffee and finish smoking our cigarettes. It is difficult to suddenly change to a new, lighter topic of conversation.

'What do you actually remember from the day of Isabel's disappearance?' I ask.

'Not that much,' he says, 'apart from that I had a maths exam. It was boiling in that sports hall. Luckily the exam was easy. Maths was my best subject, so I finished quickly. I didn't wait for

Robin but got on my moped and went home. That's all. Later that evening he called me to ask if I'd seen Isabel at all.'

'Robin called *you*? Why?'

'Isabel's mother had probably just called you.'

'But why would you have known where she was?'

'No idea. Robin knew that I knew her too. Isabel used to go out with…what's he called again? That bloke in my class, the one with the denim jacket and black hair. Bart! Yes, Bart de Ruijter. I told him he should call Bart.'

I'm shocked, but I try not to let anything other than interest show on my face. 'And did he?' I ask.

'He gave Bart's telephone number to Isabel's mother but Bart had been sweating away at that maths exam all afternoon, he hadn't seen Isabel at all. He was interviewed by the police later though.'

The waiter sets down two tiny cups of coffee in front of us.

'Espresso,' I say in disgust.

'Don't you like it?'

'No. Here, take mine.' I push my cup towards Olaf.

'What would you like? A milky coffee?'

'No, don't worry. I don't really feel like coffee. Do you think they've got anything stronger here?'

Olaf laughs. 'There are tonnes of pubs around here. We'll go soon, okay.'

The blue of the sky takes on a darker tone. The neon lighting feels almost aggressive. I light a cigarette and watch Olaf drink his coffee. He stares into space.

'Robin was really mad about her,' he says after a while.

I look up with a start. 'What, Robin? In love with Isabel? No!'

Olaf looks at me in astonishment. 'But you knew that, didn't you?'

'No, and I don't believe a word of it. Robin and Isabel? That's ridiculous!'

'Why? She was good-looking. If you'd said she was eighteen, I would have believed it. I didn't realise that she was so young until Robin told me that she was in your class. But I know for sure that he had his eye on her, even if he didn't do anything about it. No one could understand it because she made such a play for him.'

'Didn't he do anything about it?' I ask, moved.

'No,' Olaf's eyes are soft. 'No, he didn't do anything about it, but I could see that it was a real struggle for him. He was attracted to her and she knew it. If she liked someone, she had to have them, even if it was only very briefly.'

I remain paralysed in the red bucket seat. Robin was in love with Isabel. He was in love. With Isabel!

'He hated her,' I say. 'He told me so himself.'

Olaf empties his cup.

'Yes,' he agrees. 'He hated her too. Love and hate are quite close to each other. Why does it affect you so much?'

I look at him with dull eyes. 'You know why.'

Olaf leans forwards and lays his hand on top of mine. 'Yes,' he acknowledges, and after a short silence adds, 'Was it that bad for you?'

I look away, at a tram ringing its bell at a cyclist.

'Yes,' I hear myself say. 'Until Robin got involved. But before that it was really bad.'

The relaxed feeling seeps away and the familiar pains in my shoulders and stomach return. My hand shakes as I put out my cigarette.

Olaf notices. His eyes meet mine, but he doesn't speak. I'm grateful to him for that.

12

I'm twenty-three and I haven't had a boyfriend, apart from Bart. When I was a student I noticed plenty of boys and they noticed me too, but one way or another a night out never developed into a relationship. It was my fault, I've since realised. I just don't like being hugged, or feeling a possessive arm around my shoulder, or being pushed against a wall to be kissed. I feel like pushing them away.

The psychologist I saw during my depression tried to find out if I'd had a sexual experience in my childhood, something that disturbed me. She was quite convinced of it; all my symptoms pointed in that direction. But she didn't find anything in our sessions and eventually let it drop. Everything there works as it should. It's just that since Bart I've not come across anyone worth bothering with, or who was interested in me.

The first time I became conscious of sexual feelings was when I was around fourteen. A film based on a book had recently been on at the cinema. I'd been really taken by it. It was the story of a forbidden love affair between a girl and a much older man. I wondered whether the book would be as beautiful and got it out. In the film the sex scenes had been quite subtle; in the book they were anything but. I lay on my bed with flushed cheeks. My body seemed to have a life of its own.

Even though my parents never interfered with what I was reading and wouldn't have forbidden it, I hid the book in my wardrobe. I was embarrassed by what it brought out in me.

From then on, I couldn't look at boys in the same way. I wasn't interested in the boys in my class who were mostly a head shorter than the girls, but I watched the older boys who Isabel hung out with. Bart de Ruijter was one of them – the best looking and most popular boy in school.

He was two years above me, the same age as Olaf and Robin. He belonged to the group they hung around with a lot. Of course I'd noticed him before, but I'd thought I didn't stand a chance. Why would he pay any attention to such an unremarkable, shy girl? Yet he did.

It was at the school Christmas disco when I was fourteen. I didn't want to go, but my parents knew it was on so it was impossible to stay home. The idea that I was different would have hurt my parents. Having them feel sorry for me seemed more painful than the disco itself.

My father dropped me off and gave me some money to get a taxi home. He could have picked me up of course, but that was the last thing I wanted.

I mingled with my classmates and tried to stay away from Isabel's gang, but they were everywhere, shrieking and laughing. I danced with no one in particular, like everyone did. The music was pounding. In the middle of a song the whole group appeared on my right, some of them rolling their eyes. Isabel was copying me dance and trying to get Bart to join in. Bart and I barely knew each other and I saw him turn from Isabel to me with a look of non-comprehension. Isabel pulled a sulky face and made a few clumsy dance moves, which the others laughed at. I felt myself blushing and my movements became even more wooden.

'Yep, I'm on a diet,' Isabel said, and ran her hands over her hips. 'I've already lost two kilos.'

'Really?' Bart said. 'Then they must have sunk to your arse.'

Everyone burst out laughing and Isabel kicked Bart in the shins. I caught his wink.

After a while, they all went outside and I stayed behind. Then Bart was standing opposite me, smiling. He offered me his hand and pulled me towards him. We danced. We drank. Alcohol was banned but many students had brought small bottles of whisky with them and were adding it to their cokes. There was something intimate about the way we poured shots of whisky into our glasses and drank it huddled close together so the teachers couldn't see what we were doing. The butterflies in my stomach got stronger.

As the evening progressed I lost more of my shyness; the whisky must have contributed. Isabel's group came back but didn't notice anything about us because we had separated and were dancing with the others.

The evening was almost over when we came together again. That's to say, Bart gripped my elbow, led me from the dance floor and we went outside. At the beginning of the evening he'd been a stranger and now we were walking with our arms around each other to a deserted corner of the bike stand. Then we were kissing, hard. He was a fantastic kisser. I barely knew what I was doing.

'Open your mouth a bit more,' he said. The sensation of his tongue slowly exploring my mouth was breathtaking. I was kissing the most popular boy in school!

Just then it struck me that this might be a practical joke. I didn't know in which way I was being teased but I opened my eyes and looked past Bart to check if the others were around. The bike shed was empty. Bart's hand moved to my trouser zip, but I pulled it off. He didn't mind.

'No?' he said. 'Okay.'

We kissed some more and then finally walked hand in hand back to the main entrance. I was in seventh heaven. The party was over. Most people had already left. The group had also gone, probably into town.

It wouldn't have surprised me if Bart had said goodbye and gone off to find them. But instead he asked me where my bike was. When I told him that my father had brought me, he got his bike, a rickety old rust bucket, and said, 'Hop on the back.'

He took me home. It was a ten-kilometre ride, and for him another lonely ten kilometres back. At the front door, we said goodbye so slowly that an hour passed before I finally slipped inside. I lay in my bed with a thumping head, in no fit state to sleep. Bart, Bart, Bart, the voice inside sang.

I hoped that things would be different from now on. Bart would defend me, protect me and draw me into the group. Isabel would treat me with respect and we would be friends again. It would even be enough if she left me alone.

I'd forgotten that the Christmas holidays had begun and that there'd be no school for two weeks. But Bart would call me and we'd meet over the holidays and spend them together.

He didn't call.

For two weeks I moved between hope and despair. Christmas passed me by totally and on New Year's Eve, I looked outside at the fireworks in the starry sky and made a half-hearted wish that he'd show up in the new year.

After the holidays, I returned to school and the first person I saw was Bart. He was near the bike shed, next to Isabel. He looked in my direction but didn't see me. At least, he didn't seem to. The school bell rang and the mass of students began to move, streaming through the main entrance into the large red-brick building. Isabel's group passed me as I was leaving the bike shed, my canvas school bag slung over my shoulder. It was fate that had me come out next to Bart, or perhaps he'd arranged it himself. I was never sure. But it didn't matter. Bart smiled at me, held out his hand and tapped the tip of my nose with his finger. It was a sweet, tender gesture that affected me more than if he'd kissed me. But that was all that happened and he ignored me for the rest of the day. I was totally confused.

Later that afternoon, I saw him through my bedroom window. He was on his bike.

I ran downstairs to open the door. 'Hi,' he said, swinging his leg over the crossbar of his bike. 'Shall we go to the beach?'

We lay in the cold, kissing in the hollow of a sand dune, and went to the cafe at the beach entrance to eat chips with ketchup and mayonnaise to warm up again.

The next day at school he ignored me again, but I found a note in my bag.

Cinema on Friday? – Bart

Then I understood – our relationship was secret. I didn't ask the reason, I didn't actually mind. My relationship with Bart would have created a lot of shake-ups and I could do without them.

For about six months we met up, always in places where there was little risk of running into anyone we knew. I don't think anyone ever found out about it, although I'm sure Isabel suspected something. She would look from Bart to me sometimes, sharp and disbelieving. And she was all over Bart in public, running her hand through his thick dark hair, teasing him and laughing. She had to have him, if only to prove that she could.

But he was mine. Until the day that Isabel vanished. That was when our relationship came to an end. Bart took his final exams and left school, and as much as I have fantasised about it, I haven't seen him since.

And now Olaf is sitting opposite me. He reminds me of Bart. Is that why I feel so attracted to him? I haven't had sex with anyone since Bart and it only occurs to me now just how strange that is.

Tonight it's going to happen. I know it, I feel it, I want it. I've been alone for long enough.

After a few glasses of wine in the cosy pub, I let Olaf take me home. At the front door I read the question in his eyes. I smile, gesture towards my flat and kiss him with full abandon.

13

I'm woken up by snoring. I turn over alarmed and almost get an elbow in the eye. Olaf lies on his front, his arms under the pillow. I'm wide awake instantly.

Olaf. So I didn't dream it.

It is already light so it can't be that early. I roll over and look at the alarm clock. It's a quarter past six, but I'm happy for the day to begin. My thoughts return to last night and the butterflies in my stomach chase away the last remnants of sleep.

At first Olaf seemed only to have kissing in mind. We lay against each other on the sofa, whispered, cracked jokes and kissed in between. Then Olaf's hand on my leg crept upwards, gliding over my hip. There was something sensual about being stroked with my clothes on, if only because of the promise that it would be even nicer if they were off.

It wasn't long before our clothes were strewn around the bedroom.

We didn't get much sleep. I wonder how I've managed all this time without sex. I close my eyes and feel it throughout my entire body.

A louder bout of snoring finally chases me from bed. It follows me into the shower, into the kitchen as I put the coffee on and toast a few slices of old brown bread.

At the moment the toast pops up, Olaf appears in the door-way, wearing only his boxer shorts. He yawns, looks crumpled.

'Morning,' he says sleepily. 'You're up early.'

'I couldn't sleep anymore. Do you know that you really snore?' I spread jam on my toast.

'You should have given me a shove, then I stop.' Olaf crosses over to the counter and pours himself a cup of coffee. 'You've already got a coffee.'

'And toast. Would you like some?'

'No, I never eat breakfast. A cup of black coffee and a fag is enough for me.'

'I couldn't survive on that.' I get the newspaper and spread it out on the kitchen table, I have no intention of changing my morning ritual. I need to have a good breakfast and read the paper for a while.

'I'm going to have a shower, is that alright?' asks Olaf.

'Make yourself at home.'

I immerse myself in the paper but can't avoid hearing the sounds coming from the toilet. He's left the door open but doesn't seem at all embarrassed. Then the shower begins to splatter and I hear Olaf singing.

A little later we walk over to the car which he'd managed to park in front of the door the night before. Olaf climbs in and opens the passenger door for me. I get in and put my bag down at my feet. It's a mess. The morning sun shines onto the medley of CD boxes, Mars bar wrappers and half-empty cigarette packets. It smells. I put my on sunglasses and wind down the window.

'They'll suspect something when they see us arrive together,' I say.

'Sorry?'

'At work. They'll suspect something.'

'Oh,' says Olaf.

'Doesn't it matter to you?'

'No.'

We drive into The Bank's carpark. Olaf reverses into a space and we climb out. It's busy; everyone arrives around this time. Olaf puts his arm around me and pilots me through the revolving doors as if I couldn't get inside on my own. In the reflection of the panels, I see Renée walking behind us.

'I have to stay downstairs for a bit. I'll email you,' Olaf says. He takes me in his arms and kisses me. I break free from him, annoyed. He winks and strides away through the lobby.

Renée and I arrive at the lift together. Our greeting is brief.

The lift fills up and in the crowded silence of strangers forced to breathe in each other's toothpaste and deodorant, we zoom upwards.

As soon as the lift stops on the ninth floor, Renée forces her way out and into the office. When I enter she is already setting up for the day. She switches on the computers and the coffee machine and picks up the keys to open the cupboard doors.

The computers come buzzing to life with animated start-up tunes.

'Sabine, did you send that authorisation to Pricewaterhouse yesterday? I've got an email here asking where it has got to.'

'Authorisation? Which authorisation?' I ask.

'The authorisation I asked you to send yesterday. I left a note on your computer because I had to leave. You did see it, didn't you? It was right in the middle of your computer screen.'

'I didn't see a note.'

Renée stares at me speechless for several seconds. 'You must be joking!' she says at last. 'So the authorisation was never sent?'

'If I didn't know about it, I couldn't have sent it, could I?'

'Oh shit!' Renée puts her hand to her head, opens her mouth, shuts it again and paces.

I look at the pile of faxes on my desk. There's a note paper-clipped to them: *Please send before 10.30am.*

'Good morning!' Walter goes to his pigeon hole.

'Walter!' Renée swoops at him. 'We've got a problem. Sabine forgot to send the authorisation to Pricewaterhouse.'

'What?' Walter turns around with a start.

'Don't worry, we'll sort it out. If you give me your car keys, I'll take it over to them in person.' She holds out her hand but Walter's eyes flash over to me.

'I said several times that it was very important that they got that authorisation *today*. Before ten o'clock. I said it several times.' His voice is calm. Too calm.

'Everyone makes mistakes, Walter,' Renée says.

'Pricewaterhouse are our biggest customers.'

'Give me your keys and I'll take the authorisation over.' Renée looks at her watch. 'I can make it.'

Walter places the keys to his BMW in her hand. 'Hurry then, but drive carefully.'

'Of course,' Renée says. She picks up her bag and leaves. She doesn't give me a second glance. Walter and I are left alone together. The silence hangs over us.

'I didn't know anything about it,' I say. 'Renée says that she put a note on my computer, but there wasn't one.'

Walter runs his hand tiredly through his greying hair.

'At ten o'clock some clients from Illy coffee are coming in,' he says. 'Do you speak Italian?'

'No, but I speak German and French.'

'They're Italian,' Walter says. 'Can you make sure that everything is ready in the meeting room?'

I nod and look at the pile of faxes in my hand which all need to be sent before half past ten. 'Where are Zinzy and Margot?'

'How should I know?' Walter walks out of the office.

I click open the Outlook calendar and read the entry for Friday 14 May: *Zinzy day off. Margot dentist.* Brilliant.

If only I'd put on runners this morning instead of these elegant, new high heels. I twist my ankle on my way to reception where the delegation of Italians are waiting. I greet them with a wholehearted *buon giorno* then I switch to English.

I take the men into the meeting room where I've hurriedly set out milk, sugar and a plate of biscuits. The coffee is on but they'd rather have tea.

I tell Walter they've arrived and run back to the coffee machine to get hot water for the tea. I rinse out the thermos flask of coffee and pour in one cup of hot water after another. Now, tea bags and I'm ready.

Walter gives me an irritated look when I finally return to the room. I spill tea on the saucers.

'Leave it, Sabine. We'll pour ourselves. Do you have coffee too?' Walter asks.

No, not anymore.

'Of course,' I say. 'Coming up.'

'Bring a cloth with you,' Walter says with a glance at the rings on the beechwood table.

'Will do.' I smile at the Italians and they smile politely back.

After I've taken the coffee, I bump into one of the sales assistants in the hall outside the office.

'Don't you ever pick up? Those phones have been ringing for an hour,' Tessa says.

All the phones are going. Flustered, I go over to my desk and pick up the first telephone.

'The Bank's administration office, good morning. You're speaking to Sabine Kroese. One moment please, I'll put you through.'

'The Bank's administration office, good morning. You're speaking to Sabine Kroese. I'm sorry, I'm afraid he's in a meeting. Shall I ask him to call you back? I'll pass that on. Have a good day.'

'The Bank's administration office, good morning. You're

speaking to Sabine Kroese. Bonjour, madame Boher. *Un moment, je vous le passe.*'

It doesn't stop. Margot comes in, sees the chaos and starts answering the phones. At eleven o'clock it finally quietens down and we can get a coffee.

Tessa wanders into the office. 'Has Signor Alessi called yet?'

'I haven't had him on the phone,' I say.

'Me neither,' Margot says.

Tessa looks worried. 'I really need his response right now because I'm about to go into a meeting with the shareholders. Are you certain?'

She leaves through the book of sent faxes. 'The fax to Alessi isn't in here. It has been sent, hasn't it?'

I shoot upright. The faxes!

'Damn,' I say. 'It was so busy the whole morning, I never got to them. I'll send them right now.'

'They haven't even been sent?' Tessa looks furious. 'Renée was right,' she snaps as she leaves the office.

'I'm positive I didn't see a note on my computer screen,' I tell Olaf later that evening. We've ordered pizza and are sitting on my balcony eating them in the sunshine.

'Could it have fallen on the floor?'

'I didn't see anything,' I say.

'Maybe it fell under your desk. Or she's lying.' Olaf picks up the bottle of Frascati from the table between us and refills our glasses. 'I think she's lying,' he adds.

'Me too,' I say.

We sit outside until the sun goes behind the buildings and then we move to the bedroom. We make love, chat, joke about Renée and make love again. I smile but I don't feel happy. When Olaf leaves – he has to go round to a friend whose computer has crashed – I switch on the TV and finish the bottle of Frascati.

I drink too much. Far too much, but at least I know it. I promise myself I'll do something about it, but not yet. I'm getting better. In spite of work, I feel stronger and have more energy. But that evening I relapse. An advert about friends on the television, the news, even an emotional scene in a soap – everything – makes me cry. And then I can't stop. An old grief breaks free and comes to the surface.

It is past ten when Jeanine calls.

'You're not in bed, are you?'

'No, I was watching telly.'

'Oh, good. It wasn't until I was calling that I realised it was already after ten. How did it go?'

'With Olaf, you mean?' I ask, and switch off the television with the remote.

'Yes, of course with Olaf.'

'It was nice,' I say neutrally.

'Now, come on! Tell all! Did you sleep with him?'

'Don't you want to know how our evening went?'

'First I want to know whether you slept with him, then you can tell me all about your romantic evening. Or was it not romantic?' Jeanine asks.

'Well, if you consider a pancake stall the height of romance…' I say.

That knocks the wind out of her sails. 'He didn't take you to a pancake stall? Is he mad?'

'Next time I'll dress for McDonald's.'

We giggle.

'So there is going to be a next time,' Jeanine says.

'I think so, I don't actually know. We didn't mention it this morning.'

'This morning at work or this morning at your house?' she asks.

'This morning at my house, nosey parker. And he came

around tonight too. And to answer your next question, yes I did sleep with him.'

'Just as well you bought that lingerie!'

'Yes,' I'm forced to admit. 'Thanks to you.'

'Do you feel like going to the beach at Zandvoort tomorrow?'

'Are you telepathic or something? I was planning to get a bit of colour on this white skin of mine.'

'Great. Don't forget your sunscreen. And you're warned, tomorrow I want to hear everything. Everything!'

14

The beach is busy, but not over-packed. We choose a spot near the entrance, spread out our towels, build sand pillows for our heads and get the sunscreen and sunglasses out of our bags. We rub the cream into each other's backs and then stretch out.

Jeanine lets out a sigh of satisfaction. 'Sun, sun, do your work! Isn't summer wonderful. I want to be really brown. I'm going to spend every free minute sunbathing.'

'Then you'll look like an old leather handbag in ten years' time,' I say, resting my head on my arms. It *is* lovely to feel the sun on your skin, it makes you feel so much better.

'So, I'm ready for the juicy details,' Jeanine says, just as I am dozing off. 'Tell me, what was the sex like?'

'Well, normal. Good, I think.'

'Good, you think? Jesus, did you come or not?'

'Yes,' is all I say. That counts as pouring out my heart for me. I'm not planning to go into the details. But Jeanine carries on pestering and within ten minutes she's prised even the most sordid parts out of me. That's quite an achievement.

'He's nice,' Jeanine says, satisfied. 'Are you in love with him?'

'I really don't know.' I raise myself up, pull my knees to my chest, wrap my arms around them and gaze out to sea. 'He is nice, but being in love feels different from this. I do think about him a lot, but without feeling the need to go running to him. And I did feel like that once about somebody else.'

I can still recall the feeling of longing I used to get when I looked at Bart, the pleasure I felt when he would touch my hand when we found ourselves walking alongside each other in the busy corridor. That was deep longing, even though I was young, and I haven't felt it again.

'Who were you really in love with?' Jeanine asks.

I tell her about Bart. The longer I talk about him, the more recent it seems. Then Jeanine begins an account of her own love life, and that takes up much more time.

I lie on my back, listen to her and feel my face nourished with the warm sunlight. As I dig small hollows in the sand with my heels, the seagulls cry overhead, circling in the bright blue sky.

A memory wells up. I'm thirteen and I'm lying on the beach. It's summer and I'm on my own. I often go to the beach alone. It's nearby and I love reading with the surf in the background.

A little further up, a group of girls arrive on the beach. Isabel, Miriam and a few other classmates. At that point, my friendship with Isabel isn't what it used to be, but she is not yet bullying me.

I claw myself up, collect my belongings and walk over to them. I stand in front of them smiling, shading my eyes from the bright sun. In an apologetic tone, I ask whether I can come and sit with them. I should have just sat down with a confident 'hiya', but I sense that the leaders of the group won't accept that kind of cheek.

Isabel looks at me. We stare at each other for a few seconds and then I look away. The girls stick their heads together, confer and after a short discussion tell me that I can't.

I go back to where I'd been, my towel over my shoulder. I look at the hollow I'd dug for myself. The wind blowing over the beach has turned chilly. I turn around and leave the beach, for home.

Jeanine sits up, puts her hands out behind her and leans on them while she lets her eyes roam over the beach. I do the same and follow her gaze to two boys walking towards the sea. They're good-looking and fit and, from their manner, they know it too.

'Shall we go for a swim?' Jeanine proposes.

'The water will still be very cold.'

'You just have to get through it. Come on!' She jumps up and pulls me up by my arm. The two boys are standing up to their ankles in the water but when we approach they dive in instantly.

'Oh, wow,' says Jeanine. 'Come on, Sabine.'

The two boys come to the surface and smile at us. Their smiles are challenges. Jeanine dives. She's so graceful. And there's nothing for it but to join her.

We stay on the beach for the entire afternoon. It's seven o'clock before we carry the cooler box and our beach bags back to the car. Baked by the sun, our shorts and tops full of sand, we drive to Amsterdam.

'Pizza at your place?' Jeanine suggests.

'I'd better watch out with all these pizzas,' I say, ' Olaf and I had one last night.'

'Where do you know Olaf from? You said you used to know him.'

I undress, step under the warm water and tell Jeanine that Olaf was a friend of Robin's. Jeanine sits down on the closed toilet seat and listens. Before I know it, I'm talking about Bart again, and then about Isabel.

'It's unbelievable that you knew her,' Jeanine says. 'That you were friends. I saw her so often on the news back then. Do you really remember nothing from that time?'

'No, not much in any case.'

While Jeanine showers, I paint my toenails.

'I read something about that once,' Jeanine calls out. 'I don't know where, in some newspaper. It was about people who had been sexually abused and didn't know about it. Much later their memories came back. They'd completely suppressed them because they couldn't cope with the psychological trauma. For one reason or another they ended up in therapy, became better adjusted and then the memories came back.'

'I wasn't sexually abused,' I say.

'No, I know, I'm not saying that. The article was about repression. Maybe you've banished something from your memory, something too nasty to leave in there.'

I pay great attention to the painting of my nails and see Isabel's face reflected in each shiny surface. When I'm myself once again, I see that not just my nails but also my toes are red.

The water stops and Jeanine steps out of the granite shower cubicle with a towel wrapped around her.

'Have you ordered the pizza?'

15

A month before my fifteenth birthday, my father was taken to the hospital in Den Helder from his work. He'd had a heart attack.

I was called out of my German lesson and Mr Groesbeek drove me to Gemini Hospital. Mr Groesbeek was the school caretaker. He was rough; always stomping around and shouting. We were all in awe of his enormous hands, which he used to separate fighting boys, to repair punctures and to look after the plants in the classrooms. At the time, Mr Groesbeek seemed ancient and also a bit creepy, with his wild grey hair and his thundering voice. He had a little delivery van which he drove from Callantsoog where he lived to Den Helder every day. On his way he sometimes picked up a student struggling to ride through the gusts of wind and pouring rain. I'd got a lift from him several times myself.

On the way to the hospital I sat staring out of the dirty window. I could feel Mr Groesbeek watching me.

'You haven't had it easy recently, hey?' he said.

I turned my head, not understanding.

'At school,' he said. 'And now this.'

I didn't know what to say so I just nodded my head.

Mr Groesbeek slapped my leg and let his hand rest there a

while. He had a large, hairy hand and I stared at it, feeling its weight pressing into my thigh. It was ages before he took it away again. We drove on without any further conversation until he dropped me off at Gemini Hospital.

'Good luck,' Mr Groesbeek said. 'Wish your father a speedy recovery from me.'

I scrambled out of the van and watched it drive away. Then I turned around and went into the hospital.

A heart attack is serious but I didn't actually feel that my father's life had been in danger. I couldn't imagine it and his behaviour during the visiting hours strengthened my feeling of disbelief. Each time I came in, he greeted me with a broad smile and a quip, as if it was really funny that he was lying there. He could really rattle my mother by waving around the hand which had the heart monitor attached to it so that it would beat crazily. Robin would laugh but I didn't find it funny either. I just sat there quietly looking at my father's pale face, that strange blue smock he was wearing and the electrodes stuck to his chest.

Over that time I realised how much I loved my father. I forgave him for the times he'd clapped too enthusiastically when I'd played the piano at school concerts. I even forgave him for shouting 'bravo!', much to the hilarity of my classmates. I forgave him for getting up and making my sandwiches in the morning, from the healthy brown bread bursting with grains that my mother got unsliced from the baker. My father cut thick slices and stuffed them with hunks of cheese carved from a round Edammer. I could barely get them in my mouth and was teased because of it, but I still let people think I'd made the sandwiches myself rather than having them laugh at my dad. My father got up early especially to make my sandwiches. I didn't even consider making them myself because he enjoyed doing it. It was the only part of the day that we could spend together, just the two of us in peace, he always said. My mother was not much of an early bird and Robin didn't have breakfast. He got up far too late every morning and left right away. My father would make a big pot of tea for me and get the chopping board out ready on the counter.

He was used to getting up early. He used to work as a driver on National Rail and often had to leave as early as 5 a.m. I would wake up. I was little at the time, about six or so, and I'd hear him creeping downstairs in his stockinged feet. I would slide out of my bed and go and stand in front of the window ready to wave him off. It was never that long before my father left the house, but it would feel like I was waiting for ages and I was always desperate to go to the toilet. One time I ran to the toilet, then back to the window. I was disappointed when I realised I'd missed my father. I imagined him gazing up at the window and then finding that I wasn't there to wave him off. The next morning I was at my post, jiggling on crossed legs.

After that first heart attack, he had a second, lighter one while he was still in the hospital, but he survived that as well. I visited him frequently, after school or when I had a free period. Often I skipped school.

After visiting him once during a free period, I returned to school to find my classmates huddled in the canteen. Isabel had been in an exuberant mood all day because of a white leather jacket she'd got for her birthday. She was attracting a lot of attention with it.

When the group saw me they fell silent. It was a tense silence with repressed giggles and exchanges of glances. To delay the start of the teasing, I stayed by the soup machine and bought a cup of tomato soup from it. I headed towards the other corner of the canteen but the group ambled over to me.

'Hey Sabine, you're back then,' Miriam began. 'Where do you keep disappearing off to?'

'In the Dark Dunes,' somebody said, 'with the other sluts.'

They laughed.

'My father had a heart attack,' I said. 'He's in the Gemini.'

There was silence.

Isabel recovered first. I thought I saw a flash of shock in her eyes, but she said, 'A heart attack? Are you surprised, what with that fat belly?'

It made me think of how concerned my father had been about Isabel when she came away with us to a holiday park in Limburg. We were ten years old and she had a fit. My father drove her the three hours back. I remembered too the countless times he'd cooked us pancakes, taken us to amusement parks, done magic tricks for us which we'd seen through straight away.

There was an intrusive buzzing in my head. It increased until it became a banging behind my eyes and troubled my vision. My heart beat so fast my chest hurt and my hand clamped like a claw around my cup of tomato soup.

I threw the contents over Isabel's new leather jacket. I can still recall the expression on her face. She looked at me so shocked, so taken aback that I almost felt sorry. Until she stared into my eyes. Then I knew that I had a big problem. I had declared war, and war it would be.

The girls from my class blocked my way and pinched me when I squeezed past them. They punctured my tyres. They threw the contents of my bag around the school grounds and they tore up my homework.

They waited for me after school, made a fool of me, cut up my new jumper, held me down and cut a chunk out of my 'stupid bitch's haircut'. I ran inside, into the school, to Mr Groesbeek. He took me home in his van and said I should come to him if they did anything else. He said he'd take my bike inside and fix the tyres. He said they must be out of their tiny minds, or maybe they needed their heads seeing to. But he never said anything to them about it. Perhaps he was afraid of the power of a group, or perhaps he just thought that he couldn't do much about it.

After that I didn't use the main entrance. Sometimes I used the teachers' entrance with one of the teachers, but then I still had to cross the school grounds to get to my bike.

Often I went to Mr Groesbeek's office, but that was an emergency measure. Mr Groesbeek had a particular way of consoling me. He sat with his arm around me and let his hand dangle in front of my breast which he'd touch now and again, as if by accident. Or he'd pull me against him and stroke my neck with his rough hand. In Mr Groesbeek's office, I felt trapped in a different kind of a way. Once he felt that he'd consoled me enough, he let me escape out of the window. Then I hid in the bushes, waited until the gang had given up waiting for me and walked home, steering my broken bike.

One night at home Robin repaired my tyre for the second time. He asked no questions but copied down my school timetable. From that moment on, whenever he could he'd be waiting for me, standing next to my bike with his moped. We rode home together, me hanging onto his arm, overtaking Isabel on the way.

How is it possible for everything you are, everything you believe in and everything that makes you feel safe to be swept away? Until you are a person who walks around with hunched shoulders, has to pluck up the courage to utter a single word and jumps at the shrill sound of your own voice. Insecurity steals up on you, and then it conditions your behaviour – you become what you exude.

One person learns quickly, the other needs time. It took me a long time to realise that I didn't have to put up with everything that was being done to me.

16

That night I can't sleep. My mind roams, over images of Isabel, over things my mother used to say. 'You're too loyal in your friendships, Sabine,' she once said. 'You should look out for yourself more.'

Since that time, all my friendships have remained very superficial. Jeanine was the first person to break through. We'd both just started at The Bank when she received a phone call from the hospital. Her father had had a stroke. I saw her face turn as white as chalk, pushed her into a chair and gave her a glass of water. I explained to Walter what had happened, arranged for one of the sales people to look after the office and took Jeanine to Emergency. When I turned to leave, she took my arm and said, 'Sabine…thank you.'

That was all she said, but the quaver in her voice affected me. It felt good to be able to offer help instead of to receive it. In the evening I called her and kept on doing so until she came back to work. It was strange to see that someone needed me and appreciated my support.

Jeanine's father survived the stroke, although he was partially paralysed and never his old self again. From then on, Jeanine and I were more than colleagues. While she was completely occupied with caring for her father – her mother had died and she didn't have any brothers or sisters – memories from my childhood were dragging me down into a black hole, though it wasn't until months later that I could no longer get out of bed. Aside from the sessions with the psychologist, I didn't leave the house. At that time, the future felt so bleak that I'm amazed that now, a year later, I feel so much better. I'll be even better once the past finally leaves me in peace. My psychologist didn't get everything out of me but since I've met Olaf there's no holding me back. The door is open and I have to walk through it and deal with each memory in turn. The psychologist was right: you can run as fast as you like but one day your past will catch up with you.

After tossing in bed for two hours I give up and swing my legs over the side. The kitchen windows loom large and black and reflect my pale face and crumpled T-shirt. I open the fridge to get a glass of milk but my eyes fall on the half-full bottle of wine and soon I'm pouring myself a glass. The first sip is always the best. I feel the cold liquid run down my throat, close my eyes and sigh with pleasure. Another sip.

I lean against the counter and gaze out into the dark night. There's a draught, my feet grow cold and goose bumps appear on my arms. The wine is cold too but it warms my heart, chasing away the images that appear in the black window.

I pour a second glass and drain it quickly. The alcohol begins to do its work and after the third glass I stagger back to bed and fall asleep at last.

The next day I've got a headache, stomach ache and terrible nausea. At first I think I've just got a hangover but the following day I still feel as sick as a dog. I call work.

'A tummy bug,' I tell Renée, who picks up the phone. 'I've got a terrible stomach ache.'

'Oh,' she says. 'It came on all at once, did it? Well, get better soon.'

I crawl back into bed and pull my knees up to assuage the cramps. Instead, a wave of pain drives me out of bed and to the toilet. Everything is coming out of both ends: my toasted sandwiches from last night, wine and still more wine. I hold my hair out of my face with one hand, vomit into the toilet bowl and then swap over to sit on it. I'm just too late and an unbearable stench begins to spread around me. When it's over, I come to, panting and sweating, take a bucket from the hall cupboard, fill it with water, pour in plenty of Spring-fresh cleaning liquid and mop the floor. I've just finished when the next cramp comes on.

Someone rings the bell.

I blunder to the door. I press the intercom button and say, 'Yes?'

'Health and Safety. May I come up?'

Health and Safety. They got here quickly. I press the button, hear the downstairs door spring open and heavy shoes clatter up the stairwell. A dark, heavily built man comes in carrying a file. 'Sabine Kroese?'

I turn around and run back to the toilet. The man waits in the hall, but after a while, I hear him come in and go into the sitting room to wait.

It is awful to sit on the toilet with a stomach bug and all the sounds and smells that go with it, while a few metres away a total stranger is patiently waiting until you've finished. I wash my hands and hardly dare to enter the sitting room.

'Now, now,' the man says when I finally emerge.

'Stomach bug,' I say.

'So it seems. Your employer asked us to do an urgent check. She wasn't convinced that you were sick, but obviously there's no reason for her to worry. When do you think you'll be able to return to work?' The inspector consults his notes.

'How should I know? I've only just called in sick.'

He writes something down and looks at me in a paternal manner. 'Stay at home for a few days.'

I was planning to. The inspector leaves and I let myself sink into the sofa like an old woman. An urgent check! That vote of no-confidence is enough to bring on a new attack of cramps.

It's not until two days later that I can keep anything down, and then it's only small quantities at a time. When the phone rings, I stagger over to it with legs of jelly,

'Sabine, it's Renée. I was wondering how you were doing.'

'Not too well,' I say brusquely.

'It's not over yet then?'

'Not really, no.'

Silence.

'That's strange,' says Renée finally. 'I've just called my GP and he told me that type of thing usually only lasts a day or two.'

'You called your GP?' I repeat, flabbergasted.

'Yes, I thought it seemed to be going on a bit too long, so – '

'This is only the third day I've been off.'

'To be honest, I'd expected you back at work this morning. But fine, let's agree that you'll be back after the bank holiday.'

I can hardly believe what I'm hearing. 'I'll decide when I come back to work, Renée. If you don't believe that I'm sick, why don't you come round? There's been a lovely smell around here for days and it is hardly worth cleaning the toilet every time, so the splatters and the bits of sick are still there under the rim. I'll leave them a bit longer, then you can come and see them. And the bed linen I threw up on is still in a corner somewhere, so…'

Beep, beep, beep. Renée has hung up. I put the phone down. It's at least half an hour before my hands stop shaking.

Olaf calls in the afternoon and is sweet and caring. He wants to come over but I won't let him. My house is a tip and I look dreadful.

I do feel better at last though. The sandwich I nibble stays down, the bowl of tinned soup too and then an enormous pang of hunger comes over me and I make a raid on the fridge. I eat everything that isn't past its use-by date. The cheese looks like it's wearing an angora sweater and the milk comes out of the carton in lumps. I take a bin bag out of the kitchen cupboard and throw everything away. I fill the sink with soapy water and scrub the fridge clean. I set about the bathroom with all the cleaning products I can find, throw all of the windows open, change my sheets, put the washing machine on, pour bleach down the toilet. Then I go into a frenzy. I throw away all the shoeboxes piled up at the bottom of my wardrobe and attack the dust bunnies which have gathered in the corners. I clean the fingerprints off the wardrobe door, clean the dust from the skirting boards and then I lie on my stomach to reach under the bed. I don't have much storage space and have shoved boxes and plastic bags under my bed. I actually don't have any idea what's there. I only know that there's a thick layer of dust over it, which hasn't bothered me for years, but has now become unacceptable. I pull everything out, wipe off the boxes and bags and open them. Old walking boots, text books, a brand new karate suit that I bought during the brief spell when I suddenly decided to learn some self-defence, a tent, a deflated airbed, a bag full of rods.

And then I see the box with the diaries. I thought they were in the loft. The sudden confrontation with the familiar homemade covers makes me freeze.

My diaries. Naturally I hadn't forgotten that they existed, but it has never occurred to me to look at them. I know approximately what's in them. At least, I think I do.

But curious, I pick up the top diary. It is covered in a rose print fabric. I see myself still sitting at my desk making it. How old was I then? Around fourteen or fifteen.

It begins on 1 January, typically methodical of me. If I could, I'd puzzle it out so that I could begin each new diary on that kind of date.

And I was fourteen then, I see as I leaf through it. The diary covers quite a long period of time, I didn't write lengthy entries. The entries are so staccato and frugal, it's more of a notebook.

I go into the sitting room with the diary and stretch out on the sofa.

My school timetable is glued into the front, which reminds me that the timetable for the following year is stuck in the back. The subjects and classrooms vanished from my memory years ago, but now I see them I get the urge to do my homework. As I leaf through the pages I tumble back in time. Next to each date there's a little cloud, or a little sun, both or streaks of rain. That's what I used to do at the time, I don't know why.

My eyes glide over the familiar round handwriting, over things I've confided in blue fountain pen. I read a passage here and there, afraid of what I might come across.

Nothing special.

Things about the storms that made me late for school, about the wind that had changed so it was against me on the way home too, about the books I'd taken out of the library after school. Not a word about Isabel.

I turn to Monday 8 May, the day Isabel disappeared.

Crap day. Shame that the weekend is over already. I've just got home and am about to have a bath. I rode home so hard I'm covered in sweat. If only we lived nearer the school.

That's all. Not a word about Isabel. But why would there be? I didn't yet know that day would be significant. But there's nothing about her the following days either, just little suns and clouds, nothing else.

The little sun I'd drawn next to the date catches my eye. It was

95

warm for the time of year. I remember that Olaf had said that too, that it was hot in the gym during his maths exam.

I suddenly feel restless. There was no wind at all that day. Why had I ridden so fast?

17

The question keeps me busy for the rest of the afternoon and the entire evening. I try to ignore the floral diary on the table. I even throw it back in the box, but I take it out again. Reading the diaries accelerates what was already in motion. The dive into the past has become unstoppable. It seems like it was much less than nine years ago. Has so much time passed already since Isabel disappeared?

Has it been so long since I last saw Bart? All at once, I begin to miss him. I know that's crazy but I do. I've always had a nostalgic streak, and once I give over to it, there's no going back. The longer I spend reading my diary, the worse it gets. I snap the book shut, put it back in the box and shove it under my bed. Back to the present.

I go to bed early, but the night brings no rest. Isabel turns up repeatedly in my dreams. I relive the day in question, but now everything is recast strangely. I'm in a maze of tall trees whose thick canopies block out the blue sky. The sky must be blue because it's warm even in the shadow of the trees. Birds warble and the surf pounds in the distance. I'm alone and wandering around, without knowing what I'm looking for.

Then I'm face to face with Isabel. She stands in a clearing and smiles at me. I don't know why she is smiling. I'm scared. And then I realise that she isn't smiling at me. She doesn't even see me – I've become invisible. I glance around and see the shape of a man between the trees. Isabel says something to him and he says something back. His voice is low and attractive. I know it well. And still, there's something different. The birds stop singing. He comes out from between the trees and walks towards Isabel. I know what he's planning to do. I'm so certain it's like watching a film I've seen before. He goes up to Isabel, flings her to the ground and grabs her by the throat. He holds her down with his full weight. And then he begins to press, press.

I can't see Isabel's face, but I can hear the choking noise she is making, I see her tug at the strong hands around her throat. I don't know what to do, whether to raise the alarm, throw myself onto the man's back, do something.

I do nothing. I stand there, watch, then shuffle slowly back to the shelter of the trees. I'm not scared. I know the man, and I can't imagine that he'd do anything to me, but it's better that he doesn't know that I've witnessed it.

Once he's disappeared back into the woods for good, I stand there looking at the motionless body in the clearing. At the contorted, dead face in the sand, at the empty shell that until a few minutes ago housed Isabel. I run away, further into the woods, with heavy, leaden steps, as if my shoes were stuck to the floor. Every time I look around, I see the clearing and Isabel's body. However fast I run, I can't get away.

And then I wake up. I open my eyes and lie still in the rushing silence of the dark. A dream, it was only a dream. My T-shirt is wet with sweat and my hair is stuck to my forehead. I throw off the covers, feel the night-time coolness and slowly come to. The darkness goes from pitch black to dark grey and the familiar forms of my bed, wardrobe, chair covered in clothes and the framed photos on the wall appear.

It was only a dream.

Oppressive and frightening, but no more than a dream.

I get a glass of water. I was thinking of a glass of wine. But first I drink water to rinse my dry mouth.

Leaning against the counter, I sip the cool Frascati and think about the shape in my dream. I'd known who Isabel's murderer was, but on wakening it escaped me. What does that mean? That I was witness to a murder and that my unconscious is trying to let me know it? If I barely remember anything from that day, why shouldn't I have been somewhere nearby when she was attacked?

On the other hand, if everything you dreamed might have actually happened you'd be scared to dream. If the murderer really had walked away from Isabel, I'd have found her body. Something in the dream doesn't make sense.

I finish the last mouthful of wine, switch off the light and go back to bed. I crawl under the covers and try to put the dream behind me. But I can't.

The next day I awake early. Much too early, but as soon as I open my eyes, I know that I'm not going to be able to sleep anymore.

It's Ascension Day, a public holiday. That's lucky as I have to get out of here. I have to go back to Den Helder. I don't yet know what I'm looking for but I feel the centrifugal pull of the past.

Something tells me that it's not for nothing that I don't remember 8 May, nine years ago. Was I there? Did I know the murderer? Is that why I've blocked the memories?

I don't have any air conditioning in my car and feel the sweat patches under my arms before I even reach Alkmaar. When I drive into Den Helder, it is only half past nine and already boiling. I wind the windows down, and crawl through the centre of town. Where now?

My old school.

A long, familiar street takes me towards the school building. I can't yet see it, but I can see the park where we used to hang out in the break and where we lay on the grass in the summer. That's to say, when I was in Year 12 and had some friends again.

I turn left. A tall red-brick building rises up before me and the years fall away.

I park my car in the street and get out. A great part of my life took place here. The day my parents left this town I swore I'd never return. But here I am again, and my heart is racing just as it did before.

I cross the street and walk into the school grounds.

The girl is here. I feel her presence before I see her. There she is, sitting on the luggage rack of a bike, her heavy book bag at her feet. She looks engrossed in her diary, but she's just pretending. She's acutely aware of the group just a way off and the space around her. If she smoked, she could have lit up a cigarette to conceal her unease, but she only has her diary. It probably wouldn't have made much difference. There's an intangible *je ne sais quoi* that has driven her to the edge of the group, right from the start.

My urge is to put my arm around her. Instead, when I cross the school grounds I stand next to her as if by chance.

She looks up but doesn't say anything. Her eyes wander over the school grounds.

Should I speak to her?

I look at her, hesitating. Her eyes catch mine, look away and then return. Her face is guarded.

'Hello,' I say.

'Hello.' Her voice is suspicious.

'You don't know me,' I say. 'But I know you well. I wanted to ask you something.'

She just looks at me, nothing but wariness. 'What?'

'Something about Isabel Hartman.'

Silence.

'You do know her, don't you?'

She turns her head away.

'What happened the day Isabel disappeared?'

'I don't want to talk about her!'

'Why not?'

'She's dead! What's the use of talking about it?'

'How do you know she's dead?'

She shrugs her shoulders. 'She must be. She's been gone so long.'

'What do you think happened to her?'

'Who knows. Maybe her boyfriend knows something.'

'Which boyfriend?'

'The boy she'd arranged to meet at the beach.'

'Did she have a date? On the day she disappeared? Who with?'

She looks at me with her clear blue eyes. 'You know who.'

How is it possible that I could have forgotten? Isabel was meeting someone that day at the snack bar by the Dark Dunes. I heard her talking about it to the group. She said she was done with him. She was going to end it. How terrible he'd find it. She laughed at that and I stiffened. I thought I'd heard who she was meeting, but I hoped I'd misunderstood. Isabel could have her pick of the boys, but I hoped with my heart and soul that two of them were immune to her powers of attraction. That was why I followed her that day. Not because I was so keen to ride through the dunes. I wanted to see who her boyfriend was. Or, to be more accurate, who her boyfriend used to be. I took a small detour and arrived at the snack bar but there was no one to be seen. I looked over at the children's farm at the entrance to the woods and caught a glimpse of someone in a familiar white leather jacket going round the corner. Someone was with her. I rode to the point where I'd seen the two of them disappear.

An enormous pain shoots through my head. The picture disappears. The girl has also gone, swallowed up while I wasn't paying attention.

I walk back to my car with a banging headache. An ice cream van is driving past the school and I signal it to stop.

'Ice cream, young lady?' the man says.

'Yes please, vanilla,' I say.

'Cream on top?'

'No,' I say. 'We can't have that.'

I pay him and walk back to my car. With the door open so that the heat can escape, I eat the ice cream, turn on the radio, start the engine and drive away, towards home.

18

The next morning I have to drag myself to the office. I arrive late but no one is there. Just as well, then nobody will know what time I got there. I pick up an envelope on my desk. *Sabine* is written on it in slanting letters.

I open the envelope and take out the note. It's not signed but I recognise Renée's handwriting.

Sabine,
In the future will you send your private correspondence from home and not from work. It seems to me that you don't have enough to do.

I stare at the note for some time and then tear it up. I put the pieces in an envelope, address it to Renée, and throw it into the in-tray on her desk.

So, the first bit of mail has been answered.

Meanwhile, my mailbox has filled up. Most of it is work-related, but there are also three emails from Olaf – two jokes and an invitation to go out for my birthday.

I send him an email back.

How did you know that my birthday was coming up?
It was on your calendar.

What are we going to do?

Surprise…

Exciting!

I begin sorting the post that is lying on my desk in big piles. Zinzy comes in, engrossed in an old file.

'Where's Renée?' I ask.

'Gone with Walter.' She perches on the edge of her desk. 'Sabine,' she says. Her expression is uncomfortable. 'I just wanted to warn you,' she says.

'About what?'

'There's some talk about you. They think that you don't show enough commitment. The fact that you only work half days and there are still tonnes of mistakes in your work is annoying people.'

I have no idea what to say. A tight band encircles my chest.

'They think you're faking it. Taking the piss.'

'I work half days on the advice of the company doctor.' After every second word I have to take a breath. 'I totally collapsed for a year. These mornings at work take up all of my energy.'

'I know,' Zinzy says, full of sympathy. 'But for a lot of people you're only sick when you're on a life support machine. If you're not, then you keep on working. That's what Renée thinks and she's getting the others on her side. What's the matter? Do you want some water?'

'Please.'

Zinzy fetches me some water and I take a couple of sips.

'Are you alright?' she asks. 'You went so pale all of a sudden.'

'I'm okay now.' I draw my chair up to my desk. 'Thanks, Zinzy.'

At the end of the morning, Walter and Renée return, laughing and chatting.

Zinzy is in the archive. When Renée sees me alone in the office, her smile falls and she sits down at her computer. She opens the envelope with the shredded letter from her in-tray.

She doesn't say a thing. I don't say anything either. The silence hangs like a lead weight between us.

It's true, there are too many mistakes in my work. I send faxes to the wrong addresses, file things in the wrong place and my memos are full of typos. I banish all the other thoughts from my brain and concentrate on my work. For a while things go okay. I double-check the faxes that I send, and make tidy piles on my desk in order of priority.

And then Roy comes flurrying in, asking in a loud voice why that courier delivery has been lying around in reception for the whole morning.

'I did ask you to pick it up, Sabine,' Renée says. Roy is looking at me, red with wound-up frustration. 'I'll get it in a minute, Roy. I should have checked whether it had been done.'

'It's not your fault,' Roy grumbles. 'You should be able to trust her to do at least one thing.'

Renée makes a soothing noise and walks out of the office. Roy goes with her. I hear their hushed voices in the corridor. My hands shake.

Zinzy and Margot work on behind their desks, their faces expressionless.

'I really can't remember her asking,' I say.

'I heard it,' Margot says, without looking up from the computer screen. 'It was when you were standing by the fax machine.'

'And she asked me? Me specifically? Did she look at me and say my name?'

Margot swivels her chair round. 'Jesus, Sabine, is that how it has to be from now on? Do we have to stand right in front of you, look you in the eyes and say your name before anything goes in?'

'Apparently,' I say.

'Then I don't understand what you're doing here.'

Zinzy gives me an apologetic look. 'You're really not focused, Sabine. Everyone has noticed.'

I bite my lip to hold back my emotions. 'There is a reason for that.'

'Still?' Margot says. 'After having stayed home for a year? Some people are just work-shy.'

Her comment hangs in the air, between the printers, computers and bulging cupboards. Just then Tessa and Luke arrive and pause. They look around and disappear just as quickly. I hear them talking in the corridor.

I walk to the toilet, turn on the tap and hold my wrists under the cold water. I can't stop shaking and I feel more and more dizzy. My head begins to pound, spots appear before my eyes and my lungs gasp for oxygen. I breathe more and more quickly and find myself more and more desperate for air. I grab a plastic bag from the bin, stumble into the toilet cubicle, collapse onto the seat and blow into the bag. In and out, in and out.

It's half an hour before I return to my work space.

'Sabine, could you come with me,' Renée says when I'm back at my computer. 'Shall we pop into the meeting room?'

'Okay.' I save the document I've just made, push my chair back, rummage in the paperwork on my desk and only then do I look up at Renée, as if I'd half forgotten her. She is already a few steps away from my desk, expecting me to have followed her. She looks back in irritation.

'What do you want to talk to me about? I don't have much time.'

'I'll tell you that in a minute,' Renée snaps.

We go into that same room in which I'd interviewed her. Renée holds open the door for me in a way that suggests I'm being taken into custody and closes it behind us. She makes the mistake of pulling out a chair and sitting on it. I go to sit on the edge of the table so that I can look down on her. This clearly annoys her but I can sit where I want after all.

'I'll get to the point straight away. I want to talk to you about your performance,' Renée says. 'I know that you were sick for a long time and it takes a while to get used to being back in the office again. That's why I gave you some time to acclimatise. It's understandable that you should take things easy at first, but what bothers me is that you continue to do so. You're more often at the coffee machine than at your desk and I've noticed that you nearly always pack your bag at a quarter past twelve. And now those sick days…'

Blood rushes inside my head and my mouth becomes dry. I have to think of a response, a retort, tear down Renée's well-constructed accusations.

'And I'm not the only one who thinks so, the others do too,' Renée says. 'And by the others I mean Margot and Zinzy. We've agreed to examine your performance and to report back in a fortnight.'

I can't believe my ears. The fury that fires up in me makes my voice sharper than I'd intended. 'Didn't you trust your own critical ability?'

'That's got nothing to do with it. We are colleagues, we work together here as a team,' Renée says. 'I was afraid you'd have a problem with my promotion. That is precisely the reason I've asked Margot and Zinzy to monitor you as well.'

It stings. It stings so much.

'Believe me, it's not what I want,' Renée says.

I wonder how she'd react if I hit her in the face. She must be enjoying this display of power against somebody who had trained her personally, who took her under her wing and taught her some French so that she wouldn't look stupid when she got a French client on the phone, who supported her against Walter.

I feel regret. Terrible regret.

'If you've got a problem with something, you should say it, Sabine,' Renée says. 'I know that you've worked here longer than me, but that doesn't mean you would have got my job if you hadn't been sick.'

'I wasn't aware for one second that your job existed.'

'We needed someone to do it and Walter thought I was the most suitable person,' Renée says. 'You'll have to learn to live with it. So, I've said what I wanted to say. Take a different approach to your work and things will be fine. We'll talk again in two weeks. Anything else to get off your chest?'

I've got so much weighing down on my chest that I can hardly bear the burden of it.

19

On Monday I'll be turning twenty-four and to get into a birth-day frame of mind, I make an apple tart the day before. I love baking. I used to bake a lot but it's a long time since I went to the trouble of peeling apples, sifting flour and breaking eggs.

I put on Norah Jones and sing along while I potter about in my kitchen. This room gets the full sun and when I heat up the oven, I have to open the door wide to keep the temperature bearable. I step onto the balcony with a tub of apples and sit down in the white basketwork beach chair to peel them.

My balcony is great. Because I don't have a garden (which I miss terribly), I've invested all my creativity in these two metres of concrete. Boxes of geraniums and fuchsias hang on the rail-ings and there's almost no room to sit down for all the terracotta pots of herbs and lavender. The sun blazes down, releasing Mediterranean smells.

I could have bought a few cakes of course but there's nothing better than using your own recipe and ingredients. Following my mother's recipe, I pour a generous shot of cognac over the chunks of apple and the raisins.

Smells have the ability to take you back to a particular period in your life. I only have to smell running shoes to be transported back to the gym, standing on the side and waiting in vain to be picked for a team. But the smell of homemade apple tart takes me back to my fourteenth birthday.

My mother prided herself on always making tarts rather than buying them. That year, we entertained the whole week because first one person and then another couldn't come, so we had guests every day and she had to keep on baking. Towards the end of the week, I couldn't bear the smell of apple tart anymore.

I'd been planning on letting my fourteenth birthday slip by unnoticed at school when something happened that changed everything.

At the beginning of the week, Isabel had a fit. She began to pull funny faces, smacking and licking her lips, and her breathing faltered. She collapsed in the middle of the school grounds. The other girls pulled back shocked, some squatted down next to her convulsing body and looked on helplessly. The whole episode lasted less than a minute, but in that time I'd laid my coat under her head and had a nearby bike taken away so that she wouldn't hurt herself on it.

I sat beside her for the whole time and spoke to her. It wasn't such a bad fit and I could see in her eyes that each reassuring word was getting through to her.

Gradually her arms and legs stopped convulsing and her whole body relaxed. I helped her to get up when she made a move to stand and gestured, as I had done for many years, to the trails of saliva in the corners of her mouth. She wiped them away. She usually preferred to get up as if nothing had happened, crack some joke about it and then go back to dominating the conversation. This time she needed quite some time to come round in Mr Groesbeek's little room.

I led Isabel to his room and wiped the cigarette ash and half-dried-up chewing gum from her denim jacket.

'Should I take you home?' Mr Groesbeek asked.

Isabel didn't want to be taken home. I stayed with her until she felt better and was given permission to miss the English lesson.

'You're a good friend,' Mr Groesbeek said.

Isabel and I didn't look at each other. We didn't speak either when Mr Groesbeek briefly left us alone. We stayed there for a full period. I kept an eye on her and got her a cup of water so that she could take her medicine. We only spoke when necessary: 'A cup of water, please.' 'Thanks.' 'Feeling better?' and 'Yes, I'm feeling better.'

Afterwards we went to maths and I was left alone for the rest of the day. I even gained a certain respect from my classmates. I didn't hear any sniggering behind my back, my books remained in my bag and my purse was still full when I went to buy a biscuit during the break. They left me alone for a whole week. I could hardly believe it. Slowly but surely I approached the edge of the group. They tolerated it.

I tested out my new position by walking out of the main entrance after school. The group stood smoking and chatting at the foot of the stairs as usual. Isabel looked up. Her eyes met mine but she didn't say anything.

The invitations to my birthday party were burning a hole in my pocket. I'd thought about posting them but found that a bit pathetic. I gathered my courage and took out the neatly addressed envelopes.

'It's my birthday next week,' I said. 'I'm having a party. See whether you can come.'

I gave them an envelope each, raised my hand in farewell and walked to my bike. I didn't dare to look around until I was leaving the school grounds. There was silence behind me.

I worried about my birthday party all week. My father did the shopping. I brooded over how I could convince him that there had to be wine and beer in order to give the party a chance of working. My parents weren't keen on alcohol. Still, my father was surprisingly understanding. He added cans of beer and a few bottles of cheap wine to the supermarket trolley and didn't complain either when I added some expensive French cheese.

On the day of the party, Robin spent hours with a couple of friends – I think I remember Olaf being there – hanging up lights in the garden and tidying up the shed so that it could be used as a bar.

They put out torches that we could light after dark, and a marquee tent in case it rained.

I was happy that Robin went out that evening.

That his friends didn't witness how dead my party was.

I would have preferred it if my parents had gone out too so that they didn't have to spend the evening hovering around me making cautious gestures.

I waited.

Nobody came.

I've bought croissants for my birthday breakfast. I put them in the oven and get dressed while the lovely smell intensifies around me. I squeeze a few oranges, pour myself a glass, and set the steaming croissants down on the table. The first one is nice, but I feel sick after the second. I leave for work earlier than I'd planned.

When it's your birthday it's customary to either bring in something tasty to eat or to circulate a list from the baker's and have the cakes delivered. I circulate the letters that need signatures, that's all.

The day is not a great success. The harder I try, the more mistakes I seem to make. My hands shake all morning and I jump each time someone says my name. It becomes harder and harder to concentrate on my work. I'm conscious of everything – a look of irritation, a repressed sigh, Roy's furtive little chat with Renée.

He goes straight to Renée after I've made a pile of photocopies, got them in the wrong order and missed out various pages. I hear them murmuring while I'm tapping coffee from the machine.

'Just give them to me,' I hear Renée say. 'It is a complicated job, Roy.'

I hear them laugh, then Roy comes into the corridor. We look each other in the face. The smile disappears from his lips and he hurries on.

At the end of the morning, I see Olaf in the corridor.

'Hey!' he calls. 'Happy birthday!'

He comes up to me, and kisses me.

'I've booked a table for us in De Klos tonight.'

The dark colours in the corridor suddenly seem to lighten. I return to the office smiling, as Roy is passing by.

'What was that about? Are you celebrating something?'

'No.' I don't give him a second glance. 'Not a thing.'

20

When I get home that afternoon I can still smell the apple tart. There's a card from my parents: *Happy Birthday. What a shame we can't celebrate together. We'll see you soon though.*

I prop the card on the mantelpiece, press play on the answering machine and hear my brother's deep voice. While I take off my coat and make tea I replay the message a few more times to have Robin's voice around me again.

While I'm washing, the phone rings. I let it go to the answering machine. It's Jeanine. 'Hey, Sabine, happy birthday! I'll come round tonight, okay? If you have other plans, ones beginning with an O perhaps, call me back. Or, no, send me a text – I'm about to go into a meeting. Oh yes, another thing – I was looking at missing.com and there's a website about Isabel. Her father set it up. I thought you might want to know.'

Did I want to know? I sink into a chair at the dining table. I pick up my mobile from next to the computer and text Jeanine

Eating 2nite with Olaf. Come 2? Will ask Zinzy as well.

It takes a while for my computer to come to life. I spot Isabel's face among the black and white photos on www.missing.com

almost instantly. I click on her photo and the circumstances of her disappearance come up on the screen. Other missing people have photos next to them of suspects who have been arrested. One in particular attracts my attention. It's a man of around thirty, blond, with a narrow face. The deep lines running between his nose and the corners of his mouth make him look prematurely aged.

I read the accompanying text. Jack van Vliet, sentenced for the murder of Rosalie Moosdijk, whom he'd raped and strangled in the dunes near Callantsoog in the summer of 1997. After that, he died in prison without confessing to the murders of other missing girls he was believed to have committed.

My eye falls on a link to the website that Isabel's father has made. I click on it.

Isabel's name appears across the full width of the screen. On the right there's the most recent photograph of her, which looks like it was taken in their back garden.

This is our daughter, Isabel Hartman. She disappeared without trace on 8 May 1995, aged fifteen. Since then we've heard nothing from her. We've set up this site in the hope that it will stir up some trace of our daughter. We'd kindly ask anyone who thinks they may know something about Isabel's disappearance to contact us.
Luke and Elsbeth Hartman.

On another page there's an account of the day on which Isabel went missing. She was last seen at two o'clock in the afternoon by her girlfriend M. After that they went their separate ways and there are no further clues.

I study the map of the route from the school to the dunes. I hear the wind in the treetops and clear, lifelike images rise up like bubbles. I'm reliving everything as if it were a film with me playing the lead role, only I've forgotten my lines.

The moss is springy underfoot, branches scrape against my skin. It's dark under the trees, but there's a clearing in front of me. I can't quite place the anxiety that comes over me. It's as if my mind is keeping a secret from me.

I'm on the edge of the sandy clearing, hidden beneath a green canopy. I take a small step forwards.

Stop.

Don't go any further!

Stop this film.

With trembling hands I shut down Isabel's website and disconnect.

In the kitchen I tell myself, just one glass. I drink slowly, my eyes closed. Then another. It is my birthday, after all. The wine slides down my throat and my anxiety is shrouded in a reassuring mist. In the sitting room I collapse, head spinning, onto the sofa.

Wine in the middle of the day; that bodes well. The solution to all my problems. As much as I'd like to stay lying down, I go back to the kitchen to make coffee. As I stand next to the percolator and watch the thin, brown stream trickling into the pot, the image holds me in its grip. I'm still in the woods, standing frozen on the edge of the clearing. I shake my head fiercely and pour myself a mug before the coffee has finished percolating.

The strong coffee brings me back. To my relief, the images recede, although I know that I'm going to have to watch this film sometime.

The phone rings. This time I pick it up straight away.

'Happy birthday to you, happy birthday to you, happy birthday, dear Sabine, happy birthday to you!' roars the voice into my ear.

I hold the telephone at a safe distance and laugh. 'Robin!'

'Are you having a good day? I can't hear the party.'

'Everybody's at work, you idiot. The party's tonight.' With three people, I fail to add.

'A shame I can't come. But I've got good news! I'll be finishing up here in ten days and then I'm coming back to Holland.'

'That's fantastic! You have no idea how quiet it is with you all away.'

'Are you coping?' He sounds concerned.

'Yes, really. I'm good.'

'What were you doing?'

'Making coffee, surfing the web.'

'Are you still working half days?'

I remain silent, weighing up how much to tell him. 'Yes.'

'What is it?'

'Nothing. What do you mean?'

'You sound a bit depressed all of a sudden.'

I can't keep anything from Robin for long. It takes up less energy coming out with the whole story than foisting him off with excuses. I give him a short summary of my glorious return to The Bank. The name Renée crops up remarkably often.

Somewhere in England, Robin sighs. 'And now?'

'I have to leave that place, Robin, and fast. But it's risky just resigning and looking for another job.'

'Yep, that's true.'

We fall silent.

'But now for a nicer subject – do you know who I've just started going out with?' I ask.

'Who?'

'Olaf. Olaf van Oirschot.'

'No! Does he live in Amsterdam?'

'Yes. He works at The Bank too. That's where we ran into each other.'

'What a coincidence,' Robin says.

'You don't sound too enthusiastic,' I say.

'We grew apart in the last year of school. I don't know what it is with Olaf but he always went just a bit further than the others,' Robin pauses. 'He wouldn't take any shit when we went out,

117

and there was always some row or other in a bar. It got to the point that there were so many fights it wasn't fun anymore. From then on I let things slide between us.'

'Oh,' I say, astonished. 'I didn't know that at all. How strange, I really didn't get the impression that Olaf was an aggressive type.'

'Perhaps it was just a phase,' Robin says. 'Maybe he's calmed down now.'

'Do you know what I've just discovered?' I say. 'Or rather what a friend told me – there's a website about Isabel.' There's a long silence. So long I feel forced to carry on talking. 'And her disappearance was recently featured on *Missing*. And there's going to be a school reunion soon. I'm thinking about it a lot, Robin.'

'Don't,' Robin sighs. 'Let it go.'

'I can't do anything about it. I'm beginning to remember things.'

Another silence. 'What exactly?'

'Oh, I don't know. Scraps I can't make much of.'

'And it's suddenly coming back? After all these years?'

'Things used to pop up before, but I've always ignored them.'

'I've always thought you knew more than you said at the time. Mum and Dad too.'

'I really don't know. Perhaps I do know more, but if it's important or not…By the way, Olaf said that you had something going with Isabel.'

'Me? God, no! What made him think that? She was a good looking girl, you know, but I knew how things were between the two of you. When I went out, I used to bump into her, but not much happened.'

'But something happened?'

'One night we kissed. I hadn't seen her for a while, it didn't really sink in who she was. When I realised, I lost interest at once. I told Olaf at the time what a bitch she was, and that she'd dump him.'

'Dump *him*? Olaf?'

'Yes, he went out with her for a while. She had quite a grip on him.'

'I didn't know anything about that. Why didn't Olaf tell me?'

'He probably didn't want to rake up the past. Don't worry about it.'

I'm not worried, but once we've hung up, the conversation leaves a nasty taste in my mouth.

'It didn't mean much,' Olaf says. 'You could hardly call it a relationship. We met up a few times, that's all. I think Robin is confusing me with Bart. Didn't Bart de Ruijter go out with Isabel for quite a long time?'

'No,' is all I manage to say.

We're out having dinner: Olaf, Jeanne, Zinzy and I. I texted Zinzy as well and now we're sitting here, all four of us. We're in a restaurant where you don't sit around tables but on a long wooden bench, at a sort of mediaeval table. I feel more at home here, in this relaxed environment surrounded by my best friends, than anywhere else in the world.

'The police spent ages questioning him because he was her last boyfriend,' Olaf adds.

'The police?' Zinzy asks.

'Did they interview many people?' I ask.

'Only the ones that Isabel hung out with. Not that much came out of it.'

There's a short silence. 'How nice that your brother's coming back,' Jeanine begins. 'You've missed him, haven't you?'

I nod. 'Robin and I have always been really close.'

'Did he know that Isabel was making your life a misery?'

'Yes. If he could he'd wait for me after school. If I finished early, I'd wait for Robin in the caretaker's room.'

'What was the name of that guy again?' Olaf wonders.

'Groesbeek,' I say.

'Groesbeek! That was it. God, that man used to give me some trouble! He always knew when I was skipping school. I think he knew our timetables off by heart.'

'Or those of the worst offenders,' Jeanine says. 'We had a Dean who seemed to know absolutely everything. It seemed like magic. He probably only read our faces, but we didn't realise it at the time.'

'I never skipped school,' Zinzy says. 'I didn't dare to.'

'I knew the menu of the snack bar on the corner off by heart,' Jeanine says.

Out of the window, a pale green van goes by. A van the same colour green as Mr Groesbeek's.

'Earth calling Sabine!' Jeanine waves a chicken leg in front of my nose. 'Are you still with us?'

I turn back to the others. 'Mr Groesbeek often used to pick us up when we were riding home in a gale force 9. He'd drive his van onto the kerb and load up our bikes. You could fit quite a few in there. Sometimes he'd go back to give other students a lift.'

'How sweet of him,' Zinzy says.

'He lived close by, didn't he?' Olaf says.

'Callantsoog.' I look out of the window again. My thoughts are darting all over the place.

The van. A dirty green.

Wasn't I just behind it, at the traffic lights? The traffic lights where I turned off, and Isabel went straight on. The van went straight as well. Yes, I was behind it. I didn't want her to see me. But how many of those vans would have been driving around in Den Helder?

'Was Groesbeek questioned by the police too?' I ask.

The conversation has already moved on to something else. Everyone pauses, surprised that I am taking them back again.

'I don't know. I don't think so. Why should he have been questioned? He was always at school during the day,' Olaf says.

'Not always,' I say. 'Sometimes he'd to take us home if we were sick, or he'd run an errand for the school.'

There's silence.

'He really had it in for people like Isabel,' Olaf says.

'Yes…' I look out of the window again.

'Who is this Isabel then?' Zinzy asks.

The next day it takes an enormous amount of will power to get on my bike, to ride to The Bank and to go inside. I walk through the revolving doors on spaghetti legs, through the hall, to the lift. The closing doors remind me of prison doors shutting, the zooming noise of the lift taking me to the ninth floor builds up until it's an alarm going off.

'Hello,' I say as I enter the office.

Renée doesn't even turn her head. Margot looks up and then refocuses on her work.

'Good morning, Sabine,' Zinzy says. 'It was nice last night, wasn't it?'

Renée looks at her in amazement. Zinzy gives her a challenging look. Thank God for Zinzy. If she wasn't there, I'd go crazy. I know how lepers must have felt in the olden days. They'll be giving me a bell next.

The whole morning there's an unearthly silence around me. Conversations fall dead when I enter a room, meaningful glances are exchanged and drafts land in my in-tray with a slap.

I return to the office with a post book full of signed letters and see Renée and Margot drinking coffee together, their heads bent towards each other. I hear my name and then Zinzy's, and then they transform before my eyes into Isabel and Miriam. The next moment the image has disappeared.

'If I can just interrupt you…I've got a book full of letters for the ten o'clock courier,' I say.

'And?' Renée says.

'Well, it's obvious. I could use some help, otherwise I won't get it done in time.'

Renée looks at her watch. 'If you go a bit faster than usual, you'll easily make it.'

I just make it, but only with a sprint to the postroom. When I return, the office is full of colleagues who've gathered around a box of cakes. Tessa is being sung to and congratulated. They've just finished when I come in.

'Where did you disappear to for so long? The postroom isn't that far,' Renée says.

She is sitting on the edge of my desk which is loaded down with horrible little jobs. Piles of faxes, illegible drafts and tapes with dictations which need typing out.

'Have a cake, Sabine,' Walter says.

The cake box is full of globs of cream and fallen bits of fruit. No cake.

'Sorry,' Tessa says. 'I must have miscounted.'

21

Mr Groesbeek used to live in Callantsoog, but these days he lives in a small street near Den Helder docks. I drive there in the afternoon on the off chance and park my car in front of the door. The houses don't have a front garden but open directly on to the street. A sign, I'M ON GUARD HERE, with a picture of a black dog, gives burglars something to think about.

J. Groesbeek is printed on the sign below this.

I ring the bell.

At first it seems like there's no one home. I ring again and then hear shuffling footsteps in the hall and a voice which grunts, 'Coming, coming.'

A key turns in the lock and the door opens. A bent figure, dressed in a dark blue jacket and grey trousers, looks at me in annoyance. That's the look. That was the look he used to give to latecomers. The wreath of grey hair has become as white as snow and has slipped even further down. His face looks like a map of rivers. He's very different to how I remember him, but it is him.

'Again? But I've just donated!'

I raise my eyebrows.

He looks at my empty hands and says, 'I thought you'd come to collect for the Asthma Society.'

'Of course not,' I say with my friendliest smile.

'They think they can milk pensioners because they're forgetful but I've got their number.'

'I'm sure you do, Mr Groesbeek,' I say.

He glares at me. 'Don't be so familiar. I don't know you. What are you here for?'

'I'd like to ask you something.'

He appraises me. 'Are you from the police or the newspaper?'

'No, absolutely not. I used to be at your school. Where you were the caretaker.'

'You don't have to tell me that. I know what I used to be.'

'Perhaps you remember me? Sabine Kroese?'

He looks at me without bothering to disguise his lack of interest.

'There's going to be a reunion soon,' I continue.

'I read about it in the paper.'

'Are you going?'

'Why should I?'

'Wouldn't it be nice to see all those students again?'

Groesbeek shrugs. 'They all know who I am. They think I'm an old fool, and who can blame them. I'll just see a load of adults I don't recognise at all. What's so nice about that?'

'You wouldn't recognise anyone?'

'There were five hundred students at that school, young lady. And each year new faces.'

'Yes,' I say.

'So...' Groesbeek says.

'I'd still like to try to refresh your memory, Mr Groesbeek. I'm collecting stories, anecdotes and special memories from people who were at the school at the same time as me. I think it would be nice to put all that together in a book that people could look through at the reunion.'

Groesbeek looks at me with disinterest.

'May I come in?'

He shrugs again, turns around and shuffles into the hall. He leaves the door wide open which I take as an invitation. I follow Groesbeek into the sitting room. It's small and stuffy with its dark furniture and there's an indefinable smell which makes me want to throw open a window. Then I see where the smell is coming from – cats.

Not one or two but, five, no six cats, curled up in the corners or walking along the window seat. There's one on the coffee table and another comes up to me and nudges me with its head. I'm allergic to cats. If one touches my skin, I come out in itchy spots.

'Would you like a cup of tea?' Groesbeek asks.

'Please.' I shove the cat aside with my foot.

Groesbeek trudges to the kitchen and stays there forever, clattering cups and a gas kettle. I sit down in the chair nearest the door.

The cat jumps up into my lap all the same and gives me a penetrating stare. I push it off with my bag. It miaows in complaint and looks at me accusingly. That's what I find so irritating about cats – that look in their eyes.

'Kssst,' I hiss.

The cat jumps onto the coffee table, just as Groesbeek shuffles in with two china tea cups. He puts them down on the table and takes a kitsch sweet tin from the dresser. Greying chocolates garnished with a layer of dust. Thanks but no thanks.

'Sure?' Groesbeek places the tin on the coffee table. '*You* want them though don't you?' he says to the cat on the table. The animal inspects the contents of the tin, licks at them and then turns away.

'So,' Groesbeek says. 'You're called Susanne.'

'Sabine. You often helped me when I had problems. You repaired my tyre, you gave me a lift when the wind was too strong.' I hesitate. 'And you let me slip out via your office when they were lying in wait for me.'

Groesbeek doesn't say anything. He picks up his cup of tea, sips, and looks at me over the rim.

'Don't you remember anymore?' I ask.

He puts down his tea and strokes the cat, which is in the middle of the table next to my cup. Hairs whirl downwards.

'I might have,' he says. 'Yes, I might have done that.'

'It made a big difference to me, you know that?' I say. For a while I think he's noticed that I'm sucking up to him, but for the first time a smile replaces his defensive look.

'Your tea's getting cold,' he says. 'Are you sure you don't want a chocolate?'

'No, really not. Thank you.'

The cat sniffs around the chocolates once again, until Groesbeek lifts it down from the table. 'Get away, Nina, those aren't for you.' He chuckles at me and I smile back.

'To be honest I've forgotten a lot of the past,' Groesbeek says. 'I know that I haven't got a screw loose, but I forget things. If somebody is coming to visit today, or if it's tomorrow. If I've already sent my grandchildren their birthday cards. Or where I've put my pillbox.'

He stops talking and strokes two cats who've jumped up onto his lap. His grey trousers are slowly covered in white and black hairs. 'It's difficult sometimes, Susanne. Do you understand? No, of course you don't. You're still too young.'

'I understand better than you think, Mr Groesbeek.'

'Sometimes I sit on the sofa and wait for my wife to call me for dinner,' Mr Groesbeek says. He nods at a photograph in a silver frame on the dresser. 'That's Antje. She's been dead five years. No, six.' He knits his brows, does some mental arithmetic, frowns again and strokes the cats. 'Approximately,' he says.

'Do you still remember Isabel? The girl who went missing?'

'No, her name's Antje,' Groesbeek corrects.

'I mean one of the students, Isabel Hartman.'

'Hartman,' Groesbeek repeats.

'She was in my class.'

'Oh?'

'She had epilepsy. You once took her home after a fit.'

'I saw something on the TV about that recently, epilepsy. It's terrible, if you have that.'

'Do you remember her?'

'I can only remember faces, not names.'

I take a photo of Isabel out of my bag and lay it on the table. Groesbeek looks at it, but his expression remains the same. One of the cats jumps off his lap onto the table, onto the photo. I pull it out from under its front paws and give it to Mr Groesbeek.

'Terrible,' he says.

'What is? What's terrible?'

Groesbeek makes a useless gesture with his hands. He opens his mouth as if he's about to say something, changes his mind and frowns once again. 'It's terrible,' he says at last.

'What is terrible, Mr Groesbeek?'

'Epilepsy. It looked like she was going to die.' He illustrates this by screwing up his face and opening his eyes wide.

'Did you see her look like that?' I can't remember Isabel ever having had a fit in Mr Groesbeek's presence.

Mr Groesbeek turns his attention to the cat which is still on his lap.

'Cats are wonderful creatures,' he says proudly. 'They're my best friends. But they can't come with me to the retirement home. *No, you're not allowed.*' His voice turns high-pitched, the tone that mothers use to speak to their babies.

'You do know that Isabel disappeared? She went missing without a trace?' I change tack, hold the photo up high, in case he's already forgotten what we were talking about.

'Do you hear that, Nina?' Groesbeek says to his cat. 'Just like Liz. We haven't ever seen her again, have we?'

I let the photo drop.

'Gone is gone,' Mr Groesbeek says.

'Yes,' I say.

'Sometimes you never find them again. Then they're dead.'

I zip up my bag and look at my watch.

'I have to go now. Thank you for your time, and…'

'It's no use looking,' Mr Groesbeek says. 'They've been really well hidden.'

'Goodbye Mr Groesbeek. Nice to see you again. I'll let myself out.'

I stand up and glance in passing at the back garden. It's an overgrown jungle between three high fences. The grass has grown tall and big piles of soil that look like giant molehills line the fence.

Mr Groesbeek sees me looking and says, 'Antje is dead.'

I nod and walk to the door. At once four cats come up to me and join me as I go into the hall. Mr Groesbeek stands up.

'Belle and Anne, stay here!' He chases the cats back into the living room and closes the dividing door. We're alone in the hall.

'How many cats have you got?' I ask.

'Six,' he says. 'I'm a cat person. Some people are dog people, others are cat people. I hate dog people. Which are you?'

He stands too close to me. Far too close. I can smell his old man stink. I can see the flakes on his bald scalp. He stands between me and the front door.

I smile weakly. 'I'm mad about cats.'

He nods, satisfied and steps aside. I rush past him.

'Come again sometime!' he calls.

I drive to the corner of the street and get out again. I feel ridiculous as I creep into a dark alleyway and sneak around the back of the housing block. I count the houses until I'm standing in front of Mr Groesbeek's back garden. I try the rickety gate; it's locked. I contemplate the fence, but the planks look too rotten to climb up. The container next to the gate makes a more suitable step. It's a little bit high but if I lay it on its side I can just see over the fence. What a wilderness. If Antje was the gardener it's clear she's been dead a few years. There really aren't any flowers in the garden, just weeds, even the mounds are overgrown with them. The mounds of soil puzzle me. Are they borders?

A boy on a bike rides down the alley and looks at me so surprised that I jump down from the container. I set it back upright, smile at the boy who is looking back over his shoulder, and walk back to my car. My arms and legs itch. I scratch and red spots appear. Ideally I'd drive home, take a shower and rinse off all this cat hair but I'm not done here yet.

In the car, even though I've opened the windows, the smell of the cats persists.

'You should have telephoned,' the lady from the *Helder News* complains. 'Then I could have got the information ready for you.'

'I'm sorry,' I say. 'I didn't know. Can I take a look at it now? I've come all the way from Amsterdam especially.'

The woman pulls a resigned face, and picks up the telephone.

'Nick? The cuttings file with the missing persons – can you send it up?'

She listens to the answer and hangs up. 'If you'll just wait fifteen minutes…'

'Sure. I'll go outside for a cigarette. Just give me a shout.'

She looks as if she's going to say she's got better things to do, but then nods. I go outside and light up my last cigarette. I try to wipe as much cat hair off my skirt as possible. After ten minutes there's a tap at the window. I go inside and follow the woman to a room with long rows of hanging archive files. Along the side there are tables where you can study the files. A young man sets a thick one down on the table.

'That's your one. All of the missing persons cases from the past twenty years.'

The woman and the young man leave me on my own. I open the file and a musty waft of print and old paper rises up.

Murdered girl found

No trace of 16-year-old Anne-Sophie

Lizette, where are you? Emotional plea from parents of missing girl

I study all of the yellowed cuttings. Most of them are from years and years ago, but the uniformity of the panic and the incomprehension hits me. I look at the smiling faces in the photos, at the out-of-date hairstyles, at how young they look, and how confident.

Since 1980 at least ten girls have gone missing – three in Den Helder and close by. Four girls were never found, the others were murdered. Raped and strangled. Only one of the girls' murderers was found – Jack van Vliet raped and strangled sixteen-year-old Rosalie Moosdijk in the dunes near Callantsoog in the summer of 1997. He was picked up after six months of intensive detective work and confessed. Yes, I remember that, but from where? I read something about that recently. Then it comes to me – there was a piece on the internet about Jack van Vliet. It was in the newspaper articles on Isabel's website.

I leaf through knowing what I'll find but I still get a shock when I see Isabel's face in black and white. I look at her for a while, then pick up the article about Rosalie Moosdijk. She disappeared in the summer of 1997 and went to the same school as us. Could there be a connection? The police thought so; that's why the article about Jack van Vliet was on Isabel's website. There was probably too little evidence to pin anything on him.

I start when the young man walks past me unexpectedly.

'Can I copy these cuttings?'

He nods at a photocopier in the corner. 'Ten cents a copy.'

I pick up the pile and get to work. I'll read through everything at my own pace at home. It's quite likely that a number of the girls were attacked by the same person. Perhaps I'll find a link between all of these cases. The copies glide into the sorting tray.

Police ask public to join in search for Nina

Missing Isabel still a conundrum to the police

Search for Lizette at a standstill

While the photocopier does its job, I scan the articles. Three more of the missing girls were at the same secondary school as me – Nina, Lydia and Isabel. The other girls were not from Den Helder but from the north part of the county, suggesting that the perpetrator lived in the same area.

I put my copies in my bag. As I go outside, I feel them burning through the leather – it's as if the headlines are screaming the answer at me.

22

I've just left Den Helder when it hits me. Without thinking, I go to hit the brakes but stop myself in time. I look in my rear view mirror and see no vehicles behind me; there's nothing oncoming either. Time to do something rash.

I do a U-turn. The tyres go onto the shoulder slightly but then I'm on the right side of the road. Back to Den Helder.

My God, I was there in the house. I asked questions about Isabel and not only that, I pressed the point. And he let me go. Has he really forgotten? Is that what saved me?

I break out in a sweat. I can't sort this out on my own. I've got to go to the police. However reluctant I am, I have to tell them about this. But I first have to double-check.

I park my car again on the corner of the street, out of sight and walk along the pavement to number seven. Mr Groesbeek's neighbour opens the door. She's an elderly lady with carefully tended grey hair and a sweet grandmotherly face. She's got grandchildren she spoils terribly, I think, or otherwise she'd really like some.

'Yes?' she says.

I look at the name plate on the door. 'You're Mrs Takens?' I ask.

'Yes?'

I smile. 'I've just visited your neighbour, Mr Groesbeek. He used to be the caretaker at my old school and I'm compiling a book with anecdotes from the time.'

'Oh, how nice.'

'I'm writing a piece about Mr Groesbeek because so many of the former pupils remember him.'

'I couldn't tell you anything about him, you know,' Mrs Takens says. 'What Joop wants to tell, he'll tell you himself. I wouldn't want gossip about him to be published.'

'Oh, no, that's not my intention at all. Mr Groesbeek has told me enough, it's not that. What it's about is the cats. I found it so funny that he's got so many of them.'

'Yes,' Mrs Takens says.

'And that he's given them names of his old pupils. That's so original! I wanted to list them in my article.'

'And now you want to know what his cats are called? Why don't you ask him himself?'

'He's asleep,' I say. 'We had to finish our conversation because he was so tired and I don't want to bother him any more. I thought that you, as his neighbour, would certainly know what his cats were called. I think one of them is called Nina.'

'Yes, and there's one called Anne, and Lydia, and Belle.'

'Belle?' I take out my diary and write down the names.

'Apart from that I'm not really sure. There are so many of them.' Mrs Takens concentrates. 'He stands there every evening calling them, but right now I can't think of them. Oh yes, Rose. But the last one I really can't recall.'

'That doesn't matter, I'll call round at Mr Groesbeek's another time. Thank you so much, Mrs Takens.'

'It's a pleasure. Good luck with your article.' Mrs Takens closes the door.

In the car I take out the copies of the newspaper cuttings from my bag and read through them. Not all of the headlines give the names of the missing girls, but they are in the articles themselves, of course. I write them down, next to the names in my diary. Straight afterwards, I drive to the police station.

The police station has disappeared. It used to be in the middle of the town. I went there once to report my bike stolen, after the yearly carnival. The bike was leaning against the police station wall. I see myself and Lisa going in again. The poster of Isabel on the pinboard in the waiting room. All those missing faces.

I got to know Lisa in Year 12, the summer after Isabel disappeared. She came to sit next to me and we got on immediately. That whole class was like a breath of fresh air, friendly and with no obvious rule-led clique. A year without Isabel's tormenting had brought about a complete metamorphosis in me. The rest of the group left me alone after she disappeared.

When you're young, you feel compelled to show just one personality from all of the possibilities in your deck. They're all there, hidden under your skin, but the circumstances affect which 'you' is brought out. For years I showed Sabine One and repressed Sabine Two, although she screamed out for attention. In the last year of school all the attention was on her. Sabine Two was witty in class. She talked back to teachers almost to the point of rudeness but still had them laughing. With her exuberance and loudness, Sabine Two was a popular girl. Lisa was exactly the same and together we wrought havoc at the school. It was a wonderful time but halfway through the year, Lisa moved and we quickly lost touch.

I drive around, spot a pedestrian and wind down my window.

'Could you tell me where the police station is?'

The middle-aged woman stops and leans in through my window. 'Yes, it's on Bastion Drive. That's quite far from here, you know,' she says, and explains how to get there.

I thank her and turn around. I know Bastion Drive well, it's not far from Lange Vliet. Ten minutes later I park my car in front of a particularly beautiful building. I admire the stream-lined facade before going in.

It's not busy. There's only one man in front of me, come to report that his car has been damaged. I'm prepared to wait patiently until he's given his lengthy account, but before that, another police officer gestures me over.

'I've come to report something,' I say.

The officer gets out a form. 'What kind of thing do you want to report?'

'It might sound a bit strange, but it's about a missing persons case from nine years ago. Isabel Hartman. Does the name mean anything to you?'

The officer nods but doesn't speak. She looks at me attentively.

'I went to school here,' I continue. 'Isabel Hartman was in my class. She went missing a long time ago, but I think I've got some new information.'

The officer, her colleague and the man with the damaged car all look at me.

I look back.

'Well,' the officer says. 'Do you know who's looking after the Hartman case these days? Fabienne?'

'Rolf,' her colleague answers.

'Do you have a moment?' the officer asks me.

I nod and she walks off. After a while she returns and gestures for me to follow her. She opens the door to a small room. 'Would you wait in here? Mr Hartog will join you shortly. He's just getting the file.'

'Fine.' I settle in and wait.

It's not long before the door swings open and a man comes in. I guess that this is Rolf Hartog and that he's an inspector if he's in charge of Isabel's case. He's tall and dark with a few unsightly spots on his neck. Probably unmarried, otherwise his wife would

135

have told him that his mint green tie clashes with his pale blue shirt. He's carrying a large file.

He holds out his other hand and introduces himself. 'Rolf Hartog. And you are…?'

'Sabine Kroese.'

'I can't offer you a chair since you've already got one.' He smiles at his own joke and I smile back. 'Would you like coffee?'

'Please.'

He puts the file down on the table and goes out. It is so long before he returns that I regret agreeing to the coffee. The file is so close, tantalising me. I'm just reaching for it when the door opens again.

'I'm sorry it took so long. The coffee tin was empty.' Rolf Hartog puts the coffees on the table and sits down opposite me.

'Go on then, Miss Kroese. I believe you have new information about the disappearance of Isabel Hartman?'

'Possible new information,' I correct. 'In any case, it seemed important enough for me to report it.'

'I'm curious. I've had a quick look through the dossier, even though I know it very well. You say you were a friend of Isabel Hartman, but I didn't come across your name in the file.'

'We weren't friends, but we were in the same class. We had been friends once but we'd grown apart,' I say. 'In primary school Isabel and I hung out with each other but at secondary school we stopped. At the time she went missing we didn't have anything to do with each other anymore. But her disappearance has always bothered me. We'd know each other so long…'

Hartog nods. 'That's understandable.'

'There's going to be a reunion soon,' I continue. 'Perhaps that's why I've been thinking about Isabel. I dream about her. I remember things I'd forgotten years ago. And then I suddenly remembered about Mr Groesbeek.'

I give Hartog a probing look, but his expression gives nothing away. 'I'm wondering whether he was ever questioned.'

'Yes,' Hartog says, without needing to open the file.

'Oh, and what came out of it?'

'Miss Kroese, what is the new information you were talking about?'

'It's to do with Mr Groesbeek. He was the caretaker at our school. He was a nice man, but quite strange. Very loud and gruff, but…' I hesitate. Hartog nods and I continue. 'He was a bit odd. I never knew whether to feel safe when I was on my own with him, you know. It wasn't that he did anything to me but there was always a possibility. He used to give students a lift to school in his van when the weather was bad.'

There's silence. Hartog coughs into his hand, leafs through his file and says, 'We know that, yes. That was the reason we interviewed him, but Mr Groesbeek said that he was at the school the whole day when Isabel disappeared. Various teachers and students can vouch for that.'

'Mr Groesbeek was always round and about in the school building. He'd move between various locations. One minute he'd be in his office, the next he'd be tearing off in his van. It was impossible to say for sure where he was.'

Hartog checks the file. 'Isabel Hartman left the school at ten past two. Between two and three, Mr Groesbeek was spotted at various times around the school building.'

'Around the school building. That's not one place. He could have nipped out at some point.'

Hartog leans back in his chair and closes the file. He stretches his back as if he's tired.

'Miss Kroese, what is the information you've come here about?'

'I was riding behind Isabel the day she disappeared.'

At once I have his full attention. The exhaustion disappears from his eyes and he puts his arms on the table and leans towards me.

'She was riding with Miriam Visser,' I tell him. 'I thought she

137

was going home with her. Miriam lived somewhere near the Jan Verfailleweg, I'm not sure exactly where. But Isabel carried on, towards the Dark Dunes. She was meeting someone by the snack bar at the main entrance.'

Now Hartog is all ears. 'Did you see who she was meeting?'

'No,' I say. 'I turned off earlier because I didn't feel like riding alongside Isabel.'

Hartog looks at me silently for a few seconds and opens the file again. He spends a while studying its contents and I peer with him. I see the name *Miriam Visser* a few times.

'For years we've thought that Miriam Visser was the last person to see Isabel Hartman alive,' he says. 'But in actual fact it was you.'

'No,' I say. 'It was whoever she was meeting.'

Hartog nods. 'Of course, if we assume that we're dealing with a crime. Around that time, let's say between half past two and three o'clock, did you see anyone you knew at the snack bar?'

'Not at the snack bar, I wasn't there, but at the crossroads where I turned off.'

Hartog clicks out his pen. 'Which crossroads was that?'

'At the intersection between Jan Verfailleweg and Seringen Avenue. That's where I turned off.'

Hartog makes a note. 'And who did you see there?'

'I didn't so much see someone as something. A green delivery van, a very dirty one. It was exactly the kind of van that Mr Groesbeek drove.'

Hartog leafs through his file and reads for a while. 'What time was it approximately when you reached the traffic lights?'

'I don't know,' I say. 'But I know I rode home as soon as school finished. Not that quickly, but I'd say we must have been there around half past two.'

Hartog continues to look into his file. 'At that time, Mr Groesbeek was collecting the empty coffee flasks from the sports hall where the exams had taken place.'

'You mustn't count on my timing exactly. He could easily have driven there afterwards. I remember him overtaking me.'

Hartog claps the file shut. 'Thank you for your information, Miss Kroese. We'll certainly look into it. We now know which direction Isabel Hartman was going. That could be important.'

He doesn't sound like he finds it important.

'That's not what I came to tell you,' I say. 'I mean, that too, but it wasn't the reason I came here.'

Hartog lays his hands in resignation on the file. 'What else did you want to tell us?'

'Mr Groesbeek has got six cats.'

Hartog stares at me.

'Six cats,' I repeat. 'I went round to his house this afternoon, you see. That's why I'm covered in cat hair.'

Hartog opens his mouth to speak, but I get there before him.

'Most people give their cats stereotypical names,' I say. 'Ginger, Fluffy, Blackie, you know. But Mr Groesbeek is more original than that. Much more original than you'd expect from that sort of a man. What were their names again?'

Hartog listens with the face of somebody who has had to listen to crazy stories for years on end and can no longer work up any enthusiasm for them.

'Miss Kroese…'

'No, wait a minute.' I fish my diary out of my bag, even though I know the names by heart. 'These are the names of the cats: Nina, Liz, Anne, Lydie, Rose and Belle.'

I take the pile of copies out of my bag and push them across the table towards Hartog. 'You'll certainly be familiar with these missing cases, the names of the victims too. Nina, Lizette, Anne-Sophie, Lydia, Rosalie and Isabel…'

Hartog looks at the papers, but doesn't touch them. He knows these names, I see it in his face. 'You've got good powers of observation,' he says finally. 'I must compliment you on that. But it doesn't mean anything, of course.'

'It doesn't mean anything? Groesbeek has named his cats after those girls, or in any case, given them the names of people who have then been abducted!'

'That's not an offence.'

'But it is rather remarkable. Too remarkable.'

Hartog reclines in his chair a little.

'Hmm,' he says.

I straighten up. 'What are you going to do now?'

'There's no law against naming your pets after missing persons you've seen on the news. At the most, it is remarkable, as you call it, but it is also not that extraordinary. It's getting more common for people who are affected by the news to react in this way. Especially old people. They haven't got anything other to do than watch television and follow everything that happens in their area. Often that's the only link they have to the outside world, which they feel cut off from.'

'Mr Hartog, Isabel went missing nine years ago, Lydia van der Broek five years ago. Those are the most recent cases. The other girls have all been missing for much longer. Now if they were more recent cases, I'd agree with you. But now...'

'According to you, Rose must be for Rosalie,' Mr Hartog interrupts me. 'That's the only name that fits. And Rosalie Moosdijk was found a month after she disappeared.'

'I know,' I say. 'She was strangled by Jack van Vliet.'

Hartog raises an eyebrow. 'You've done your homework,' he says. 'Then you can see for yourself that Mr Groesbeek hasn't got anything to do with Rosalie Moosdijk's death. Jack van Vliet admitted murdering her.'

'Perhaps Jack van Vliet wasn't working alone,' I suggest. 'Only Rosalie has been found. If he's also guilty of killing the other missing girls, he surely can't have operated on his own. He probably had an accomplice. Somebody who came into contact with girls of that age, somebody who could get them into his van without suspicion.' I shuffle to the edge of my chair.

'Those are all suppositions,' Hartog counters.

'Doesn't an investigation begin with suppositions? You have to have something to investigate, haven't you?'

Hartog discreetly checks his watch but remains patient. 'Investigations get a lot of attention, Miss Kroese. They shake things up at the time, and they're regularly dusted off with yet another program on television which brings back memories for people. Those programs are watched by lots of people and they get people thinking. Especially old people, like I said. It's more common than you think.'

I don't say anything for a while, drink my coffee and think it over. Rosalie Moosdijk was murdered in Callantsoog, where Groesbeek lived. Is there a connection or did he just feel really drawn to the case? So intensely that he even named his cat after her? It's quite possible he knew Rosalie. But what about the girls who didn't come from Callantsoog and weren't at his school?

'There has to be a link,' I say. 'Perhaps it is getting more common, but I still find it strange that Mr Groesbeek of all people named his cats after those missing girls. Half of those girls went to my school!'

'I find it remarkable, I must admit, but I think you're going too far when you accuse him of being a criminal.' Hartog's tone is that of someone who wants to stay reasonable, but is wondering when the conversation will end.

'You can find out whether he had any connection with Jack van Vliet,' I insist. 'Do you know what you should do? Go and look in Mr Groesbeek's back garden sometime. It's full of strange mounds of earth.'

Hartog says nothing, just looks at me like he's never come across anyone like me before. 'We'll certainly direct our attention to it, Miss Kroese, but don't expect too much.'

'In what way?' I insist.

'What?'

'In what way are you going to direct your attention to it?'

Hartog lifts up his hands in surrender. 'We'll talk to Mr Groesbeek.'

'Isn't it enough for a search warrant?' I push. 'Aren't you going to dig up his back garden?'

'I'm afraid not.'

'He's forgetful. You won't get far by just talking.'

'We can't do much more than that, I'm afraid.'

23

I spend the first day of the bank holiday with Jeanine. When I turn into my street that evening, Olaf is standing in front of my door. I beep and he comes over to the car and waits until I've parked.

'Hi,' he says when I open the door.

'That's lucky! I've been out the whole day.'

'I know,' Olaf says. 'I've come round a few times.'

'Why didn't you call me?'

'I did call you. A few times, but you didn't answer. Why was your mobile switched off?'

'Was it off?' I fish my mobile out of my bag and look at the display. 'You're right. How silly of me.' I smile as I open the downstairs door but Olaf stares at me.

'What is it?' I ask.

'Nothing.' He pushes the door open and precedes me up the stairs.

'You don't really think I turned it off deliberately? Why would I do that?' I say to his back.

'I don't know,' Olaf says. 'Maybe you needed a day to yourself.'

I really don't know how to respond. On the one hand I find his jealous behaviour rather funny, on the other hand it annoys me. I open the door to my flat and we go inside. 'Do you want a drink?'

In response, he pulls me towards him. With his arm around my waist he looks at me. 'Sabine…'

I look up at him.

'Is everything alright between us?' His breath mixes with my own. I feel a pinching grip around my waist.

'Yes,' I say, surprised. 'Of course.'

His breathing speeds up. He bends towards me and kisses me, but it's not a nice kiss. It's too hard, too aggressive. He manoeuvres me in the direction of my bedroom, I push him away. A flash of anger crosses his face and I begin to feel uneasy.

'Do you want a drink?' I offer again.

'No.' With gentle pressure he pushes me into my bedroom and undoes my bra under my top.

'Olaf, I don't want to.' I fend him off. 'I've had a long day. Let's just have a drink and watch telly.'

He shoves me so that I fall down onto the bed. 'What's going on?'

'Nothing, I'm just tired. Can't we just kiss for a bit? Open a bottle of wine?' Actually I'd rather he left but something in his eyes stops me from asking him to go.

Olaf looks at me for a long time. 'Okay,' he says at last.

I get off the bed and go into the kitchen. Wrestling with the corkscrew, I think about Olaf's strange behaviour. He's jealous, I conclude. He's terrified of being dumped, just because I've been away for the day and had my mobile switched off. Jesus.

With an irritated tug, I pull the cork out of the bottle and take it to the sitting room. Olaf has got two glasses ready on the table and sits with his arms spread over the back of the sofa. He still looks grumpy and I feel like sitting somewhere else. But I sit next to him and let him kiss me. Now he is sweet and tender again, but I can't readjust so easily. I extricate myself and fill the two glasses.

When the bottle is almost empty, Olaf is in a good mood again and clings to me drowsily.

'You know, sometimes I wish I believed in God,' he says with a bit of a slur in his voice.

'Where did that come from?'

'Nowhere in particular.'

'Why do you wish you believed in God then?'

'Because the Catholic faith offers a lot of support. And forgiveness.'

'And what terrible sin do you need forgiveness for?' I ask, amused.

He draws his cigarettes from his pocket. He lights up and blows the smoke up towards the ceiling.

I can't stand cigarette smoke in my home. I do smoke sometimes, but always outside or in a café. This is not really the moment to bring it up though. I put up with the smell and look at Olaf with a smile on my face.

'So tell me, what dark secrets are you keeping from me?'

He inhales deeply. 'I've done something awful.'

'What?'

He shakes his head and looks away.

'We all do things we later regret,' I say.

'But that's the point, I don't regret it,' Olaf says.

'Oh.' I'm daunted by this for a moment. 'Well, then you don't need to worry about it, do you? It can't be that bad.'

'Sometimes it's difficult to see the consequences of things you do. Things get out of hand and you'd best keep them to yourself. No one would understand that you didn't mean it that way. No one. That's why it's so serious.'

A chill creeps up my legs. Goose bumps appear on my arms.

Olaf turns to me and uses a finger to wipe a lock of hair away from my face. 'Apart from you,' he says. 'You would understand.'

I don't want him to sit so close to me, so close that I can't get away. I don't want his face so close to me. I don't want him to kiss me, or his hands to stroke me.

What in God's name does he mean? What has he done that he feels so sorry about? Do I really want to know?

'I must go,' Olaf says unexpectedly. He stands up, goes to the toilet and pees without closing the door. I want to get up so that I see him out but I change my mind. It might seem too eager. I remain on the sofa and pour the last bit of wine into my glass. Olaf finishes and goes into the hall.

'So, see you tomorrow at work then,' I say with false cheer.

'Have you forgotten it's bank holiday weekend? We've still got another day,' Olaf says.

'Oh, yeah. That's good.'

'What are you planning on doing?' Olaf asks.

'Oh, I don't know. Have a bit of a lie-in.'

'And after that?'

'We could do something,' I say.

'We'll see,' Olaf says. 'I'll call you, alright?'

'Okay.' I stand up with the glass of wine still in my hand, kiss Olaf and let him out. When the door closes behind him, I breathe deeply, in and out.

24

Olaf doesn't call. I spend the whole bank holiday Monday waiting for a phone call that doesn't come. On Tuesday I ride through the morning sunshine to work. When I walk into my office, the conversation stops.

Renée and Margot, and even Zinzy, look at me as if I've caught them out. I look from one to the other, don't say anything and turn my computer on. With as much calm as I can muster, I go to the coffee machine in the corridor. Zinzy comes over at once.

'I wasn't joining in,' she says with a grave expression.

'Okay.' I'm not sure what to think. I can imagine that Zinzy wouldn't want to openly take my side, but if it had been me I would have turned away and carried on working. I avoid Zinzy's eyes and say that I'm going to get a biscuit from the vending machine.

On my way to the lift, I bump into Ellis Ruygveen from the HR department. 'You look happy,' she says with a grin.

I pull my mouth into the semblance of a smile.

'Still got problems with Renée?' she asks.

I look at her surprised.

'Walter talked to Jan about it,' she says.

Jan Ligthart is the head of HR. So they know about it too. I look away from her, tired of this.

'Not everyone is as enthusiastic about Renée as your boss,' Ellis says. 'She applied to work in HR but I don't think much of her.'

'She applied…?'

'I'm pregnant.' Ellis smiles.

My eyes travel to her stomach, which is indeed much larger.

'I want to come back part-time,' Ellis continues, 'and given that we already needed extra help in HR, we're looking for someone to join us full-time.'

'And Renée applied for that position?' I free myself from the wall of the lift and look at Ellis with great interest. 'Do you think she'll get the job?'

'God forbid. I'd rather work with you, Sabine. Are you interested in applying?'

The blood rushes through my veins in top gear. 'Yes,' I say. 'I'd definitely like to.'

'Well then, write a letter. Today. Renée is the only suitable candidate, apart from you.'

'I'm not that suitable. Renée is head of the department.'

'Head?'

'Yes.'

'Where did you get that from?' Ellis asks. 'That position doesn't exist. That's typical Walter, making up a position like that. He's done that before, dangling carrots in front of their noses. It's a load of bullshit.'

We look at each other. Suddenly the day doesn't seem so long anymore.

'Now that you're working full-time again, I want to make a few things clear,' Renée says, her hands folded on top of her desk. 'Your manner and the effort you make had better drastically improve and you…Are you listening?'

'What?' I stare at my computer screen.

'I was saying that your manner had better drastically improve. And I think…'

'I feel like a coffee,' I say, and shunt my chair backwards. 'You too?'

She looks at me speechless. In the hall I pour myself a cup of coffee with malicious pleasure. When I return, Renée is still sitting in the same position.

'Sabine,' she says. 'We were having a conversation.'

'No, you were going on at me,' I say. 'That's something quite different. And officially you've got fuck all to say to me, so I'm not planning on listening to you. Get it?'

I squeeze in behind my computer and take a sip of coffee.

Renée stands up. 'I'm going to speak to Walter,' she says.

I smile.

When it's past six and everyone's leaving, I hang back. As soon as I'm alone, I write an application letter and a CV. I print them out, delete the documents, put the two sheets into an envelope and walk to the HR department. Ellis has already left. Jan's jacket is hanging over his chair, but he's not at his desk. I put the letter on his keyboard and go home.

That evening Olaf calls and I tell him about my application.

'You'll get the job,' he says.

'You sound a bit sure of yourself,' I laugh.

'I am. If the choice is between you or Renée, isn't it obvious who'll get the job? Don't think she'll stand in your way.'

I hope he's right. He doesn't say why he didn't call, and I don't ask.

They are still there, flashbacks, fragments of memories, images out of the darkest depths of my mind. They come over me at the strangest moments and I don't stop them anymore. That's what I've been doing all this time, I realise. But it's so long ago. Now I'm older, I must be able to get through this.

And then I feel the wind in my hair.

My arms rest on the handlebars of my bike. I pedal like I'm possessed, hear my own panting breath, feel the lack of oxygen in my lungs. Fear is chasing me like a sudden squall. I can't go on much longer. Each time a flashback invades my vision, I shake my head and pedal as hard as I can.

I come home to an empty house. Robin's moped is not in front of the door and neither is the car – my mother has just left for the hospital.

I climb the stairs, to my bedroom. I've buried what I've seen behind a thick, defensive mist. But the fear and desperation remain and nestle deep in my heart.

I walk around in circles, barely conscious of what I'm doing. Only when the mist dissolves and my teenage bedroom gives way to my familiar flat, do I stop.

I study myself in the vintage mirror hanging above my dressing table.

I don't look like a young woman with a weighty secret. Perhaps if you look into my eyes where there's no spark of life. Eyes are the windows to the soul. I press my nose against the glass and look. The blue eyes look back without relinquishing their secrets.

'You shouldn't look for solutions to problems, but causes,' my psychologist said when I was still being treated. 'Your unconscious contains all the answers, all your motivations are there. You need to become conscious of your inner self. I know for sure that there's something hidden in that unconscious of yours, but I can't get to it. Not without your consent.'

At the time I'd let her speech flow over me, but now it comes back to me word for word. My flat becomes suffocatingly small. I grab my bag, run down the stairs and wheel my bike outside.

It's nice weather. Hot. The outside air and the sun on my face do me some good, the pain in my chest subsides and the noise of the city is reassuringly familiar.

I dismount in front of the public library on the Prinsengracht and use all three locks to secure my bike. If I can find answers to my questions anywhere it's in the library; there's a psychology section that will keep me busy until closing time. The books I look through are about the workings of the memory. I read, copy, choose what to borrow and go home with a whole stack of books.

I settle on the balcony with a cup of tea and begin to read. *Where is the consciousness located?* is the title of the first chapter. I was wondering that too. I read about the cerebral cortex, nerve cells and the lobes of the brain, but it seems you can't deal with this kind of problem in such a biological way. Consciousness is a neurological process. It's like a piece of music, with contributions from all corners of the stage, according to American neurologist Antonio Damasio. Imagine an orchestra with many musicians. Where is the music located exactly?

I'm less interested in this. I leaf through until I find something more appealing to me.

Memory.

I read with interest. 'Memories are constructions; they grow and mature as our lives progress. Be on your guard against the certitude of "I remember it like it happened yesterday,"' warns the writer.

And a few pages further: "That memories sometimes need a prompt, was something William James realised in the nineteenth century. "Suppose I am silent for a moment, and then say in a commanding voice: 'Remember!' Does your memory obey the order, and produce a definite image from your past? Certainly not. It stands staring into space, and asks, 'What *kind* of a thing do you wish me to remember?" It needs in short, a *cue*. The memory doesn't recall to order, but allows itself to be guided by stimuli. It's no use asking the memory what prompted it, it can seldom identify the hidden hint.'

I leaf through, my eyes flying over the lines.

'When we begin to search the memory for something we've forgotten, we enter a strange psychic realm called repression. The idea of repression derives from a certain strength of the spirit. Supporters of this theory believe in the ability of the spirit to defend itself against emotionally overwhelming events by removing certain experiences and emotions from the consciousness.'

The book feels heavy in my hands.

'Our mind seems to open doors, or in fact to close them. This occurrence is called amnesia. Part of the memory, the explicit memory, doesn't remember the events, while another part of the memory, the implicit memory, functions independently and memories of the trauma surface in the form of dreams or feelings of anxiety.'

I think of riding. I pedal like a mad woman, hear my own panting breath.

'Repression is not a conscious choice. It is associated with an emotional, psychological or physical situation that is so overwhelming that it is unbearable. We don't consciously decide to banish the images from our spirit, we just do. We protect ourselves by using repression. It is the way in which our spirit protects itself from something we can't look at.'

I feel the wind in my hair.

All of the propositions and conclusions are backed up with real-life examples of things that actually happened. I read them with a growing feeling of discomfort. I drop the book, reach for my tea from the side table next to me and take a sip. Deep down inside, a voice I have long kept silent cries out.

That night in bed I test my memory by closing my eyes and trying to open myself up to everything I've apparently been repressing. It doesn't work. It's as if there's a shadow crouching inside me. It disappears without trace at the moment when I am getting close to something. I slip away cowardly into my dreams. They are disturbing dreams, which disappear at daybreak and leave me drenched in sweat.

Exhausted, I go to work. It's raining. The heat from the past weeks is driven away by a cloudburst that releases earthy smells from the parks. My colleagues' spiteful comments run off me like the drops of water running down the windows. I see myself, as if from outside my body, spurned and isolated.

My psychologist taught me to console myself. She advised me to visit that lonely, unhappy Sabine from earlier and stand by her. I did that. I looked for and found the girl from the past. She was in the streets of Den Helder and the school grounds.

And now I see her sitting in the changing room after PE. She has had a shower, after the others in order to get some privacy. The group are ignoring her while they get dressed, laughing and talking loudly. Everyone has left when she comes out of the shower room unnoticed and slips into the changing room.

It's noisy outside – recess. Another five minutes and the bell will go, and then the next PE class will come in.

She wraps the small towel tightly around her to stem her rising panic. Her eyes dart around the room, over the wooden benches and the clothes hooks. Not only are the girls gone, so are her jeans and top, her coat and shoes, and her sports clothes. She looks everywhere through the cubicles, under and behind, but all of her clothes have disappeared.

She walks along the corridor to the gym and calls for the sports teacher. There's no answer. Finally she slides into the room where the basketballs, hockey sticks and lost property is stored. She looks in the basket of lost property and takes out a T-shirt and tracksuit bottoms. They fit her perfectly.

Before the bell goes, she walks barefoot along the corridor and leaves by the emergency exit, something that is strictly against the rules.

At that instant the bell goes and the school grounds empty. She goes to her bike and finds her clothes strewn across the ground, kicked and trampled into the mud. She gathers everything up: her new jacket, her favourite jeans, her shoes, her top which has been cut to shreds.

She puts on her shoes and jacket, watched by many eyes behind the classroom windows, and rides home. Nobody's there. She puts her jeans into the washing machine, scrubs her shoes in a bucket of soapy water, examines the holes in her top and the tears in her coat. She throws them away.

Everything comes back at once.

Later on, it was Robin who took her into town on his moped to buy a new coat. Robin, who'd come home unexpectedly and had caught her in her bedroom with her ruined clothes.

'Just don't tell Mum,' she said when they got back home. 'She's got enough to worry about with Dad being in hospital.'

He nodded, his face tense and his lips pursed.

She returned to her room, lay down on the bed and wondered what she'd done to make Isabel hate her so much. She couldn't think of anything.

I still can't think of anything. Perhaps I had the aura of an easy victim and that was enough of a reason for the group to test my limits, my elastic limits. I didn't defend myself. I just became more and more withdrawn, until, totally isolated, I worked at just getting through the long days.

It still gets me by the throat, even now.

'What would you like to say to that lonely girl?' asked the psychologist.

'That things don't stay the same. I'd like to reassure and console her.'

'Do it then. Give her a hug.'

Since then I've done that regularly. It helps. Not immediately, but after a while I learned to dissociate myself from that girl. I could see myself as a different Sabine, an older Sabine and console my younger self.

But I don't want to do any more consoling.

I want answers.

25

I have to go back to Den Helder. Without any feelings of guilt I pull a sickie in the afternoon. I am sick, totally exhausted by all the memories. It's as if something magnetic has been set off, one memory bringing back another.

I can no longer stop the film and I don't try to. I know the story. I have a sense of the ending.

In Den Helder I go to Bernard Square, pull the radio out of its slot, put it into my bag and climb out. To my right there's the Kampanje theatre, and opposite me, the public library. It was my hidey-hole during those long, lonely free periods at school. I enter the familiar building, climb the steps to the top, sit down at a table, bring out my diary and thumb through it.

After a while the girl comes to me of her own accord.

'You have to help me,' I say.

She looks on with big blue eyes but doesn't speak.

'You can't keep quiet for ever,' I say.

She looks away.

'You saw her. I don't mean at the crossroads, but there. Why are you keeping quiet about it? Why won't you tell me what you saw?'

She says nothing. Her blond hair hangs in front of her face.

'Shall we go for a little drive?' I propose.

We drive around for a while. It has rained the whole morning but now the sun breaks cautiously through the clouds. Den Helder is quiet, almost dead. It is 2 June; the summer holidays haven't yet begun. Everyone is imprisoned behind glass, in classrooms or at work. We drive along the Middenweg to the school, past the school grounds glistening with bikes. We don't get out but continue to the crossroads with Jan Verfailleweg. The traffic light is red and I brake. I stare ahead in silence. The girl does the same. I try to enter her thoughts, share her memories.

'It was here,' I say. 'That's where the van was, and that's where I was on my bike. Isabel was right at the front. She didn't see me.'

'Then the lights turned green. Isabel went straight on. The van overtook her and I turned right,' the girl says.

'Yes,' I say. 'Into Seringen Avenue, and then on to the Dark Dunes.'

'She was meeting someone there,' the girl says.

My heart begins to thud and I close my eyes for a second.

'Who?' I hear myself say. 'Who was she meeting there?'

'I don't know. She didn't say his name and I didn't see anybody.'

'But you saw them going into the woods together. You followed them!'

'No, I didn't.' The girl turns away. 'What makes you say that?'

'You can tell me,' I say, with more friendliness and patience than I feel. 'I know why you followed them. I know what you were afraid of.' I look at her, but the girl refuses to look back at me.

'Is what you saw so terrible?' I ask softly. 'So terrible that you can't even talk to me about it?'

She doesn't speak.

The traffic light turns green. I accelerate and drive straight on. This isn't working. I'll have to try something else.

The Dark Dunes rise up before us like a black stripe. Then

157

we're driving past the woods. Sunlight chases the shadows between the tree trunks and lays a carpet of light over the paths. The path next to the woods is for cyclists, joggers and walkers. A few teenagers are sitting outside the snack bar. When we turn into the carpark behind it, I see a girl waiting. She fiddles with her ring, and stares at her shoes.

I take the key out of the ignition. 'Are you coming?' I sound friendly enough, but my tone is of someone who won't be contradicted. I open the door and get out, but she stays where she is.

'Come on, we're going together.'

After much hesitation she finally gets out. I lock the car and we cross over to the entrance of the woods. We pass the children's farm and go deeper into the trees. Now and then joggers overtake us. We follow the path around the duck pond, past the look-out post, and further, until the path narrows, becomes less well-trodden, and zigzags towards the dunes.

The girl stops.

I check my pace and look at her. 'It was here, wasn't it?'

For the first time she looks me in the face, with wide, anguished eyes. 'They had an argument,' she whispers. 'A terrible argument! He hit her, grabbed her by the arms and shook her. He hit her again, but she pushed him off and ran away. That way.' She stretches out her arm and points to the thick undergrowth in the woods.

I look at where she is pointing. It is so desolate here, so quiet, just like that beautiful spring day before. I stare at the place and try to travel back in time. It's a hot day and I've just got out of school. Soon I'll spend hours searching through the shelves for books to transport me to another world. But I'm not in the library, I've followed Isabel, who has gone into the woods with a man.

I see myself standing there with my bike, next to the path. The vegetation wraps me in a suffocating embrace. There are bushes everywhere, branches, logs; the two people on the foot-path can't see me. Even when Isabel breaks free and runs into the woods and her attacker screams something after her, they don't see me.

I leave the path and wrestle through the undergrowth, which is even thicker than nine years before. Like then, I'm following Isabel. Her attacker is nowhere to be seen. Has he gone away? Or has he gone to another part of the woods, planning to cut her off?

I walk towards the clearing. I could find it blindfolded. I only need to follow the shadow in the deepest part of my memory to get to where I never wanted to be. The trees recede, sand is underfoot, and there's the clearing at the point where the woods become thinner and the slope of the first dune begins.

From the shadow of two trees, I look at the sandy clearing in front of me. The sun blinds me. I squint, hold my hand up, step forwards and see Isabel lying there, her dark hair standing out against the white sand.

I brood over this recollection for the whole of the car ride home. There are holes in my memory, but they aren't black and bottomless. There's a tough film over them that I try to pierce. But it is not yet transparent.

I drive into the darkness of the Wijker tunnel and when I come out into the light at the other end, I've left Den Helder and everything that binds me to that town behind. I drive back into my familiar life and greet the signposts reading *Bos and Lommer* with a smile, as if I've escaped some great danger.

But the sight of my flat from the street gives me an odd feeling. The sun reflects in the windows and flashes warning signals.

My footsteps on the stairs sound different from normal. I'm walking quietly, instead of the way I would usually drag myself up the flight. At the front door, I stop.

Has somebody been here?

I try the door – it's locked. I put the key in the lock, turn it and push the door open. Like the heroine in a film, I stand in the doorway, careful and prudent. I've always hated those predictable moments in thrillers, when the heroine senses danger and, trembling, enters her ransacked house. That she could get a weapon, call the police or just turn on the light never occurs to her.

My flat is not dark. Nor has it been ransacked. But someone has been here.

I can see it from the doorstep, through the open hall door. A bouquet of red roses on the table, neatly arranged in a vase.

They don't look that dangerous, those roses. Still, I find it hard to go in. I can only think of one person who'd make such a romantic gesture. But how did he get hold of a key?

With mixed feelings I turn over the card hanging from one of the roses. The text is less poetic than I'd expected.

Call me, Olaf.

26

'Sabine, where are you? Call me as soon as you get this message!' Zinzy's voice sounds stressed. Still staring at Olaf's roses and holding the card in my hand, I listen to my messages.

The missed numbers function shows that work has called. The pain returns to my stomach, worse than it was when I was climbing the stairs to my flat. Shit, I'd said I was sick. I take some time to practise my excuse, 'I was in bed nearly the whole afternoon. No, I really didn't hear the phone. Well, yes, once, but I felt too wretched to get up. Yes, I do feel better now.'

I check the time – it's not yet six – and call the office. Zinzy answers.

'It's Sabine. Listen, I was in bed nearly the whole afternoon and – '

'Oh, Sabine, I'm glad you've called.' Zinzy interrupts. 'Renée's had an accident.'

My first thought is one of pleasure. I get a grip of myself and repress my initial reaction. 'What happened?'

'There was a fire in her flat. She had the afternoon off and it happened while she was taking a shower.'

'She was at home?'

'Yes. The sitting room and the hall were full of smoke, so she opened the kitchen door to the balcony and jumped off it.'

There's silence. I'm impressed.

'And what happened? How is she?'

'She lives on the first floor, so she could risk jumping, but she landed badly. I don't know exactly what she's done, but we've just had a call that she's in intensive care.'

I stare ahead, shocked. 'Is her condition critical?'

'I've no idea. We're going to visit her tomorrow. At least, if we can. It might be that only family are allowed to see her.'

She doesn't ask me if I'll join them and I don't suggest it either.

'I thought you ought to know,' Zinzy says. 'Everyone at work is talking about it. It would be strange if you walked in tomorrow without knowing.'

'You're right. Thanks, Zinzy.'

'See you tomorrow, Sabine.'

I hang up and see that the answer machine is still flashing. Another message. Olaf's voice fills the room. 'Hi beautiful! I think you must be in Den Helder again. I just wanted to let you know that I'm thinking of you and I don't think we see enough of each other. Did you like the flowers? If you want to thank me personally I'm happy to give you the following opportunity: Tonight in Café Walem, seven o'clock.'

I glance at the card in my hand. After his aggression on Sunday, I don't really feel like it. But I decide to give him one more chance.

Café Walem is a restaurant on the Keizersgracht. It's a long, narrow room with designer furniture and a granite floor, and it's permanently full. I went there once before and although the chairs were uncomfortable, the food was good and the atmosphere was even better.

I'm half expecting Olaf to be sitting at a reserved table with

162

a rose between his teeth, but I can't see him. I lean against the bar, as if I want to order a drink, take a peppermint from a full bowl and glance furtively at my watch.

Quarter past seven. I was on the late side but he's not even here. If there's one thing that winds me up, it's men who disregard arrangements.

I leave the bar, push open the door and walk straight into Olaf in the street.

'Hey. You're already here!'

'Yes.'

He puts his arm around my waist, pulls me to him and kisses me on the mouth.

'We don't see enough of each other,' he says. 'We're going to have to do something about that. Are you coming?'

'Have you reserved?' I ask. 'It's chockablock.'

'We'll find a place.' Olaf pushes the door open, leaving me outside on the street, and strides into the restaurant. I narrowly avoid getting the door in my face.

'Thanks!' I say, but he doesn't hear me.

I follow him and look around. In the narrow entrance all of the tables are taken, but at the back, near the doors to the garden, there's a couple around our age who are just putting a fifty-euro note onto a saucer.

Olaf darts to the table, just ahead of an older man and woman who've been looking around for a while. With a disarming grin, Olaf lays his hand on a chair back and says to the young couple, 'You're leaving, aren't you? That's good timing.'

The girl at the table smiles and stands up.

'You go ahead and sit down,' she says. 'We'll pay at the bar. Come on, John.'

I hesitate but Olaf sits down. The older couple stare at each other, speechless.

'Would you…' I begin, but they're already walking away.

'Sit down,' Olaf says. 'What would you like to drink?'

163

I pull my chair back, 'A white wine.'

'Frascati?'

'If they have it.'

'Tell me,' Olaf says, 'weren't you surprised when you got home this afternoon?'

'I certainly was,' I say. 'I've spent the whole time wondering how you got in?'

'Your neighbour had a key,' Olaf says. 'She gave it to me.'

I decide to have a little word with my neighbour later.

'I popped the key back through her letterbox afterwards,' Olaf explains. 'She thought the roses were really romantic.' He looks at me mischievously.

'It was very sweet of you.' I force myself to smile.

What is the matter with me? What's happened to the easy going, relaxed thing we had going? Why am I sitting on the edge of my chair searching for a topic of conversation?

'Have you heard what happened to Renée?' I ask.

'Yes, the fire. It's good.'

'What do you mean?'

'You know. That it's turned out so well.'

I look at him in incomprehension.

'She wanted that job in HR,' Olaf says. 'Ellis told me that she had an interview with Jan pencilled into her diary. Well, that won't take place. Now you'll have to get the job because there aren't any other candidates.'

'Don't jump to conclusions. They can extend the deadline, can't they?'

'But with Ellis's maternity leave coming up…'

'And the birth…No, you're right, they'll have to decide soon. Are you sure there weren't any other applicants?'

'Not according to Ellis. I don't know whether Jan might have someone in mind, but I presume he'd have discussed all the potential candidates with Ellis. After all, she'll have to job-share with that person later.'

'Yes.' I study the menu, but my thoughts are far away. I can picture myself working well with Ellis, no problem. On the other hand, I don't like the fact that Renée will have succeeded in getting rid of me.

'Renée will be out of circulation for quite some time,' I say. 'How on earth are we going to manage without her.'

Olaf laughs. 'You'll be completely lost, I'm sure.'

The waiter clears the table and takes our order. I choose a caesar salad with steak, Olaf opts for pasta. Our drinks are brought and we chink our glasses together.

'Where were you this afternoon? In Den Helder?' Olaf asks.

'Yes.'

'What have you got with that place?'

'I'm beginning to remember things from before,' I say. 'It helps if I go to Den Helder; more and more is coming back.'

'Why do you want it to?'

'Just, you know, it irritates me if I forget things which are important.'

'You don't know if they're important or not, you just think so,' Olaf says.

I look at him. His expression has changed, become almost annoyed. Why in God's name should he feel annoyed? I ask him and with a sigh he puts down his beer.

'I just don't like all this digging into the past. What happened, happened, end of story. These days, everyone seems to have had some kind of trauma they need treatment for. You have to get to know your inner self, delve into your emotions, bring everything to the surface. What rubbish! There's a reason it's hidden away. Let sleeping dogs lie.' Olaf must see that his words are not going down too well, because he adds in a gentler tone, 'We're living in the here and now. What has raking up the past got to offer?'

'The truth,' I say.

Our food arrives, so there's a tense silence for a while. When the waiter turns to leave, Olaf picks up the conversation again.

165

'And will you be happier, knowing the truth?' he asks. 'Will it add something to your life, knowing what happened to Isabel?'

'I don't know.'

'Well, I do. It will just cause more suffering, and it won't bring Isabel back.'

I say nothing.

We drop the subject and go on to talk about this and that and it's nice, but I can't shake my feeling of disappointment. It's clearly not something Olaf and I can talk about, and it would be good to talk about it with someone who was around at that time.

We decide against dessert and ride home through the city. Olaf accompanies me all the way but I don't ask him in. We kiss in front of the door, my back against the wood. His mouth moves down to my throat, his hands push under my clothes. I let him do what he wants, but I'm aware of his growing urgency and I don't want it. I push him off me as gently as possible.

'I'm dead tired,' I apologise. 'I'll be happy when I'm in my bed.'

Olaf raises his eyebrows. 'What's made you so tired?'

'Work and that...And the afternoon in Den Helder wore me out.'

'And now you're too tired to have another drink with me? Not even a little one?'

I pull a helpless face.

'Sabine, it's only ten o'clock.'

I don't like the suspicious look he gives me.

'I'm sorry. Another time.' I turn to go.

'One drink! I promise I won't stay long.' Olaf kisses my throat again.

I shake my head with a smile and see a glimmer of rage flit across his face. Or am I just imagining it? When I look at him carefully, his face is normal again.

'When am I going to see you again?' he asks.

'Tomorrow?' I suggest.

'At my house. I'll sort out some food. What would you like?'

'Chicken *roti*,' I say.

Olaf pulls a face. 'Chicken *roti*? How do you make that?'

'I'm just teasing, I don't mind what we eat. Surprise me.'

He waits until I'm inside to leave. I blow him a kiss and pull the door shut behind me.

I go upstairs and stop in the hall to listen. My upstairs neighbour Mrs Bovenkerk is seventy and hard of hearing. She watches TV until late at night. I've had to buy myself some earplugs to cut out the sounds of the advertising jingles that vibrate through the floor. Right now I can hear someone singing the praises of cat food. So she's awake. I go up to the second floor and knock on her door.

'Mrs Bovenkerk? It's me, Sabine.'

The cat food advert cuts out. There's the sound of the chain on the door, a key being turned and then Mrs Bovenkerk peers at me through the crack. 'Sabine, is that you?'

'Yes, it's me. I'm sorry to bother you so late, but I wanted to ask you something.'

The door opens wider. 'Come inside, child. Don't stay out there in that draughty corridor. I almost had a heart attack when I heard someone knocking.'

'I'm sorry,' I say again, as I enter the packed apartment. A display case full of china figurines, paintings of crying gypsy boys and a wall covered in yellowing photographs catch my eye.

'I was just about to make myself a mug of hot milk. Would you like one too?'

'No, thank you. I just wanted to ask you…' I hesitate, ill at ease, 'well, if you'd mind not giving my key to anyone. Not even to friends, boyfriends or whatever else they say they are.'

Mrs Bovenkerk looks at me in amazement. 'Of course not. I'd never do that.'

'But you did give my key to Olaf this afternoon?'

'Olaf?'

'That boy I've been dating recently. Tall, blond, handsome.'

'A nice young man, but not nice enough to diddle your key out of me.'

'But this afternoon…'

'I didn't see your friend, and I've been home the whole day.'

I look at her in astonishment. 'Are you sure? He had flowers with him.'

'No one came to my door this afternoon,' the old lady assures me. 'And if he had, I wouldn't have given him the key. I'm not very trusting, you know that yourself. Recently there was that man who said he was from the bank, he said there were fake bank cards going around and he wanted to check mine. I said to him, "Check your head, if you think I'm falling for that one." I slammed the door in his face. I might be old but I'm not off my rocker.'

I smile away my feelings of discomfort. Mrs Bovenkerk is far from being off her rocker. 'But how did he get in then?' I wonder out loud.

'He got in? To your apartment?'

'Yes, there was a big vase of roses on my table when I got home. He says he asked you for the key and put it back through your letterbox later.'

'Then your friend's a liar.'

I get out my mobile and dial Olaf's number. It rings endlessly before his voicemail picks up. Annoyed, I switch off my phone.

'Be careful,' Mrs Bovenkerk says. 'Men who force their way into your home aren't to be trusted, not even if they bring a thousand roses with them. Wolves in sheep's clothing. Just like that man who was fumbling around with your door this evening. I went downstairs and I said, 'Excuse me, what do you think you're doing, if I may ask?' Well, he jumped right out of his skin. He muttered something and left right away.'

A chill travels from my ankles up my back and arms. I don't know if I can take any more shocks of this kind.

'A man? This evening? At my door? What was he doing exactly?'

'Fumbling with the keyhole. Ringing. Standing with his ear against the door. An unsavoury type, he was. I'd just decided to call the police when he went away.'

'Did he say anything to you? What did he look like? Old or young?'

'Young. Your age, perhaps a little older. Dark blond hair.'

Around my age with dark blond hair. Who on earth could that have been? It wasn't Olaf and I don't know many other men. Certainly none who'd be fiddling with my lock and listening at my door.

I play with the key in my hand. 'Mrs Bovenkerk, if you ever hear something in my apartment, screaming or banging, will you call the police?'

Mrs Bovenkerk squints at me. 'Yes,' she says. 'One scream and I'll call the police.'

'Thank you.' I turn around and walk back into the corridor. Mrs Bovenkerk peers over the bannister as I go down the stairs.

'All safe?' she calls down.

'Yes, fine,'

'I'll wait here until you're inside. Call me if anything's wrong.'

I feel rather ridiculous and bite my lip as I open my door. My flat welcomes me with darkness and silence. I switch on the light and immediately my familiar haven returns.

'Everything alright?' calls the voice from upstairs.

'Yes, it's alright. Goodnight Mrs Bovenkerk.'

'Sleep well, child.'

I close the door, attach the chain, and turn the lock an extra time. For a while I stand still in the living room, then I fetch a kitchen chair and set it against the door. Its high back comes up to the handle. Somewhat calmer, I go to the bathroom and turn on the shower. I undress and place my mobile on the stone rim of the shower cubicle. Within hand's reach. Only then do I climb under the warm stream and remain standing there for a long time, my face turned upwards to catch the water.

27

It's lovely and quiet in my office. Several colleagues have gone to visit Renée who's out of intensive care but, with a broken leg and a ruptured spleen, is not expected back any time soon. She ended up in intensive care because she'd inhaled smoke and had trouble breathing, but that has passed.

I signed my name on the stupid card featuring a mouse with an enormous plastercast on its leg, and watched Margot, Tessa and Roy leaving with a colossal fruit basket.

'So, they've gone,' Zinzy says. 'Fancy a coffee?'

She doesn't wait for an answer but goes straight to the coffee machine. She returns with a milky coffee for me and one with sugar for herself, puts down the plastic cups, and sits down with her feet up on her desk.

'Someone telephoned for you yesterday,' she says.

'Here?'

'Yes, a man.'

The hot coffee spills over the edge of my cup and makes an ugly stain on my white trousers, but I barely notice it. I look at Zinzy tensely and ask, 'A man?'

'Yes, towards the end of the afternoon. I said that you'd gone home sick yesterday. But according to him you weren't at home.'

'What was his name?'

'I've no idea, sorry. I don't think he even gave his name.' She looks at me in concern. 'Is something going on?'

I gesture helplessly with my hand. 'According to my neighbour there was a strange man at my door last night. He was fiddling with my lock, and had his ear against my door.'

'Oh my God!' Zinzy leans towards me. 'And then?'

'My neighbour isn't easily thrown; she chased him away.' I take a sip of coffee. 'I dreamed about it last night.'

'Are you surprised? I'd dream about it too! Have you any idea who it might have been?'

'I've racked my brains but I really can't think who.'

'Maybe it's someone from the past. Someone who doesn't like the way you keep returning to Den Helder,' Zinzy suggests.

I look at her with a heavy heart. 'I did think of that. I recently visited our old school caretaker. I remembered a couple of things and I wanted to find out some stuff.'

Zinzy looks at me over the rim of her coffee cup. 'What was it you remembered then?'

I tell her about Groesbeek's van, walking into the woods and my increasing distress with every step I took.

'That doesn't sound like something you'd make up,' she says.

'No, but it's all rather vague. What's not vague is what I discovered at Mr Groesbeek's house.'

I take the newspaper cuttings out of my bag. I'd been planning on showing them to Zinzy.

'They're all missing girls,' I say, as she leafs through them. 'And these are the names of Mr Groesbeek's cats.' I thumb through my diary and hold up the address page on which I've scribbled them down.

Zinzy reads them, compares them with the cuttings and then looks at me, gobsmacked.

'If it had been an old man fiddling with my door, it might have had something to do with that, but…'

'How do you know it was a young man?' Zinzy stirs her coffee without taking her eyes off the newspaper cuttings.

'Because Mrs Bovenkerk said so. My neighbour.'

'And how old is Mrs Bovenkerk?' Zinzy looks up from the cuttings and pushes them across the desk to me.

I pick them up and put them back in my bag. 'God knows. About seventy.'

'At that age, a fifty-year-old man is young too, so it could have been anybody. Maybe it was his son or grandson. Maybe his grandson came to visit and he told him about you.'

The phone rings. I swivel around and pick up. I begin with the customary speech, and an excited voice breaks in. 'Hey sis! Hard at work?'

I jump up so quickly I knock over my coffee. 'Shit! Robin! No, I don't mean you – I've just poured coffee all over my desk. I really wasn't expecting you. You sound close.'

'So I should, I'm back in Holland. In my old house.'

'You're in Amsterdam? That's great! Shall we meet up tonight?'

Zinzy comes running with a filthy dishcloth in her hand and begins mopping my desk with it.

'Sure,' Robin says. 'By the way, I went round to yours last night but you weren't in. I waited for a while, but a crazy old witch came down the stairs with a baseball bat. I nearly had a fit.'

I burst out laughing. 'I've got good security.'

'Anyway, it's a good idea. Shall we eat out tonight?'

'Wonderful, just say where.'

'At the Nieuwmarkt, in that restaurant in the old city gate?'

'Great. I'll see you there about seven.'

When I hang up, Zinzy looks at me, curious. 'Another date already? You're hot stuff these days, Sabine.'

'That was my brother,' I say. 'And it seems he was my stalker.'

'Oh, thank God.'

'Yes and...oh no! I promised to see Olaf tonight. He was going to cook for me.'

I email Olaf. *Sorry, something's come up. I can't come for dinner tonight. Will it keep? Love, Sabine.*

His answer pops up on my screen almost immediately. *It'll have to.*

Robin is already in the restaurant when I arrive. He stands up when he sees me. We hug, kiss each other on the cheeks and cling tightly. We spend the whole evening in the wonderfully atmospheric restaurant. We laugh, eat, talk, drink and reminisce about our childhood.

'Do you remember that time you went out and came home really drunk? You threw up all over the bathroom,' I say.

'You were sleeping in the next room and it woke you up. At three in the morning you got a bucket of soapy water and cleaned the whole mess up before Mum and Dad could find out. That was so sweet of you.'

'And you picked me up from school so that I could avoid those girls.'

'We can therefore conclude that we're the ideal brother and sister,' Robin laughs. 'I missed you, you know that?'

'Me too. Why did you all need to go and emigrate? It would have been so nice if we could have stayed together.'

Robin nods, avoids my gaze.

'What is it?' I ask.

'I'm only back in Holland temporarily, Sabine. I'm going to move to London for good.'

'What?'

'I knew you wouldn't like it. Sorry, sis. I've met a nice girl there.'

'Mandy.'

'Yes. You know how it goes.'

'Fantastic,' I sigh. 'I'll be here all on my own again.'

'You've got Olaf now, haven't you?!'

I shrug. Have I got Olaf? Yes, probably, but I haven't decided whether he's got me yet.

'How's it going between you?' Robin asks.

'I'm not sure. He's good-looking and nice, but he's also got a side that I can't get used to.'

Robin nods. 'That's what I was saying.'

We talk about Olaf for a while, and then about Mandy, but finally we get back onto the subject of the past. Dad's heart attack, my problems at school.

'I felt so sorry for you,' he says. 'You always came home from school with such a white face. I could have killed those girls. And then seeing Isabel everywhere when I went out. Flirting with me, provoking me. God, what a bitch.'

'But you still kissed her.'

'I'd had too much to drink. And she was an unbelievably pretty girl, Sabine. Prettier than was good for her, and she knew it. She could've had any guy she wanted.'

'And who did she want?'

'All of them. She didn't differentiate. She kept everyone dangling. I'm glad I drew the line after that one evening. From then on she came after me continuously, she couldn't bear that I'd dumped her.'

'And Olaf? You said he'd been out with her, but he denies it. He says it must have been Bart de Ruijter.'

Robin frowns. 'Bart de Ruijter? Weren't you going out with him?'

'Maybe he was secretly seeing Isabel too,' I say. The thought that he might have cheated on me causes a stabbing pain.

'No, I'd have known it,' Robin says. 'He was mad about you.'

'Why does Olaf say that Bart went out with her and why does he deny going out with her himself?'

Robin lights a cigarette and inhales deeply. 'Perhaps he didn't want to upset you. He used to like you before. He thought you were too young at the time but he did really like you. It doesn't surprise me at all that you're seeing each other now and that he denies having had a relationship with Isabel. He's probably scared to death of losing you.' He gestures to the waiter to refill his empty glass.

'Why would I hate it so much that he'd been out with Isabel? Especially if she'd treated him the same way she treated me? Then we'd have something in common that we could share rather than it coming between us. It's completely stupid of him to lie about it.'

Robin shrugs. 'Men see things differently.'

I tell Robin about the flashbacks I've been having recently, about what I discovered in Den Helder concerning Mr Groesbeek, and about my confusing memories of the woods on the day Isabel disappeared.

'How do you know for sure that that has something to do with Isabel's disappearance?'

'Because I think I saw her right before she was murdered.'

Robin drops his fork. I see not only surprise in his eyes but something else, something vague that could best be described as dismay.

'I don't know exactly what happened, but I do know where and how.'

Robin looks at his plate, but he has clearly lost his appetite.

'You were there,' he says.

I nod.

'Are you sure? I mean, are you sure you didn't dream it or something?'

'I dream about it all the time and I see who killed her in the dreams. But when I wake up it's gone again. I don't know what to believe anymore. Which things are real memories and which are dreams?'

Robin picks up his fork and shovels chicory gratin into his mouth. The movement is robotic.

'Perhaps you should drop the whole thing. It's eating you up, I can see that.'

'You might be right.' My smile is weak. 'Perhaps I'm imagining it all. It's so easy to let things colour your memories and to link things which don't go together.'

'That's right,' Robin says. 'Call it a day.' He smiles warmly at me and looks at his empty plate.

'Would you like something else?'

'An Irish coffee would be nice,' I say.

Robin calls over the waiter and for the rest of the evening we avoid the subject of Isabel.

In the middle of the night the phone rings. I shoot upright in bed, my hand clutching my chest. My heart hammers as if an alarm has gone off in my body. The shrill sound of the telephone pierces the darkness, filling every corner of the flat. My alarm clock reads 01:12.

I swipe my hair out of my face and pick up. 'Sabine Kroese speaking.'

Silence.

I don't repeat my name, I've said it clearly enough. The sound of heavy breathing reaches my ears and every nerve cell in my body.

I hang up. The phone rings again immediately. Although I'm half expecting it, it still makes me jump. I pick up but don't speak. It's silent on the other end of the line too.

It's tempting to shout some obscenities into the receiver but I control myself. Some people get off on that. I hang up very calmly and when the phone rings a third time I pull the wire out. Fuck off, you bastard. Whoever you are.

I lie on my back in bed, my bedside lamp on, and try to sleep.

Who was that? What do they want from me? Maybe I know him. Or her.

With an irritated sigh, I switch off the lamp. It was just a crazy person.

Mere chance.

And then I see her. For a few whooshing seconds, I see Isabel's contorted face, her staring eyes, her face turning blue.

I squeeze my eyes shut but the image won't go away. I turn on the light, but I take Isabel's face with me. Her head's pushed back and her eyes are staring up at the sky. There's sand in her short, dark hair.

What is this? A memory or madness?

I sink down onto the bed and cover my face with my hands. Isabel has never been found. This has to be a fantasy, a product of my imagination.

My hands shake like those of an alcoholic in need of a drink. I can't stop them trembling. Or my teeth from chattering.

I walk, almost run through my house, but my mind is just as quick and runs with me. I pace up and down, my arms wrapped around my sides. My nails dig deep into my arms.

I dial Robin's number. He doesn't answer. The telephone rings and rings but nobody picks up. I need to speak to someone. My fingers dial Olaf's number. After just a few rings, I hear his voice.

'Olaf van Oirschot speaking.'

'I saw her,' I whisper.

'Sabine?'

'Yes. I saw her, Olaf.'

'Who did you see?'

'Isabel.'

The silence stretches out into something uncomfortable. I wait for him to speak.

'What do you mean, you saw her?'

'In a flashback. She was lying on the ground, dead, with sand in her hair.'

Olaf doesn't say anything and this time I break the silence. 'I don't know what it was, a memory or just my imagination. I wasn't asleep, I really wasn't. It just came out of nowhere. How can that happen? I can't really have seen this, can I?' My voice is shrill and faltering.

'I'll come over.'

Olaf hangs up and I stay sitting on the sofa, shivering, my arms folded around me.

After twenty minutes the door goes. I get up, peer through a chink in the curtains and see Olaf's blond head. Reassured I go to the door, press the button and shortly afterwards hear footsteps coming up the stairs.

'Are you alright?' Olaf accompanies me to the sofa. I sit and he squats down in front of me. He scrutinises me, gets up and fetches a glass of water.

I don't know where people get the idea that things will improve if you drink water, but I'm grateful for the gesture. I sip the water, clinging onto the glass like it's a life-raft.

'She's dead,' I whisper.

'Is that what you saw?' Olaf takes the glass from my shaking hands.

'Yes, just like that, all of a sudden.'

'You didn't dream it?'

I hesitate. 'No, I remembered it. All of a sudden, I remembered it.'

'Was anyone else there?' Olaf shakes me gently. 'Did you see that too? Tell me! Did you see them?'

I look at his strong hands, I see his white knuckles, hear the insistent tone in his voice.

'I...I don't know. No, I just saw her.'

He lets go of me. I daren't look at him. I pick up the glass and drink. My teeth clash against the glass.

Olaf studies me for a time.

'It's really been bothering you recently,' he says finally. 'Perhaps you should try to distance yourself from it.'

'Yes, perhaps.' I can't stop looking at his hands.

'Don't go to Den Helder anymore,' Olaf says. 'Your life's here in Amsterdam. What happened, happened. You won't be able to change things.'

'It would change things for her parents if they knew what happened.'

'Do you want to go to them with this information? Or to the police? Come on, Sabine, you know how they'd react.'

'Yes.'

'Or did you see more?'

'Just that she was lying dead on the ground.'

'With sand in her hair,' Olaf completes. 'That must have been in the dunes. But they did make a big search there, didn't they? With dogs, infra-red scans, everything. If she'd been in the dunes, they would have found her.'

Not necessarily. Lydia van der Broek's body was found on a building site in a new housing estate six months after she'd disappeared. The bushes she'd been buried under had hidden her from the infra-red scan. Tracker dogs had passed close by the place but the wind had been in the wrong direction. When the area was cleared for the development, she was found.

I don't mention this.

Olaf tips my chin with his finger and forces me to look into his eyes. 'Have a think about it,' he says softly. 'You can't do anything about it. Shall I stay the night?'

'No, I'm feeling better.'

'Are you sure? I'm here now. Perhaps you'll start dreaming again, then I can wake you up.'

I'm too tired to put up a fight. 'Okay, then.'

We go to sleep, his arm wrapped around my waist. I lie with my back to him, feel the weight of his arm on my body and stare into the darkness.

28

There's black smoke, dense like low-hanging mist, in my bedroom. I lie paralysed. I know that I must do something, call the fire brigade or jump out of the window. Invisible hands hold me pinned down to my bed. I writhe around to get free and when I finally succeed, I spring up. The smoke hangs like a curtain in my bedroom, sealing the only exit.

I look around desperately. My bedroom doesn't have a window or a balcony door anymore. This is what surprises me most. Couldn't I always get out of my room by going onto the balcony?

Behind the door I can hear the crackling of flames. I scream. The smoke takes its chance and fills my mouth, my throat, my lungs. I don't want to die. I don't want to die. I don't want to die!

I open my eyes. The white of the ceiling starkly contrasts with the dark room of just before and it takes a while to sink in. There's no smoke.

Infinitely relieved, I close my eyes and clutch my hand to my chest to settle my thumping heart.

At that same moment, I smell it. Smoke. I jump up and run into the corridor in my pyjamas.

'Shit!' shouts Olaf as he drops something.

He stands in the kitchen with a slice of burnt toast at his feet.

My old toaster smoulders on the kitchen counter.

I rub my eyes. 'What are you doing? That thing's broken, the bread doesn't jump up anymore.'

'Tell me about it.' Olaf removes the black crisp of sliced bread from the floor. 'I wanted to surprise you with tea and toast in bed.'

'You managed to surprise me. It even got through to my unconscious state.' I yawn and stretch. 'I'm going to have a shower. And to spare you the bother, I never eat that much for breakfast. Do you know what I like? Brown bread with…'

'Strawberries,' Olaf says. 'I do remember. Coming up, madam.'

He's so sweet to me. While I let myself relax in the clouds of steam and water, I try to work out why I'm not more receptive to Olaf. He is attractive, nice and clearly crazy about me. Why don't I just go for it? Why do I have such a problem with him rummaging around in my food cupboards, pottering about the kitchen, breathing in the air of my flat? It must be because of what Robin said about him, and that part of Olaf's personality does bother me. Only I've got to know a different Olaf as well and that one I do like.

Humming, I slather myself with apple shower gel. Olaf's alright. At least he's not being that pushy anymore. What other man would have the self-control to keep making breakfast instead of flinging open the shower curtain and forcing himself on me? The truth is that I'm lucky to have him, I just don't realise it.

I turn off the taps and pick up my towel.

'Would you like coffee or tea?' Olaf calls.

'Tea!' I call back, drying my hair. I wrap the towel around my hair and pick up a second one to dry the rest of my body. 'I had such a horrible dream. It came from that burning toast, I'm sure.'

'What did you dream about?'

'That my flat was on fire and I was trapped in my bedroom. I wanted to get out through the balcony but the balcony doors had disappeared.' Naked apart from the towel around my head, I go into the bedroom and open the wardrobe.

'It might also be because of what happened to Renée.' Olaf comes in through the door opening and looks at me. I feel strangely embarrassed, as though he's seeing me naked for the first time. I quickly put on my bra and knickers and pull the first white top I find over my head.

'You're right. You do think about those things unconsciously. How could the fire have started so suddenly?'

'Those old houses are like that. Bad wiring, for a start. I think it came from her television. She had an old dinosaur of a set, it had to blow up sometime.'

Olaf returns to the kitchen. I hear him fiddling with the kettle and the coffee machine.

I frown and stick one leg into a grey and white striped trouser leg. 'How do you know that? Have you been to her house?' I call out.

'No,' he calls back. 'She told me about it once.'

I try to imagine a conversation that would include televisions. Above all, I try to imagine a conversation between Olaf and Renée. I thought he hated her.

After checking myself in the mirror, I go into the kitchen and sit down at the small table against the wall. My strawberry sandwich is waiting for me, accompanied by a cup of tea.

Still in his underpants, Olaf sits down opposite me with a hard boiled egg and a cup of coffee.

'I didn't realise the two of you were so friendly.'

'We're not. I can't stand her, but sometimes we chat. It's unavoidable.'

However awful I find what happened to Renée, it's peaceful in the office. The silence here has a totally different character now. I automatically pick up my old tasks, the things Renée had taken over from me. Now that I work whole days, I'm more in touch with what's going on in the office, so I empty Renée's in-tray and place her diary on my desk.

After a few days, the sales staff, hesitant and uneasy, make their way to me with requests for help.

'I thought that Renée went a bit far with what she said about you,' Tessa says. 'We all thought that.'

I say nothing.

'But, well,' Tessa continues, 'I need your help this afternoon with a big order. There's a huge mailing to go out. Do you have time?'

'Of course.'

'It may take until late today. Around seven or so.'

'No problem. If you just give me until lunchtime to get my other work done.'

'Shall we go over it at lunch?'

'Fine.'

She smiles at me and I smile back, although it doesn't reach my eyes.

That whole morning I work hard, emptying my and Renée's work trays. Of course it's a hopeless task, so I put what's left over on Margot's desk. Zinzy grins.

I have no time for the emails Olaf sends me every fifteen minutes. I don't even open them. At half past twelve he's waiting for me in front of the canteen.

'You haven't answered me at all.'

I carry on walking to the tray trolley and he follows me.

'Sorry, we're flat out without Renée here. Did you want to ask me something?' I put a plate on my tray and lay a knife and fork next to it.

'I just wanted to chat.'

'Sorry. I really didn't have any time.'

'Shall we go to the cinema tonight? What about that movie with Denzel Washington?'

'I have to work late,' I tell him. 'I think I'll be too tired to watch a movie afterward. It's a long time since I've been so busy.'

He doesn't say anything. I study his face as he chooses between the puddings in the cooler. I'm still standing wondering what to have when he grabs a tub of peach yoghurt, walks to the check-out with his tray, pays and goes and sits with his colleagues without saying a word.

I shrug, pay and go to sit with my own colleagues. For the first time in ages they turn to me and ask me how it's going. I answer and join in the chatter. I need them as much as they need me.

Tessa sits opposite me and babbles on as if we've been close friends for years.

'Tell me, are you seeing that guy from IT or not?' she asks. Her eyes venture over to the table where Olaf is sitting.

'Something's going on between us,' I say, 'only I'm not sure what.'

'So it's not serious?' She laughs. 'I was wondering because he had a date with Renée recently.'

I look up from my cheese sandwich. 'What?'

'At her house,' Tessa says.

I put down my knife.

'She's been after him for ages. From when you were off sick.' Tessa opens a carton of milk and pours herself a glass.

'Were they seeing each other then?'

'No, not then. He didn't even look at her. It was very unfortunate. And then you came back.'

'Aha.'

'I know what you're thinking.' Tessa sips her milk. 'Do you know what he said to her once? "I don't like women with big noses." Everyone was watching. They all knew how crazy she was about him. It was really pathetic.'

Her eyes twinkle. Mine don't.

'Did he really say that? Unbelievable.'

'She does have a big nose.' Tessa laughs.

I shake my head. Friendship is so cheap.

'But why did he have a date with her if he really didn't fancy her?' I ask out loud.

'It was last week, Friday. She had a problem with her computer at home and was standing there complaining about it. It's a really old one and she was thinking about replacing it. Olaf came in and offered to go round there and take a look. That's how it happened.'

'So it wasn't really a date.'

'She thought it was.'

Deep in thought I look at the full restaurant. I think about Olaf's confession last Sunday. Tessa's voice reaches me like all the other conversations around me – an endless stream of meaningless noise. How difficult is it to set up a couple of wires in an old computer so that they can cause problems? A fire, for example. But not something that would ignite straight away.

It's a while before I realise that I'm sitting staring at Olaf. He is sitting a little back from the others, and eats huge mouthfuls with a sullen expression on his face. He glances over his shoulder as if he can sense me looking at him. Our eyes meet. I look away.

The mouthful of bread and cheese fills my mouth like a doughy ball. I can't swallow it. I push my plate away.

'Shall we get started?' I suggest to Tessa. 'Maybe then we won't have to do too much overtime.'

29

Monday morning. It's the first time I don't mind going back to the office and I work with the same enthusiasm I used to have when Jeanine sat opposite me. Even Walter notices. He smiles at me and makes jokes, something which, coming from him, is a big compliment.

'I wish Renée would never come back,' I say to Zinzy.

We stand on the tenth floor, eating Mars bars.

'It won't be soon,' Zinzy says, 'but she will come back.'

'And then the head of the department will find a lot of changes.'

'To all intents and purposes that's you now. And so it should be, you've worked here the longest.'

'Zinzy, that job doesn't exist. Ellis from HR told me herself. Renée doesn't get a cent more for it and there's nothing on paper. She only grouched to Walter that we needed a head of department and to keep her committed while I was away, he gave her the title.'

'You should have fought back at once.'

'I wanted to keep the peace. Stupid of me. But it's not too late.' I aim the Mars wrapper into the bin and give Zinzy a meaningful look.

The week flies past and by Friday afternoon I'm shattered. Everybody is exhausted and at four o'clock we begin our traditional departmental weekly drinks. Two colleagues go off to fetch beer, wine and snacks, the rest sit nattering in our office. It's a while since I've joined in with the Friday drinks. When I still worked half days there was no question of it and before that I used to invent something to do in the archives. All the way down the corridor, bent down amongst the dusty files, I would be able to hear Renée's voice dominating the conversation.

Am I imagining it or do other people feel more relaxed now too? I'm quite quiet myself. The week has taken its toll and I decline the offer to go on to the pub. Tonight I'm going early to bed, that's for sure.

Just as I'm getting ready to leave, Olaf comes into our office. His gaze meets mine at once and he comes over with a broad smile.

'Are you ready for a wild evening?' he asks.

'To be honest I wasn't really planning on going wild.' I pack up my bag. 'I'm getting an early night tonight.'

'An early night? On a Friday?'

'Why shouldn't someone go to bed early on a Friday if they need the sleep?'

Olaf's face grows more serious. 'I was going to Paradiso,' he says.

'Go on then.' I walk to the door. 'You don't need to get an early night, do you?'

He follows me into the hall, stops me and pushes me against the wall, letting his hands glide under my clothes. 'On second thoughts, an early night is exactly what I feel like,' he murmurs with his mouth against my neck.

I look around. I'd die if one of my colleagues came into the hall now. Especially now that Olaf has undone the top half of my blouse.

'Olaf, please.' I push him away and button myself up.

'If it bothers them, they can look the other way.' Olaf pulls me towards him. He begins to kiss me as if we were in bed. It's not the kind of thing I do in public. Perhaps I worry too much about what others think, but I don't like letting myself go in the office.

At first I try to wriggle out of Olaf's embrace, but he won't let me go. He tightens his grip until it hurts. I bite his lip.

'Jesus, bitch!'

I'm free at once. He slaps me across the face. We look at each other in amazement. Olaf wipes the blood from his lip and says, 'I'm sorry but you deserved that.'

'I deserved that? I thought I'd made it very clear that I wanted you to let go of me. You deserved it yourself.' I'm breathing hard. 'Don't call me again, don't ask me out again, don't email me again. I don't want to see you anymore!'

He looks at me full of disbelief. He wants to say something, but I don't wait to hear it. I pull my bag up higher onto my shoulder and storm down the corridor.

'Sabine!' Olaf roars after me.

I don't look back, turn the corner and fly into the ladies toilets. I hold my hands under the cold tap and examine my angry face in the mirror. The slap Olaf gave me was not hard enough to have left a big mark but my cheek is tingling. Robin was right. My brother broke off with him, and that's exactly what I'm doing now.

I take a sip of water, and only once I've calmed down do I go back into the corridor.

The weather was bad this morning, the kind of summer storm that chases away the build-up of heat, and I came to work in the car. It's rained all day. I walk through the wet carpark, avoiding the big puddles. As I drive out, I see Olaf's car in my rear view mirror, following me.

I change into second gear and turn onto the road. I keep my

eye on the black Peugeot in my mirror. Olaf lives in South Amsterdam so he should turn left now.

He turns right.

I change into third gear and just get through the lights on orange. Olaf drives through on red. He keeps a couple of cars between us but remains close by. What's his plan? Why didn't he just come over to me in the carpark if he wanted to speak to me?

I drive into my local area, my street, and find a place in front of the door. Thank God. Olaf double parks but doesn't get out. He sits behind the wheel. I open my door uncertainly and come out from behind the wheel. I hook my bag out towards me and hurry to the front door.

Enclosed in my flat, I feel safe. With a deep sigh, I go into the hall and lock the door behind me. I throw my bag down onto the sofa, go to the kitchen and make a pot of fennel tea. Fennel gives inner calm, something I need right now. It's become a ritual, complete with a tealight on the coffee table and pieces of chocolate on a little dish, like my mother used to do. Usually I just wait a teabag through a cup of boiling water, but sometimes I need to go through that whole tea-making ceremony from earlier.

Olaf is still double parked in front of my door, his window is open and his arm hangs out of it. He's staring straight up at my window.

I withdraw from the window and sit cross-legged on the sofa. Okay, so he's going to stalk me now. He'll soon get fed up with that because I'm not planning on leaving the house anytime soon. If he's still there tomorrow morning, I'll be the one laughing.

But I'm not laughing at all. I sip my tea, but instead of finding inner peace I burn my lip. I've broken up two bars of dark chocolate, more to look attractive than with the intention of eating it all, but within minutes the dish is empty. Scientific research has shown that chocolate contains substances which have a very positive effect on your mood. I don't know why they wasted so much money on research with such obvious results. You also wonder why they don't add chocolate to anti-depressants if it helps so much.

A little nauseated – there are some side effects – I drink my tea which has cooled down now. It's half past six, but I don't feel like eating dinner. I'll have a couple of toasted sandwiches once the chocolate overdose has worn off.

I pour myself another cup of tea, watch some telly and around an hour or so later begin to feel hungry. On my way to the kitchen I glance out of the window. Olaf is still in front of the door, but he's now found a parking space.

I put on a Robbie Williams CD and sing along, loud and out of tune, as I cut slices of cheese in the kitchen, get ham out of the meat chiller box and lay them onto some hunks of white bread.

'Come undone!' I sing.

A loud ringing tries to drown me out. I pick up the telephone but it's the doorbell.

Olaf. I daren't look out of the window to check if it is him. I can picture him, his usual pose, leaning with one hand against the doorpost, his long body bent over impatiently.

I ignore the ringing. When my mobile goes I look at the display and see Olaf's name. I turn off the phone and turn up Robbie Williams.

Olaf stands in front of my door the entire evening, rings, goes away, rings again, toots his horn for a long time and leaves messages on my machine. Later in the evening, when it's dark, I hear him drive away at last. I shower and crawl into bed. I don't know whether I'd have been able to sleep knowing that Olaf was staring up at the windows. Will he come back tomorrow? I'm not going to wait to find out, I'll make sure I'm away for the whole weekend. I'll go back to Den Helder.

30

The next morning I leave at half past eight, before Olaf can appear on my doorstep. I've slept badly. Olaf filled my dreams. I woke up feeling hounded and my cheek, where he hit me, feels sore. That was the first and last time, I think as I walk to my car. I get in, turn on the radio and push a thermos of fresh coffee into the drinks holder. It's around an hour's drive to Den Helder, and I won't make it without coffee.

I put Amsterdam behind me with a sigh. On to Den Helder. It's going to be a long day. There's not much traffic which is lucky because my mind is too busy to concentrate fully on driving. I keep to the right hand lane, don't overtake unless strictly necessary and take a big swig of coffee from time to time.

Just before Den Helder, I turn off and drive through the village where my childhood played out. All the courts and crescents of the 1970s development must be a nightmare for new postmen. The illogical numbering of the houses doesn't help anyone trying to find their way around this labyrinth, but I still know exactly how to get to Isabel's old house.

It is still early, just gone 9.30 a.m., when I park. I go up to the house. The front garden looks exactly the same with its railway sleeper plant boxes filled with geraniums. A wooden plaque on the wall, decorated with flower tendrils, announces that Elsbeth,

Luke, Isabel and Charlotte Hartman live here. I stare at the board for a long time before knocking on the door.

Nobody comes. I didn't even think that they might not be home – stupid of me. Just as I'm turning around to leave, the door opens. A petite, dark-haired woman of around fifty stands framed in the doorway. I was expecting her to recognise me. But her look is questioning and she raises an eyebrow.

'Don't you recognise me?' I ask. 'Sabine Kroese.'

Elsbeth Hartman raises a hand to her mouth. 'Sabine?' she whispers. 'Oh, now I see it. What are you doing here?' She probably realises how rude that sounds because she quickly opens the door. 'Come in. I'm quite taken aback. How nice to see you again. Were you just passing?'

'There's going to be a school reunion soon.' I step into the narrow hall.

'I read it in the newspaper. Are you going to go?'

'I'm not sure yet.'

Elsbeth walks ahead of me into the sitting room. My eyes flit around the room – lots of dark furniture, the piano that Isabel and I used to play together – and rest on a framed photo of Isabel on the wall. Her last school photo.

'Would you like some tea?' asks Elsbeth behind me.

I turn around. 'Tea, yes please.'

I sit down without being invited, thankful that Elsbeth stays in the kitchen until the tea's ready. She must need time to collect herself. It gives me the chance to look around undisturbed and deal with the memories assailing me.

Elsbeth comes in with a tray. There's a glass teapot, a plate of biscuits and two cups on it. She treads carefully and I move aside some magazines on the coffee table. She smiles at me and puts down the tray. There is a slight tremor in her hand as she pours out the tea.

'What a surprise. I'm quite taken aback,' she repeats.

I hear the question in her voice.

'I was in the area,' I say. 'I don't know why I came here. It was an impulse.'

'I'm pleased,' Elsbeth says. 'We haven't seen each other for so long. How are you?'

I take a sip of tea and burn my lip. The thin china absorbs the heat so well that the tea has cooled down more quickly than the cup. Tears shoot into my eyes and I set the cup back down on the table. I talk about my studies, my work. About my upstairs flat in Amsterdam. Each word causes her pain, yet she smiles encouraging me to go on.

I can't resist it anymore. I lean forward and lay my hand on her arm. 'And how are you? How are things here?' My eyes lock onto hers. Her smile disappears.

'What can I say?' she says softly.

Tears appear in her eyes. I gently hold her arm.

'In the beginning you still hope. You get up in the morning with the thought: maybe today…But as more and more days go by, it becomes a struggle to get up. Finding ways to fill all those useless hours. Later I tried to pick up the thread again, if only for Charlotte's sake. But you think about it, whatever you're doing. If you're shopping, you look out for her. If people ask me how many children I have, I don't know if I should answer one or two. And every year there's another birthday, and the day she disappeared…' Her voice dies away.

We drink our tea, both of us lost in our thoughts. Isabel's dark eyes look down on us from the wall. It feels like she's looking straight at me and I can't stop my gaze from straying to the photograph.

Elsbeth notices. 'Every time I look at that photograph, I get the idea that she can see me. That she looks at me and says, "Are you giving up? Are you just carrying on without me?" I don't do anything fun anymore, I feel guilty if I laugh and just for a short, short while forget about her. As if she's not immediately back in my thoughts afterwards.'

I've no idea what to say.

'As long as you don't know for sure, you keep hoping that she'll come to the door one day,' Elsbeth says.

'Has there really been no news at all?'

'Nothing. But they are still working on it. The detective who led the investigation keeps in touch with us and there was recently an appeal on *Missing*.'

'Did anything come out of that?'

'A lot of people responded, but it didn't lead to anything concrete.'

'I'm so sorry.'

Elsbeth sits up and pours another cup of tea. 'In any case, you're doing fine. I'm happy about that,' she says in a brave attempt to appear cheerful. 'It's really nice to see you again. You were always such a good friend to Isabel. I let her ride to school alone because I knew that you were with her if she had a fit. I remember at primary school you reading everything about epilepsy you could get your hands on. I always said to her how lucky she was to have such a loyal friend, always there, looking out for her, looking after her.'

'I remember that time we went on a school trip to an amusement park,' I say. 'We were about ten.'

Elsbeth smiles. 'I didn't want to let Isabel go because there'd be too much stimuli. But you swore to me that you wouldn't go on any of the dangerous rides, that you'd remind Isabel to take extra medicine and that you wouldn't leave her alone. I didn't even need to ask, you always offered to do things like that of your own accord.'

'And so she could go along.'

'And so she could go along. I heard later from your teacher that you'd spent the whole day watching over Isabel like a guard dog. He was so touched by it.'

We fall into silence again and look at each other. The memories hang heavy in the air between us.

'I think about Isabel often,' I say. 'Especially when I saw that notice in the paper about the school reunion. By coincidence I ran into someone right after that who she used to go out with.'

'Oh, really?' Elsbeth says.

'Yes, Olaf van Oirschot. Do you know him?'

'The name sounds familiar, but I must admit that I wasn't really in the loop about all of Isabel's boyfriends. She never brought anyone home with her.'

'She used to go out to the Vijverhut, didn't she?'

'Yes, I think so. And to the Mariëndal, by the Dark Dunes. I don't know a lot, she did what she wanted.'

'She was quite popular. Didn't the police ask you at the time who she was going out with?'

'Of course. They wanted to know exactly who her friends were. They questioned them all too. Not that I knew all of Isabel's friends. I used her school diary to find out.'

'Her diary? Didn't she have it with her when she disappeared?'

'No, she'd forgotten it. It was still on her desk.'

I lean forward. 'Do you still have it?'

'It's in her bedroom. Why? Do you want to see it?'

'Very much.'

Elsbeth makes no move to stand up and I feel that she's waiting for some kind of explanation. I put my teacup down on the glass coffee table.

'I'll be honest with you,' I lace my fingers together. 'For years I haven't been able to remember anything about the day Isabel went missing, but for the last few weeks more and more has been coming back. In psychology they call it repression: something that has really affected you can be banished out of your memory. I don't know why, but recently I've been getting more and more memories back.'

Something glitters in Elsbeth's eyes. I have to be careful, not give her too much hope.

'It probably doesn't mean anything, but you never know. I'm trying to recall as much of that day as possible. Perhaps it will help the police.'

Elsbeth sits dead still on the edge of her chair. She stares out of the window, then at Isabel's photo, then back to me.

'Can I help you?' she says softly.

'Yes. Could I look at her diary?'

'Come with me.'

I follow Elsbeth upstairs, to Isabel's bedroom. At the closed door, I hold my breath. What am I expecting to see? Her bedroom, like it used to be when we were twelve? Full of posters of bands, her desk covered in papers, books left open on the floor, the wicker chairs around the small table where we used to share our secrets?

Elsbeth opens the door and we go inside. The wallpaper is different. There are no books on the floor; they are all neatly arranged in the bookshelf. The wicker chairs are still here, and there's a vase of flowers on the table. Her desk is pushed against the wall next to the door, it's been kept tidy. I don't doubt that the drawers are full of Isabel's homework, pens and other personal possessions. Nevertheless, it's no mausoleum. The room is fresh, light and tidy. It just hasn't been emptied.

Elsbeth pulls open a desk drawer and removes a thick diary. 'It's full of photos,' she says with a nervous laugh. 'Perhaps you recognise these people.'

'Could I take it home with me?'

She looks shocked. 'Take it home?'

'Don't worry,' I say quickly. 'That was a stupid question. I'll look at it here.'

It would be nice to be able to do that in seclusion but Elsbeth sits on the edge of the bed and watches.

I leaf through the diary, studying each page carefully. My eyes run over the list of addresses at the front. The names, addresses and phone numbers of classmates are written one after the other in neat, small handwriting. Towards the bottom I see Robin's, and Olaf's, and some other boys I don't know.

I get my own diary out of my bag and copy them out. Under Olaf's address I draw a line.

Next I look at the photographs: Isabel in the middle of a group I don't know. They're outside somewhere, arms wrapped around each other presenting a united front. The boys are all a little bit older than the girls.

Isabel with Robin at a bar, both looking disturbed. Isabel with Olaf, kissing. Isabel in an intimate embrace with an unknown. After that, a passport photo of Olaf. On the next page, Olaf's brown face smiles out at me, younger, with wet hair and the sea in the background.

I thumb through to 8 May. There's a note of some homework assignments, and underneath, in the same tiny, neat letters: DDIO.

I look at Elsbeth. 'What's DD ten?'

'I don't know,' she says. 'At first the police thought she had a ten o'clock appointment to meet someone with the initials DD. But they couldn't find anyone in her circle of friends with those initials. Later they supposed it had to mean the Dark Dunes, but we've never known for sure.'

'Did they search there?'

'Yes, with a search party and dogs. They also used a helicopter with an infra-red scanner, but you can only use that on open ground, over the sea, on the beach, or in the dunes. The army walked hand in hand through the woods, but they didn't find anything.' Elsbeth pulls at the fabric of her shirt. 'Even when they're walking so close to each other, they can still miss someone. And if they're looking the whole day, they start off focused but after a few hours become more careless. That's why they repeated the search a week later, but nothing was found.'

I only half listen, pursuing my own line of thoughts.

'I don't understand why she would have arranged to meet

someone at ten o'clock. We were at school at that time. We didn't finish until around two. I'm certain she didn't leave school before ten.'

'I know. The police checked and Isabel had attended every lesson. She probably had a date with someone at ten o'clock at night, but we'll never find out who with.'

I look at the precise handwriting, the straight line and the round zero next to it. It's very important. I heard Isabel talking about a date after school, at the Dark Dunes. I didn't know who it was with and I didn't care. Now I wish I'd listened more carefully.

'Ten,' I say. 'What could that refer to? Did she keep a personal diary perhaps?'

Elsbeth shakes her head. 'She wasn't the type for that. Far too impatient, far too busy, always on her way to something.' She smiles but there's no happiness in it. 'She had quite a broad circle of friends she kept up with. That was the biggest problem when she went missing, we had no idea where to look.'

I keep looking at the entry for 8 May. It is dawning on me what the ten means. I feel myself tense as it sinks in. I have to force myself not to blurt it out. There's no need to upset Elsbeth or give her false hope. I pick up my bag and stand up.

'Would you like another cup of tea?' Elsbeth asks.

'No, thank you, I have to go.'

Elsbeth nods and follows me down the stairs. She sees me out, and in the doorway, kisses me on both cheeks.

'It's lovely that you came, Sabine,' she says.

'Good luck,' I say.

She takes my hand in hers to delay my departure. 'If only she was found,' she says. 'Deep in my heart I don't expect to find her alive anymore, but if she was found, we could say goodbye.'

I look at Elsbeth's prematurely aged face, at her eyes glistening with tears.

'Yes,' I say. 'She needs to be found quickly now.'

31

In the car I realise that my mobile is still switched off. I turn it on and check my voicemail. Five messages. All from this morning because when I went to bed last night I deleted everything.

9:11: 'Sabine, it's Olaf. I'm standing in front of your door but I don't think you can hear your bell. I need to talk to you.'

9:32: 'I've driven around a bit but you're still not awake. I didn't know you were such a big sleeper. Where is your car by the way? Have you gone out? Call me back when you get this. I'm going home.'

10:15: 'Sabine, Call me back.'

10:30: 'Where are you? Why isn't your phone on?'

10:54: 'I'm on my way to Den Helder and I wanted us to do something nice together, but for that you need to call me back. Where are you?'

He is really unbelievable. No remorse, no apologies.

It's almost eleven. Before he can ring again, I switch off my mobile. With Olaf's voice in my mind, I drive to the first address on the list I'd copied from Isabel's diary.

The Prince Willem-Alexander canal lies in the Golden Belt. It's a sought-after neighbourhood with expensive tall houses. I don't dare park alongside the water, so I park my car in the backstreet and walk back. I pause in front of number 23.

VAN OIRSCHOT FAMILY is written on the copper name plate next to the door. I ring the bell. Almost instantly I hear footsteps on the stairs and a moment later the door opens. An older lady with beautiful white, pinned-up hair looks at me questioningly.

'Are you Mrs van Oirschot? Olaf's mother?' I ask.

'Yes.'

I hold out my hand. 'I'm Sabine Kroese, Olaf's new girl-friend.'

With a gracious gesture she takes my hand and shakes it. She looks over my shoulder into the street.

'I'm alone,' I smile. 'Olaf had other things to do. I was coming to Den Helder today anyway and I happened to drive along this street. I don't know why I stopped. I'm a little curious, I suppose. If it's a bother, please tell me.'

A smile lights up her handsome face. 'I think it's wonderful that you've dropped by. One should always give in to impulses. The nicest things can happen as a result. Come in, Sabine. I was just about to make some coffee.'

I follow Mrs van Oirschot into the hall.

'Kroese,' she says without looking round. 'That's a familiar name. Have we met before?'

'No,' I say.

'Remarkable.'

The high-ceilinged, narrow hall leads to an oasis of light and space – the sitting room. There's a shiny, polished parquet floor, tasteful fabrics in pastel tints, white plastered walls and lots of antiques. The ceiling is decorated with what looks like authentic nineteenth-century ornamentation.

'What a beautiful house.'

'It *is* a pretty house.' Mrs van Oirschot smiles. 'Olaf thinks it's too big for me on my own but I can't imagine leaving it.'

'You're right.'

I sit down in the armchair that Mrs van Oirschot indicates. She settles down on the sofa.

'While the coffee is percolating,' she says, 'let's get to know each other. How nice that Olaf has got a girlfriend at last. Have you been together for long?'

'A few weeks,' I say. 'But why do you say "at last"? Olaf has had other girlfriends hasn't he?'

Mrs van Oirschot shakes her neatly coiffured head. 'Olaf has trouble with girls. He's rather critical.'

'But he's very popular with the girls at work.'

Mrs van Oirschot smiles. 'It doesn't seem to affect him. I ask now and again about his relationships with the ladies – maternal curiosity you could call it – but what he tells me gives me little hope of having a daughter-in-law. One's a show off, the other is too haughty, the next one is too convinced of her own beauty and I could go on. A few months ago he said to me, "Mum, there don't seem to be any girls who can just be themselves. All they do is make eyes and flirt, but you can't have a normal conversation with them. It's only about the thrill of the chase and after a few weeks they lose interest." Olaf can't stand that. He's a serious, sweet boy, not a good-for-nothing.'

'But didn't he once have another girlfriend, before me?' I angle.

'Oh yes, but I was never introduced to any of those girls. It was always over too quickly. He was so disappointed every time.'

'Do you know who they were? I might know them.'

'Dear child, I really couldn't say. As I said, I never met any of those girls, apart from the one – Eline Haverkamp. A nice, intelligent girl. A shame it didn't last. If you'll just excuse me, I'll see if the coffee's ready.' She stands up gracefully and leaves the room.

I take out my diary and write down the name. Eline Haverkamp.

'I think I know Eline,' I lie to Mrs van Oirschot when she returns with a tray. 'Doesn't she live in Amsterdam?'

A light wrinkle appears between Mrs van Oirschot's brows.

'No, I think she's from Den Helder,' she says. 'They studied together in Amsterdam, but she lives here now. But tell me, child, how did the two of you meet?'

With an elegant gesture, she pours the coffee and offers me a small dish with delicious looking biscuits. I take one, thinking back to Mr Groesbeek's chocolates.

'At work,' I say. 'But we've known each other much longer. Olaf used to be a good friend of my brother, Robin.'

'Robin Kroese! Of course, that's where I know the name from. I knew Robin rather well. So you're his sister? Gosh, what a coincidence.' She picks up a pair of sugar tongs and drops a sugar cube into her cup. 'Do you take sugar too, Sabine? No. Very sensible, sweet things are bad for your figure. Not that you need to worry about that, you're lovely and slender.'

'You too,' I say without thinking. 'You look fantastic, Mrs van Oirschot. You're very different from how I'd imagined.'

'What had you imagined?'

I feel a blush creeping from my neck to my cheeks.

'Well, I mean…Olaf can be rather unrefined. He's very different from you.'

Mrs van Oirschot stirs without looking up from her cup.

'Yes, that's Olaf. He has that from his father, he had a touch of the peasant about him too. But *au fond* he's a good, honest boy. He comes to visit me every Saturday morning.' She looks up in surprise. 'Why didn't you come together?'

'What do you mean?'

'He comes here for lunch every Saturday. He'll be arriving at twelve.'

The sip of coffee freezes in my mouth. I glance at the clock opposite me. Half past eleven. With a couple of gulps I empty my coffee cup. I'd wanted to build up to this, but I don't have time anymore.

'Mrs van Oirschot, do you remember Isabel Hartman?'

'Yes, of course I remember her.'

'She was in my class.'

'I know,' she says.

That surprises me. It surprises me so much that I don't know how to continue. I'm actually not sure what I want from this conversation. Information? Answers? But then you have to ask the right questions. With a desperate glance at the clock, I muddle on.

'Olaf was completely in love with Isabel, wasn't he?' I say.

'A lot of boys were attracted to that girl. I didn't like her. She played with their feelings. She'd reel them in and then dump them. I warned Olaf but love is blind. They went out for quite a long time, up until the day she disappeared. Olaf was devastated when she went missing. You couldn't speak to him for weeks.'

'But he was interviewed by the police, wasn't he?'

'Certainly, but he couldn't tell them anything. He hadn't seen Isabel at all on the day she disappeared.'

'I thought they'd arranged to meet that afternoon.'

'Olaf had an exam and when it finished he came straight home. That's what I told the police at the time.'

'He didn't go to meet Isabel?'

'He came home straight away.' Mrs van Oirschot straightens up. I see her transform before my eyes and there's something chilly in her voice that I don't like. I shuffle, look at the clock again and force a smile.

'I must get going. Thank you for the coffee, Mrs van Oirschot.'

'Don't get up.' Her voice is cold and at once I see where Olaf's icy expression comes from.

She leans forward, exactly like he does, and says, 'You haven't come here for pleasantries, have you?'

I don't reply, grab my bag from the floor and ignore her order to remain seated. 'I really have to go now.'

It's ten to twelve.

'Sabine!' Mrs van Oirschot cries.

I pause in the doorway. She comes to me, but I'm not afraid of her. I weigh her up as she does me. Such a frail woman can't stop me. Does she see the expression in my eyes change? She remains standing, folds her hands together and says nothing. Silence hangs like a sword between us. When she speaks at last, her question surprises me.

'Are you really Olaf's girlfriend?'

'I was.'

'I see, and does he know that it's over?'

After some hesitation, I shake my head.

She nods, reassured. 'That's what I was afraid of.'

'Why afraid?'

'As I said already, Olaf has difficulty keeping his girlfriends. I don't know why. Eline couldn't explain it. Can you?'

Twelve dongs resound through the house.

'I really have to go.' I almost run into the hall. The chain is on the front door. I wrestle with it and pull the door open. Every second I expect a hand on my arm, but then I'm in the street and the sun is shining down on my face.

At the end of the canal, I hear the sound of a noisy engine. I have to go that way but instead flee to the right. I don't care if Mrs van Oirschot is looking. I run. I'm at the corner when the car stops in front of the van Oirschot door.

It's a black Peugeot. The doors remain closed, no one gets out. I turn the corner, half expecting to hear my name being called out. But there's nothing. Just in case, I dart down a couple of side streets, hide in a small alley and get my breath back leaning against a fence.

When I've pulled myself together, I look for my car. It's quite a way away. Inside, I lock all the doors.

There are six messages on my voicemail. Without listening to them, I drive away. I'm off to the post office.

32

Haverkamp. There's a whole row of them in the phone book. I've come to the post office intending to go through the numbers one by one, but by the third I've hit my target.

'Eline Haverkamp,' says a young woman's voice.

'Good afternoon, this is Sabine Kroese,' I say. 'We don't know each other but I understand we have a common acquaintance. Olaf van Oirschot.'

Silence.

'Are you still there?' I ask as the silence lengthens.

'Yes. What about Olaf?'

'Nothing, apart from that at the moment I'm going out with him and – '

'Be careful,' she interrupts.

'Sorry?'

'He's not as nice as he seems. I speak from experience.'

'That's why I'm calling you. Could I come round for a moment?'

'Now?'

'It's important.'

'I live in the Schootens. Do you know that neighbourhood?'

'Yes, I'll be with you in fifteen minutes.'

I hang up and write down the address from the phone book.

Shortly afterwards, I'm driving towards the Schootens, a suburb of Den Helder. Miriam used to live there, I remember.

The street where Eline Haverkamp lives is not hard to find and there are plenty of parking spaces. I leave my car in front of the door and climb out. As I'm locking up, the door opens. A girl about my age smiles at me. I go along the garden path and we greet each other in the doorway with a steady handshake.

'Come in,' says Eline. 'Don't trip over the boxes of shopping, I'm just back from the supermarket.'

'That's a whole week's shop by the looks of it.' I laugh as I climb over the boxes.

'That's how you have to do it if you work during the week. Would you like a coffee?'

'No, thanks. I've just had one.' I'd like something to eat but I can't say that. We sit down in the small sitting room. Eline has the same taste as me, lots of white wood. A bookcase takes up an entire wall.

'Be careful with Olaf van Oirschot,' Eline says as she lights up a cigarette. 'I went out with him for a year, but things were only good for around six months.'

'Why was that?'

She shrugs. 'He was dominating and very possessive. From the moment that we started going out, he treated me as his own property. I had to spend every free minute with him. I hardly saw my friends anymore, and he had to come with me everywhere. If I made other plans, he sulked like a small child. He could be totally unreasonable, picked fights, made up and then began all over again. He was only nice when I did exactly what he wanted.' She tries to weigh me up. 'How long have you been together now?'

'Just a few weeks, but we've known each other much longer.'

'What's your name?'

'Sabine Kroese.'

'I know a Robin Kroese. He was a friend of Olaf's.'

'Robin's my brother. That's how I got to know Olaf. A while back we bumped into each other again and it clicked at once. But I've always had mixed feelings, I'm not sure why.'

'I do.' Eline drags at her cigarette. 'Olaf is a classic case of the handsome boy who turns into a tyrant if he thinks he's being rejected.'

'Is it that bad?'

'It could become that bad. The longer your relationship lasts, the more he sinks his teeth in. Make sure you get away from him before he becomes violent.'

'Violent?'

'He hit me,' Eline says. 'Not hard, but still…A man who hits his girlfriend is bad news. After the first time I wanted out, but it wasn't easy. He stalked me, called me endlessly and harassed my friends in order to track me down. Finally I called the police. It went as far as a court case and he was given an injunction to stay away from me. He still called me for weeks and sent me threatening letters. At last it stopped. I think once he had his eye on another girl.'

I sink back into the soft cushions on the sofa. 'I wouldn't mind a coffee after all,' I admit and light up a cigarette.

Eline gives me an understanding smile, goes to the kitchen and puts on the coffee. It's an open plan room. She leans against the bar, which forms the boundary between the rooms. 'Have I frightened you?'

'No, you've just confirmed what I suspected,' I say. 'Earlier, when he was at school, he went out with Isabel Hartman. Does that name mean anything to you?'

'Who doesn't know it?' Eline stays leaning against the bar as the coffee percolates. 'There were posters of her up in the railway station for ages. Did Olaf go out with her?'

'Didn't he tell you?'

'No. That's odd.'

'Especially as you're both from Den Helder.'

209

Eline extinguishes her cigarette in a plant pot. 'I was in Olaf's class,' she says. 'That's how I knew Robin too. So we were at school together, Sabine. It's strange, I can't remember you at all.'

'I wasn't very noticeable.' I smile. 'And I was a couple of years below you.'

'That's true. Were you in Isabel's class then?'

'Yes.'

'I wonder why Olaf never told me that he knew her so well. We even watched an episode of *Missing* which featured Isabel.'

'He didn't tell me either. According to his mother he was gutted when she disappeared. He hadn't seen her that day at all, his mother said, but I know that's not true. They arranged to meet by the Dark Dunes. Right before she went missing.'

Eline whirls around. She stares at me for a few moments then takes two mugs from the cupboard and pours the coffee. She comes back into the sitting room with the steaming mugs in her hand and sets them down on the table.

'Do you think that Olaf had something to do with her disappearance?'

'He's the last person to have seen her alive, but he denies it completely.'

'How can you be sure he's the last person to have seen her?'

'Because in Isabel's diary she wrote that she had a meeting at the Dark Dunes. I heard her talking about it at school, but I didn't know who she was meeting. Until I saw that date in her diary. She'd written IO next to it – Isabel Olaf,' I explain.

There's silence while Eline considers it. 'You're kidding,' she finally says.

We look at each other.

'Perhaps they didn't meet up after all,' Eline says.

'Isabel thought it was going ahead,' I remark. 'I saw her go that way after school. She was riding towards the Dark Dunes.'

Eline blows onto her coffee. 'That doesn't necessarily mean she met Olaf there. He might have forgotten to go.'

'Yes, perhaps. But probably not. Isabel wanted to talk to him. From what she said to her friends I gathered that she wasn't much looking forward to that meeting. I think she was planning on dumping Olaf.' I put out my cigarette and sip my coffee.

'And you don't do that to someone like him,' Eline says. She looks at me over the rim of her mug. 'I think you should go to the police.'

To give myself time to collect my thoughts, I drive to the park next to my old school. There's something reassuring about the quiet pond, the paths and lawns where I spent so much time wandering around, a packet of bread in my hand for the ducks.

The summer-green park receives me with a serene silence. I choose a path, glance over at the red-brick school building and feel just like I'm skipping school.

But I'm no adolescent now. I'm twenty-four. I've got a job, gaps in my memory and a boyfriend I don't trust. After nine years I'm hardly better off than I was. What should I do? Go to the police? It's my duty to, after discovering those initials in Isabel's diary. But who says it does mean Olaf? It's true I can't think of any other boys whose name begins with an O, but I didn't know everyone in town. And who says that O has to be a boy?

The path forks. One path goes off into a darker part of the park. The other leads to the sunny lawns. I chose the sun, lifting my face up to receive the warm rays.

A man with a dog skirts the pond. They play together, the owner throwing sticks and the dog running after them barking. When the stick ends up in the water, the dog doesn't think twice before plunging in among the waterlilies. The owner's laugh resounds over the grass field, a laugh that sounds familiar.

The owner looks to be around my age, but he's too far away for me to be sure. As he walks on, I get up and follow him. He's broad shouldered but not that big and he's got thick, dark hair. The way he stands, hands in his pockets, one foot forwards, is very familiar but I still don't recognise him until he stops in the middle of the path and turns towards his dog, which is sniffing at the bushes.

My heart jumps. He's years older and the dark hair that used to fall into his eyes is now cropped short, but I don't need to look twice to know who it is. He's been popping up in my thoughts regularly of late and now he's standing in front of me: Bart.

33

The summery park holds its breath as we look at each other. The branches of the trees rustle and the sunlight filters through the green canopy onto us.

Bart. It really is him. I take in every detail of his face – the blue of his eyes, his dark and stiff but very thick hair. He is shorter than I remember, less than a head taller than me, and a sudden memory comes: I see myself getting out flat shoes before a date so that I won't tower over the top of him.

Does he recognise me too? He looks at me for quite a long time, too long for a random passer-by I could speak to him but I don't quite trust my voice and more than that I'm afraid that this is a dream that will dissolve when I reach out my hand to him.

Bart makes a movement but it's not directed at me but at his dog. He slaps at his thigh to call his dog to him and goes to move on, but I block the way and give him a lopsided smile.

'Hi,' I manage to croak.

It's the magic word, the magic greeting that gives access to his memory. Or perhaps he just recognises my voice. In any case he remains standing there and a smile appears on his face.

'Sabine.'

'Didn't you recognise me?'

'I wasn't sure,' Bart says. 'Until you smiled at me.'

The dog looks up at me and ambles into the bushes as if it's decided that it's going to be a while before his owner gives him any attention again. Instead of the romantic reunion I've always dreamed of, Bart and I stand uncomfortably smiling at each other for a time. The more the moment draws out, the more my old feelings return. As we stand there I fall for him all over again.

'How funny to bump into you here,' Bart says finally. 'I walk Rover here every day but I've never seen you before.'

'I don't live here anymore,' I say. 'I moved to Amsterdam.'

'The bustle of the metropolis. And what are you doing there?' Bart asks.

'I work in admin,' I say, which doesn't sound as bustling as I'd have liked.

'Aha,' he says.

The dog returns from the bushes with a stick in its mouth and casts it down at Bart's feet. It sniffs my hand and pokes its nose between my legs.

'Rover, stop it! Remember your manners.' Bart grabs him by the collar and jerks him away from me while giving me an embarrassed smile. 'Do you feel like walking with me for a bit? Otherwise he'll keep at it.'

We continue further along the path that enters a shady area of the park. There's an instant air of intimacy between us and now I can't imagine that I almost didn't dare to speak to Bart. Nevertheless, we remain entrenched in the inevitable 'long-time-no-see' chat.

'And what do you do? I presume you still live in Den Helder?' I ask, trying to sound sincerely interested which is not that hard as I do want to know. Although I'd rather move on to the big question of whether he's got a wife and kids.

'I live just round the corner, in Celebes Street. I'm a journalist at the *North Holland Daily*.'

'Oh, you made it!'

He nods and kicks away a stone in front of his feet. 'Yes, that's what I always wanted to do,' he says. 'And, how are things with you? In love, engaged, married?'

'None of the above, actually,' I say, happy that I don't have to lie, happy that I'm free, that he can ask me out again. In my mind I picture us together in a cosy, intimate restaurant overlooking the harbour, hunched towards each other, his hand covering mine so that it disappears completely and…

The dog comes running up to us and jumps up against Bart. Bart picks him up, laughing, which gives me a chance to look at his hands. The narrow golden band on his finger is hard to miss.

'So.' My voice rings shrill in my ears. 'So you've completely settled down here. A dog, a great job, a wife, children…?'

'Hmm,' he says.

'What do you mean, "hmm"?' In an attempt to cover up my immense disappointment, I babble, 'That's what everybody wants in the end, isn't it? A house, a little tree, a pet. Well, not everybody, some people aren't born for that kind of life, or they're not ready for it. Young people are settling down later and later, aren't they? Women are having children much later, often not until their thirties. It used to be quite different, but…'

'I'm in the middle of a divorce,' Bart says.

My mouth falls open. 'Oh?' I say and hope that the joyous undertone isn't too obvious to the ear. Bart doesn't look at all happy about it. What a terrible egoist I am to rejoice in someone else's broken relationship. As if that automatically means he's going to get back together with me! It's not like we didn't break up for a reason.

'How terrible for you.' I lay my hand on his arm in a consoling way, which seems hypocritical to me, but Bart doesn't seem to take it that way. He looks over to me and smiles.

'Have you got children?' I ask in concern, my whole being screaming out for the answer to be no.

215

'A daughter,' Bart says softly. 'She's seven months old. We've agreed that she'll stay with her mother, but at the weekend Kim will spend two days with me, and in between I'll visit as much as possible.'

The sorrow in his voice silences me, though my heartbeat is steady, elated. A tiny little girl, just a baby. That's feasible. I love small children. She'll call me Aunty Sabine and she'll be crazy about me. When she's older, we'll take her to Efteling Amusement Park, and spend alternate weekends just the two of us.

I want it. I want it so terribly, and with every step we advance into the park, with everything that Bart confides, I believe that it's possible. I'll save him, I'll be his refuge, his old new love, and in turn he'll save me. We need each other.

'I have to go,' Bart says. 'I had this morning off but I have to be at the paper in a minute. Damn, and I still have no idea what you're doing in Den Helder.'

'It's a long story,' I say smiling and looking him straight in the eye as though to bewitch him into hearing the story later, in a cosy restaurant on the harbour.

Bart is looking at his watch when Rover jumps into the ditch with an impressive splash. 'I really don't have time for that,' he groans. 'Rover! Heel!'

The dripping wet dog claws its way up the bank and has a good shake, causing us both to jump backwards. Bart kisses me on both cheeks.

'Great to see you again, Sabine,' he says. 'I wished we could have talked a bit more.' He looks regretful and I respond with my own regretful look.

'Hey,' he says, as if he's just thought of something else.

'Yes?'

'Were you planning on going to the reunion? You do know that there's going to be one?' Bart says.

'Yes, I read about it.' I can feel where he's going with this. It's not exactly what I had in mind but it's better than nothing.

'Are you going?' Bart asks.

'Of course,' I say.

'Good! Then we can talk further there.' He kisses me on the cheek and I kiss him back. 'It was lovely to see you again, Sabine. You really must come to the reunion.'

I turn around before he can, look over my shoulder one more time and wave. He waves back, puts Rover on his lead and turns to go himself. It nearly kills me not to look back over my shoulder to see whether he looks back again.

If I want to see him again the only thing for it is to go to the stupid reunion.

34

The idea of the school reunion must have been thought up by the popular, successful people who'd ruled over the school and later found it hard to put that time behind them. They were hoping to return one more time to their glory days so they could sparkle and shine again. It goes without saying that during the night they'd surround themselves with the people they used to hang out with and the failures would lean against the wall, excluded, ignored.

But what would the failures be doing at such a reunion? What would possess them to step back into their previous roles? The intervening years might have changed them. A demonstration of their success and new self-confidence might be necessary to put an end to that period of their lives.

On the day itself, Saturday 19 June, I drive to Den Helder just ahead of a great wave of holidaymakers, and wonder what kind of person Isabel would have become. What she would have looked like, what she would have studied and what job she would have now. Whatever it was, she would still have taken centre stage. Some things never change. But I have. If she'd lived, I would still be going to this reunion.

This sudden insight surprises me. I fish a piece of liquorice out of the bag next to me and put it into my mouth.

Would I really have stood up to Isabel? Probably.

Being able to handle somebody depends mostly on how much you allow that person to reach into your soul and hurt you. You'll always come across people like Isabel in your life. The trick is recognising them from a long way off, raising your guard and trying not to make the same mistakes again.

It is already past seven and the dunes are before me, the golden glow of the evening sun disappearing over their tops. The stretches of tulip and hyacinth fields lie dreaming in the last sunlight. They bring back memories of days spent cutting the heads off tulips, a holiday job I'd started with Isabel when we'd just turned thirteen. In August a fair had come to town. Isabel and I rode there one evening. It was still light when we wanted to leave at 10 p.m., but it was rapidly getting darker. Nauseous from the attractions and fairy floss, we looked for our bikes. My bike was there, but Isabel's had disappeared. We spent almost an hour looking for it, but it really had gone. We looked at each other in dismay but then her eye fell upon a boy she knew who was just leaving on his moped. After a short conversation, she climbed on behind him, waved at me and they rode off together. By then it was eleven o'clock and the people who were still there were starting to show the first signs of drunkenness. Some men lurching between the shooting stall and the Ferris wheel spotted me and drifted in my direction. I raced away on my bike, out of the town, along the quiet Lange Vliet as it turned pitch dark. Every now and again I met a moped or a car coming the other way and my heart nearly stopped. I should have called Robin and asked him to pick me up, but I didn't think of that, I was so shocked that my best friend had abandoned me after I'd spent an hour helping her look for her bike.

You might say that I was too good a friend. My mother tried to make me stronger, tried to boost my ego, but as far as I was concerned, a friend was a friend, someone whose faults you forgave. Time and time again.

I park my car on the edge of the park where I bumped into Bart not long ago and look over at the school building. Only the expectation of seeing Bart again stops me from driving back to Amsterdam.

I look good, better than ever before. I'm wearing a new skirt, a top in different shades of pink that looks great against my summer tan. I've put my hair up in a clasp and as I check myself in the rear view mirror, I'm satisfied. That makes a difference. With a deep sigh, I throw open the door and stick out a tanned leg. With renewed self-confidence I walk to the main entrance.

I'm too early. Far too early. The assembly hall is as good as empty. I glance at the few people present but don't recognise anyone. The reunion is for the whole school, so they must be from other years.

I wander around, back to the hall, read the noticeboard to see whether I can see the names of any teachers I know and go to the toilet. As I sit on the loo, the space is filled with whispers of years ago. I read the writing scratched into the door, insults directed at the current students. My heart bleeds for them.

I get up from the loo, wash my hands by the fountain and check my make-up in the mirror. I look good, I really do. I look immaculate. Shoulders back, chest out, I can do this.

The hall is filling up with people who've left puberty long behind and are all walking around with the same sorry expression on their faces.

I recognise Miriam Visser thanks to her stout build. She's laughing rather exaggeratedly at someone and, what's happened to her teeth? They're almost falling out of her mouth. At once I'm thankful for the headgear brace that caused so much hilarity in Year 8.

I study every newcomer with a critical eye. I recognise a few people now. My eyes search for Bart, but don't find him. He can't blow me off, I've come especially for him.

'Sabine Kroese? Is that really you?'

A hand lands on my shoulder and I turn around and look into the unknown face of a girl of my age. 'Oh, hello!' I say with a weak smile.

'I thought it was you, but I couldn't really believe it. You're so…different!' she says. 'Who've you seen already?'

'Well…'

'Bart de Ruijter is here,' she confides. 'I was just talking with him. Didn't you used to go out with him? He's still really good looking, you wouldn't believe it.'

I don't waste time wondering how she knows I used to go out with Bart, but look around. 'Where did you see him?'

'By the bar. Well, I must move along, because I think…Yes, that's Karen. She looks so different. Karen, Karen!'

It is busy at the bar, but Bart isn't there. I order a wine, turn around and find myself face to face with Miriam.

'Sabine, isn't it?' she drawls. 'Wow, I'm amazed you've come.'

'I wouldn't have missed it for the world.' I've spotted Bart somewhere in the throng but he doesn't see me. When I try to attract his attention, I lose him again.

'Did you see somebody?' Miriam asks. She's wearing a blue skirt with a matching jacket. It's got a great big bow on the back. She resembles an Easter egg.

'Bart,' I say. 'Bart de Ruijter.'

Her face goes through various motions: delight, amazement and finally scorn, as though she's asking herself what the hell I'd want with Bart de Ruijter.

Wouldn't it be good if he came over and put his arm around my shoulders. But I can't see him at all and if we're not going to spend the whole evening just missing each other, I'll have to go in search of him.

'Cheers,' I say to Miriam who is in the middle of a story I'm not listening to, and I walk away.

I look from left to right, stand on tiptoes, stretch my neck looking for him. Across the room, I spot Olaf. Our eyes meet momentarily but I keep mine travelling as if I haven't seen him and press into the crowd, in the opposite direction.

And then I spot Bart. He's standing in the doorway of the main entrance, smoking a cigarette with a few former classmates I don't know. My old shyness returns and I falter. Now is the moment to lay my hand on his arm and say, 'Bart! It's good to see you!'

But I can't move.

I turn around and see Miriam on the stairs, looking over the crowd. Her eyes rest on Bart. And then she sees me and the condescending expression on her face transforms her into the teenager of nine years ago. She's not the only one looking at me. Isabel is standing next to Miriam and they're both look down at me, united in derision and scorn.

I turn away and see the girl, huddled into a corner. Her shoulders are slumped. Her gaze is directed at Bart. She's like a dog waiting to be stroked.

'Come out of that corner!' I scream at her in my thoughts. Let them see who you are.

She looks away from me skittishly. I'd like to shake her until her teeth rattle but at the same time I'm overcome by an intense feeling of sadness.

Somebody bumps into me and spills cola over my shoes. He doesn't even notice, but the sticky splash brings me to my senses. I go over to the main entrance, put my hand on Bart's arm and say, with my most charming smile, 'Hey, Bart!'

He's still talking to his old friends but when I interrupt, a pleased expression washes over his face.

'Sabine!' He squeezes my arm, kisses me three times on the cheeks and pulls me against him for a moment. I can only hope that everyone is looking at us.

'I was looking for you,' he says into my ear. 'Busy here, isn't it?'

'Far too busy,' I say, enjoying feeling his breath on my cheek.

'Shall we go?'

'Let's go.'

He takes me by the elbow and leads me outside. As we walk down the pavement, I glance briefly back at the entrance and catch Olaf studying me with the strangest expression on his face.

35

'Fresh air,' says Bart. He sounds happy. He's let go of my elbow and we walk together to our cars. I wonder what the plan is. He can't just be going home, can he?

'I don't really understand why I came.'

'Didn't you enjoy seeing everyone again? You had a good time at school, didn't you?'

'Yes, but nine years is a long time. I haven't seen most of my friends from back then. I've kept in touch with two of them, you don't need a reunion for that. Oh, you know beforehand how it'll be – blah, blah, blah. And it's always the same story.' He adopts a bored storytelling voice and rattles off his version. 'Yes, really, I do still live in Den Helder. I'm a journalist at the *North Holland Daily*. Married, divorced, one kid. Yes, it's difficult. What did you say? You've seen an old friend over there? Oh, well, see you. Hey, Peter. Yes, I do still live in Den Helder. How are things with you? Well, what can I say? Married, divorced, one kid…'

Bart sighs and I laugh.

'I'd rather just concentrate on the one person I'd really like to talk to,' Bart continues. 'What shall we do, Sabine? Get a drink in town?'

A mild breeze caresses my cheek, dissuades me from the idea of a pub.

'Actually, I feel like going to the beach,' I say. 'I think the beach bars are still open.'

'Good idea.'

'Your car or mine?' I ask.

'I came on foot, I live just round the corner,' Bart says.

'Well, my car then,' I say and point at the silver grey Ford Ka. 'I hope you'll fit in it.'

'I'll fold myself up,' Bart says.

It's just too far to walk but in the car we're soon there. Most of the beach goers have already headed home but those who enjoy their peace and quiet are just arriving.

'If I'd known I would have brought my swimming things,' I say. 'Isn't it warm? I bet the water's lovely.'

'They should have put that on the invitation – bring your bathers.'

'And your best mood,' I add.

'You'll be dropped off home afterwards,' Bart says and we both laugh.

We climb the steps. At the top there's a beautiful view of the murmuring sea. The sun rests on top of the water in a pool of reds and oranges.

'Wow,' I say.

'This was a really good idea of yours.' Bart reaches for my hand, grasps it, and just as I begin to feel nervous at the over-dose of romanticism, he hauls me down the dune, faster and faster. I shriek and run with great big strides with him. I can't do anything else. Bart accelerates and I fall. He lets himself fall too at once and we roll down the dune together. We stand up, out of breath and spitting sand. I feel fifteen again.

'That's not what happens in the film,' I say.

'It depends which film you're watching.' Bart puts his arm around me and his face close to mine. 'A comedy or a romance. Which do you prefer?'

I look into the intense blue of his eyes, a blue I've never quite been able to banish from my thoughts. 'Romance,' I murmur.

'What a piece of luck.' Bart leans in further and kisses me. Small kisses, on my top lip, my bottom lip, my whole mouth. Each time I'm about to answer his kiss he pulls back a little, until his mouth ends up in my neck and from there finds the path back to my lips. And stays there. I don't give him the chance to venture off again, I wrap my arms tightly around his neck and kiss him with all my might.

Now I know what was missing with Olaf. Now I know why one kiss isn't the same as another. I really don't care that people go past us, that they're probably watching us and laughing, or even standing staring. I've got Bart back and the rest of the world can sink into the sand.

Finally we break off because the next step is just a bit too far for the place we're in, but we remain seated in an embrace and can't stop looking at each other.

'Why did this take so long?' Bart asks. 'Nine years! I can't believe that you're here now, so close.'

I trace the contours of his face. 'I've thought about you so often.'

Bart kisses my finger. 'Me too. It really hurt when we broke up.'

'Why did you end it then?' I don't want to ask but the words slip out.

Bart drops my hand and looks at me in utter amazement. 'Why did *I* dump *you*? You dumped me. You didn't want to see me anymore.'

I look back in total confusion. 'That's not true.' My head is pounding, just a touch.

'I came to your house every day, threw stones at your window, rang the bell but you wouldn't open up. You looked outside, shook your head and that was it. You never said anything or gave any explanation. In the end it was Robin who told me that you didn't want to see me anymore.'

I free myself from Bart and press my hands against my temples. 'It can't be true, it can't be true.'

Bart looks at me with raised eyebrows. 'You do remember, don't you?' he says.

I let my hands drop and shake my head in exhaustion. 'No, I really can't remember anymore. I really can't. Did *I* finish it? Are you sure? But why? Why did I do that?'

Bart is looking at me in disbelief. 'How can you have forgotten that?'

I bite my lip and wipe the sand from my leg. 'I've forgotten so much. Too much. I've got these great gaps in my memory.'

'Gaps? What do you mean?'

'Like I say, there are whole bits missing.'

'Since when?'

'Since about the time Isabel disappeared. But I thought I'd only lost my memories of her, I'd no idea I'd forgotten stuff about us too.' I look over at Bart to see whether he believes me.

'It was a very confusing time,' he says. 'So much happened: Isabel disappearing, police investigations, the press. The whole school was turned upside down. Final exams. And then you ended it. It felt like I'd lost everything I was sure of.'

'When did I end it? When Isabel went missing?'

'That same week. From one day to the next you didn't want to see me anymore. I've never understood why, I just had to let it go.'

I'm overwhelmed with guilt, but I still don't understand. Why did I do that? Why did I end things with a boy I was so in love with?

'I've read a few books about the workings of the memory,' I say hesitantly, afraid of what he will think. 'It seems that you can repress traumatic events. I don't know exactly how it works but it's possible to banish them from your memory out of self-protection. That makes it sound like you have some control over it, but there's a certain part of your consciousness that makes that

227

decision for you. I think, no, I know that this is what happened to me. I must have seen or heard something that I couldn't cope with emotionally, something my memory has hidden away. But it's still there, and I'm getting more and more pieces back.'

'To do with that bullying?'

'No, I remember that all very clearly. It's got to do with Isabel's disappearance.'

'Oh?'

'It's not very spectacular,' I say, wanting to evade him. 'It's also difficult to put into words because there are no concrete images. It's more…a feeling.'

Bart stretches out on his back in the sand and folds his hands under his head. 'I do believe the memory is capable of such things. I saw something about it on the Discovery Channel once.' He gives me a sideways glance, his eyes serious. 'Don't worry that I'll think you're crazy, I won't.'

I don't hesitate any longer. It's so good to be able to talk about this with someone, someone who takes me seriously and who knows the people involved. 'I'm in the Dark Dunes and I see somebody walking. Suddenly that person is gone; they've disappeared. I carry on past but then go back. I must have noticed something but I don't know what. I get down from my bike and leave the path. I go into the woods. I'm cautious, as if I sense that there's something going on that I'm not supposed to see. The woods quickly turn into duneland. On the edge of a clearing, I stand hidden in the trees.'

I stop and wipe some sand from my leg.

'And then? What do you see?' Bart puts his hand on my arm.

'Nothing. The sun is shining in my eyes and it blinds me. I blink but I can't get rid of the spots in front of my eyes. That's when the memory stops.' I stare at the sea rolling backwards and forwards onto the beach. 'To be honest, I'm not even sure it is a memory. Perhaps it's my imagination playing tricks on me and I only think I'm remembering this.'

Bart rolls over onto his side, supports himself on one elbow, squinting as he considers me. 'But deep inside you believe you witnessed something terrible. Something that happened to Isabel in the woods. The only way to be certain is to tell the police and have them search there. Do you still know where you entered the woods?'

I picture myself sitting in front of DC Hartog. 'I remembered walking into the woods and seeing a clearing.' 'What did you see there then?' 'Well, actually nothing. I'm not sure if it's a memory or a dream. But why don't you dig a hole with the entire police force?'

I push my toes into the sand. 'They'll never believe it. I need to go to them with more, be more definite about it, be able to pinpoint the exact spot.'

'Can you do that? Do you know where it was?'

'That's what I was just saying. Not exactly.'

That's not true. I could walk there now if I wanted to, but something stops me from sharing that information with him. He might decide to take me to the Dark Dunes right now and that's the last thing I want.

'I went to see Mr Groesbeek,' I say, changing the subject.

'Groesbeek? What did you want with him?'

'I remembered something. It was very strange, remembering it suddenly like that. On the day Isabel disappeared I was following her on the bike, and I saw her stop at the crossroads between Jan Verfailleweg and Seringen Avenue. What I hadn't thought about for a long time was the delivery van I'd hidden behind. It was a green, dirty little van, just like the one Groesbeek had. And that van went the same way as Isabel.'

'The van was following her?'

'No, it overtook her, but that doesn't mean anything. He could have waited for her a bit further up.'

Bart lets the information sink in. 'Did you confront Groesbeek about it?'

'No, I didn't mention it. I don't actually know why I went to see him, or what I hoped to gain from it. He didn't recognise me and Isabel's name didn't ring any bells either. But I did discover something extraordinary.'

I give Bart a short resumé of my meeting with Mr Groesbeek and a lively description of making the acquaintance of his cats.

'They all had girl's names,' I say. 'Anne, Lydie, Liz, Nina, Rose, Belle. Liz could be short for Lizette. Anne comes from Anne-Sophie, Lydie is Lydia, Nina stayed Nina, Rose stands for Rosalie and Belle could be Isabel.'

'Are you winding me up? Were those really the names?'

'Yes.'

'You have to tell the police.'

'I did. They're going to talk to him, although they weren't that bothered.'

'Are they blind? Those are all the girls who something happened to!'

It strikes me that he made the connection immediately. I'd never heard of those girls until I read the newspaper cuttings.

'You're very well informed,' I say.

'I'm a journalist, I keep up with the news.' Bart stands up and holds out a hand to me. 'Shall we walk a bit?'

I let him pull me up and am happy that he doesn't let go of my hand afterwards. We zigzag along the tideline for a while and then Bart gives me a serious look. 'I don't like it that you went to see Groesbeek completely on your own, Sabine. If he's really got something to do with the case then you could have got into real trouble.'

'I sat right next to the door,' I say.

'So you did feel uneasy. Why did you go then?'

'Because my memory is coming back. One recollection brings back others. I've always had the feeling that I know more about Isabel's disappearance than I could say, and now I know it for sure.'

I glance over at Bart who is standing looking out to sea. 'Why do people repress events from their lives?'

I don't know whether he's expecting an answer or whether it's a rhetorical question. There's a long silence, until Bart looks at me.

'Because they're too shocking to live with,' I say.

'And what could have happened that was so shocking to you?' Bart continues.

'I don't know.' I avoid his gaze.

Bart takes hold of my chin and forces me to look at him. 'I think you know full well. In any case you have an idea. Why don't you tell me what you think happened?'

I sigh. 'Because I'm not yet sure of it.'

'Of what?'

'That I did witness whatever happened to Isabel.'

'I think you did, too. But why have you repressed it? If she was murdered, I can well imagine that would be a shocking thing to witness. I can also imagine that you'd be dead scared and in the first instance you might shut yourself off from the outside world. You might not even want to see *me* anymore. But why didn't you go to the police later on, why did you repress everything with such force?' Bart's voice becomes more urgent and his hands hold my upper arms so tightly that it almost hurts.

His eyes are really close, so close that I can't escape their magnetic effect.

'I don't know,' I whisper, but that's a lie. I begin to cry. We both know that there's one reason I wouldn't want to face the truth – because I knew the murderer. Because it was somebody I liked.

36

The atmosphere has changed completely. All of the romance is gone and there's something indefinable in its place. Bart holds my hand tightly, so tightly that my bones almost meld together.

'It wasn't me, if that's what you're thinking,' he says. 'I didn't like her that much but I didn't have a problem with her.'

'Olaf van Oirschot thought that you had something going with her,' I say.

'Do you think so too? While I was going out with you? Come on, Sabine, you know better than that.'

It's true I hadn't noticed anything, but do we always see what's going on under our noses? He correctly interprets my silence.

'With Isabel, you would know,' Bart says. 'She was a slut. If a guy even looked at her she'd try it on, just because she could. She did come after me – who didn't she go after – but it didn't work.'

I'd pictured our walk along the beach quite differently. I want the romance back, but it's too late to retrieve it.

'She tried to seduce me right up until the day she disappeared,' Bart tells me. 'In the meantime, she satisfied herself with everyone she could get, and there were quite a lot of them.'

I think of Olaf and Robin. How sure can I be that Bart didn't fall for her too? Not that it matters much after all this time, if you discount a lover's tiff as a motive for murder.

'Why was our relationship a secret?' I ask. 'Why couldn't anybody know? And will you let go of my hand please, it's beginning to hurt.'

Bart draws my hand to his lips. 'Sorry, why didn't you say so before?' He kisses my hand a few times and says, 'I didn't want to cause you any more problems. Isabel was already after me because she couldn't have me and if she'd found out that I was in love with you, she'd have ruined your life completely. I thought that you'd understood that.'

'I thought you were ashamed of going out with me. That you didn't dare tell anyone,' I say. 'But I was so in love that it was enough for me as it was.'

'It bothered you?' Bart sighs. 'God, what a lot can go wrong if you simply take it for granted that the other person understands you.'

I lay aside this reason for our break-up. Mind you, I *don't* know why I ended it. I really can't remember anything. There could have been hundreds of reasons, of which one is quite obvious. But no, I don't want to believe that.

How can I fall for this man if I don't even know our own past? And yet I want him. I look at Bart's handsome, powerful profile and feel myself irresistibly attracted to him, something which has never changed. In all the tumult of emotions and memories, I can trust only that feeling. It's all that I have.

Shattered, I lean against Bart and he wraps his arms around me at once.

'And now?' he says, with his chin on the crown of my head. 'What are we going to do?'

The sun is long gone, it's getting cooler and darkness is creeping over the beach.

'I'm cold and tired,' I say.

'Do you want to go home?'

'That's quite a drive,' I mumble into his T-shirt.

'My house is nearby.'

I break away from him and push him backwards a little in order to get a better look at him.

'Hmm, I'd better sleep at yours,' I say.

Bart nods.

'Sleep,' I repeat.

'Sure, I heard you. Anyway, we'll have to sleep at some point.'

The tension is broken. We walk back along the beach hand in hand. There's not a swimmer to be seen. For that reason, the one other car at the top of the steps is instantly noticeable to me when we get into my Ka. I start up the engine, drive out of the carpark and look once more in my rear view mirror. In the darkness under the dunes, I can just make out a dark-coloured Peugeot driving after us.

I accelerate, keeping an eye on the dark-coloured car and indicate right. The Peugeot follows us at a safe distance. At the crossroads I go to drive straight on but at the last moment I swing the wheel and turn left.

'You're going the wrong way,' Bart says.

'Sorry,' I say. 'My mistake.'

I shoot into a side street and take a few more random turns.

'What on earth are you doing?' Bart asks.

'I thought we were being followed,' I say apologetically.

Bart looks over his shoulder at the empty road and grins. 'Women,' he says.

For the rest of the drive, I see no further sign of the Peugeot but it's a while before it stops following me in my mind.

37

It might sound unbelievable but we don't do anything other than sleep that night. Okay, we kiss, whisper and laugh too, and it's the middle of the night before we stop reminiscing. We collapse into sleep, entwined, as if we'd never been separated.

Waking up with Bart is totally different than it was with Olaf – I lie relaxed on my side and listen to Bart's breathing, the sounds he makes in his sleep. I resist the urge to stroke his face. It is still early, much too early. Let him enjoy his sleep.

I snuggle up to him, and sink back into a slumber. When I open my eyes again I find myself staring right into Bart's.

'Good morning,' he says.

'Good morning. What time is it?'

'Not that late. We've still got plenty of time.' He kisses me softly, tenderly and I feel the awakenings of desire.

'Plenty of time for what?' I respond to his kisses.

Bart rests on his elbow and looks down at me. 'To repair the damage of earlier. Do you know, there must be a reason I met you again now. Six months ago, I was still married.'

He shouldn't have said that. Some of my blissful feeling ebbs away. We can do our best to repair the damage, but there are nine long years between us, years that have formed us, turned us into completely different people. This is not the Bart I know;

this is a man with a marriage behind him, the father of a small girl.

Bart senses my mood, something he was always good at. 'Sabine?' he says. 'I'm serious about you, you do know that don't you?'

I feel a warm flood of happiness wash my worries away. 'I'm serious about you too.'

We kiss. The sun creeps through a chink in the curtains and reminds us that everyone else is starting to get up now, but we stay in bed. Desire grows and then kissing and touching isn't enough anymore. When the phone rings it is worse than irritating.

Bart is not concerned by the shrill ringing and turns his full attention back to me, but the phone keeps going. Finally Bart rolls off me with an irritated sigh and picks up.

'Bart speaking.'

On the other end I can clearly hear a woman's voice. Bart listens, nods a few times as if she can see him and says, 'Hmm,' and 'I understand' and 'No problem, I'm on my way,' and then hangs up.

I look at him, uneasy. 'Do you have to go?'

'Yes, sorry.' Bart buries his head into my neck. 'Sorry. I wanted to do all kinds of nice things with you today but Dagmar has got flu and her parents are on holiday. She asked if I could look after Kim today so that she can recover.'

'Oh,' I say.

'I couldn't say no. How can she look after Kim properly when she's in bed with a fever?'

It's gutting but I've got to get used to it, better still, I'll show how well I can handle this.

'No, don't worry,' I say in an understanding tone of voice. 'Go round quickly, we'll see each other another time.'

'You're a sweetheart.' Bart gives me a long, grateful kiss. 'Let's quickly have breakfast and then I'll call you later. Give me your address and phone number.'

We exchange contact details over the breakfast table and then Bart becomes restless. He wants to go to his daughter, perhaps also to his ex. They loved each other, married each other, will always be linked by the birth of their daughter. How many of those feelings remain secretly dormant, even when you're divorced?

We say goodbye slowly, one last kiss, and another. A caress, a wave, and then I'm in my car and Bart's in his.

Despite the abrupt end to our night together, I sit behind the wheel with a blissful smile. I drive out of the centre, turn onto the North Holland Canal and remember that my mobile is still switched off. Perhaps Bart has sent me a text message.

I grab my mobile and turn it on. There are five urgent messages from Olaf on my voicemail, all of which say that he wants to speak to me, and which dampen my mood.

I'll have to make it clear to him once again that I'm really not interested. If he was standing on the beach steps last night, he must have got an inkling of that. How will Olaf take the fact that I went home with Bart? Not very well, I imagine.

I worry the whole drive back to Amsterdam and when I turn into my street, I make a quick check of the cars parked there. No black Peugeot.

I park, climb out, close the door and cross the street. I open my front door feeling very uncomfortable and slam it shut behind me. My footsteps sound hollow on the worn wooden stairs. I hesitate in front of the door to my flat. I stare at the wooden surface as if hoping that supernatural powers will be able to tell me what's waiting behind it.

Legs trembling, I go one floor further and ring Mrs Bovenkerk's bell.

'Who's there?'

'It's me, Sabine. Could you open the door, Mrs Bovenkerk?' I shout.

'I'm coming, child. Just a minute.'

237

Jigging from one leg to the other, I wait. The door opens and Mrs Bovenkerk smiles out at me.

'Hello dear. What can I do for you?'

'I just wanted to know whether anybody has been to my door,' I say.

'I didn't hear anybody,' she says. 'But I did hear your phone ringing constantly.'

'And no one asked for my key?'

'No, no one. And that would have been pointless as they wouldn't have got it.'

I smile. 'Thank you. That's all I needed to know.'

She looks at me, curious. 'Is something going on? Are you being harassed?'

'A bit,' I say.

'Put another lock on your door,' Mrs Bovenkerk advises. 'Or put a couple of chairs against it. That's what I always do in the evenings. They won't get into my flat! And if they do manage to force their way in, I've got my grandson's baseball bat under my bed.' She peers into the stairway with a combative expression, as if she's half hoping to use the bat. 'Oh yes, child, I'm going to my daughter's for a few days, so I hope you can keep an eye on my flat.'

Perhaps I should move in there.

Reassured I return downstairs and open my flat door. The sun shines into the living room, giving my familiar, loved possessions a warm glow.

No flowers on the table, no surprises, no Olaf.

I let the tension slide away from me and lock the door behind me. Now for a shower, clean clothes and a cup of coffee on the balcony.

I ignore the answering machine which is blinking at me. Once I've had a shower and am nicely freshened up, I listen to it.

'Hello my lovely, beautiful Sabine,' I hear Bart's deep voice. 'I just wanted to tell you how wonderful I found it to wake up next to you this morning. A shame our Sunday together didn't work out, but we'll repair the damage as quickly as possible. You're not home yet, I'll call you later.' His message ends with a series of kissing noises, but the smile is wiped off my face as messages from Olaf follow, one after the other. Their tone progresses from reproachful to outright fury. I delete them and check that I've locked the door. I save the message from Bart so that I can listen to it again.

The rest of the afternoon I spend reading on my balcony and in the evening I put a pizza in the oven. I've still got lettuce and tomatoes, so I don't need to leave the house. I eat all those calories in front of the TV, mildly entertained by a dumb comedy. When the film is almost over, the doorbell goes.

I shoot up and switch off the television as if a burglar alarm has gone off. The bell goes again, followed by a banging at the door.

'Sabine! Are you home! It's me!'

Olaf.

'Sabine!'

I sit on the sofa in silence, the remote control pointed in front of me as if I can zap Olaf away with it. In the meantime, he thumps on the door even harder with his fists.

'Sabine! Open up!' The anger in his voice is terrifying.

I tiptoe to the telephone, but when I go to call the police, I hesitate over the keypad. What was it again? 122. No, 112, or do you have to put something before it? Shit, why does your memory let you down when you need it the most?

I hurry into the bedroom where my handbag is. The phone book in my mobile says 112. I hold my finger above the call button and listen to Olaf pummelling the door. If he breaks in, I'm going to call.

He doesn't break the door down. There's silence in the hall and I hope for a moment that he has gone away. I listen hard then tiptoe out of the bedroom. I'm standing rigid when the door swings open and Olaf comes in, a key in his hand.

It's such a big shock that blood rushes to my ears. I stare at him. He looks back and we just stand there.

'Olaf,' I say at last.

He looks at me. 'So you are there. Why didn't you open the door?'

'I didn't hear you,' I say with my sincerest expression. 'How did you get in?'

He walks up to me and waves my spare key in front of my face. 'I found this,' he says. 'Some time ago.'

'You found it? You stole it, you mean. I can't remember giving you that key.' I grab the key from his hand and try to look confident, but fear trickles from behind the mask.

'I took it, yes,' Olaf says.

Irritation competes with fear. Stay calm, he's inside now, don't make him angry. He has such a strange look in his eyes; don't make it worse.

I turn away from Olaf with a light laugh. 'Well, now that you're here, would you like a drink? A beer?'

I'm already on my way to the kitchen. Olaf follows me and stands in the doorway. He leans against the doorframe, his arms folded, and watches every movement I make. It's a real effort to crack open a bottle of beer. I could do with a sip myself. I pick up another bottle, turn around and give Olaf his. He takes the bottle but doesn't drink. My back to the counter, I avoid Olaf's gaze which is still focused on my face.

'Why didn't you open up?' His voice sounds calm but I can see a muscle in his neck throbbing.

'I didn't hear anything,' I repeat.

'What were you doing then?'

'I had my iPod on,' I say, and go into the sitting room where I'll be closer to the telephone.

Olaf follows me. 'I heard that you went to visit my mother recently.'

240

'Yes.' My voice is shrill. 'I was in the area and thought, what the hell, why not go and see where Olaf used to live. When I saw that your mother still lived there, I dropped in.'

'Why?'

I inject some surprise into my voice. 'Isn't it normal to meet your boyfriend's parents?'

'I'd imagined we'd visit her together,' Olaf says.

'Sometimes it's nice to have a girlie chat.'

'What did you chat about then?'

I reflect. It's quite possible that his mother has given him a full account of everything we said.

'You,' I say. 'And Isabel, and Eline. I wanted to know who else you'd been out with.' I accompany this with a smile, the apologetic grin. I'm the perfect jealous girlfriend.

Olaf relaxes. 'You could have asked me that.'

'Yes,' I admit. 'Are you very annoyed?'

He pulls me towards him. I don't resist, even though his eyes remain hard. 'Did you have a nice time with Bart?'

My eyes don't leave his. 'At the reunion, you mean?' I say. 'Yes, it was lovely to see everyone again.'

'Not that you stayed very long.'

I don't know what to say to this. Why should I say anything at all? What difference does it make?

'You followed us.' My voice is equally cold. 'I saw your car. Why did you do that?'

He lets go of me. Or to be accurate, he pushes me away from him. 'Because I didn't believe you'd go with him.'

'What's wrong with chatting with an old friend? We were only going for a walk along the beach.'

We both pause, our gazes locked, weighing each other up.

'You used to go out with him, didn't you?' Olaf says. 'Robin told me once. And now you've met up again. Isn't that romantic? But what did that guy mean to you? You had a relationship that nobody could know about. True love?'

'He kept it secret to protect me from the others,' I say.

Olaf sniffs. 'Do you know what I would have respected? If he'd openly admitted that he liked you. If he hadn't given a shit what the others thought and had brought you into the group. That's what he should have done. That's what I would have done.'

I believe him. Yes, I believe that he would have done that right away. We stand staring at each other for a while. Every part of me screams for him to leave, but instead Olaf ambles into my sitting room and downs his beer in one. He slams the empty bottle down on the dresser. 'Do you have any more?'

I nod and disappear into the kitchen. I wrestle with the bottle opener with shaking hands. I hear him walking around, pacing backwards and forwards, backwards and forwards.

When I peer around the kitchen door, he is standing over my answering machine. Bart's voice fills the room and my skin crawls. 'Hello my lovely, beautiful Sabine. I just wanted to tell you how wonderful I found it to wake up next to you this morning. A shame our Sunday together didn't work out, but we'll repair the damage as quickly as possible. You're not home yet, I'll call you later.'

The kissing noises that had given me such a warm feeling this morning, make me stiffen now. I creep to the kitchen door, into the hall and glance into the sitting room. Olaf stands with his back to me in front of the dresser, his hands pressed to it, his head bent down, like somebody doing his utmost to retain his self-control. His finger returns to the answering machine and Bart tells him again how wonderful it was to wake up next to me. Olaf presses delete, Bart shuts up and Olaf turns around.

I slip into the toilet and lock the door. Olaf's footsteps go past and I hear him enter the kitchen. 'Where are you?' he asks.

I swallow, take control of myself.

'In the loo,' I call. 'I'll be there in a minute, help yourself to beer.'

He doesn't take his beer. I hear the bottle splinter on the kitchen floor and I crumple. More bottles are being broken.

I turn the lock on the toilet door, millimetre by millimetre, and peer around the corner. Olaf is throwing a chair at the glass of the balcony door. I fly into the hall, grab my bag from the bedroom and run to the front door. In the kitchen, he is making too much noise to hear me. My plates and bowls are being broken. I tug open the door, go into the dark hall, shut the door behind me and lock it. That will hold him back a bit once he discovers I've gone. There are a couple more spare keys around the house but he won't find them that easily.

I run down the stairs and pull open the front door. The cool evening air rushes over my hot face. My car is in front of the door. I run to it, fumble with the lock and almost fall inside. Central locking, start the engine, drive.

38

I'm always amazed how many people are out late at night, walking, riding or driving around. It's a Sunday night and it's busy at
this time on weeknights too, out on the street.

I ring Jeanine's bell endlessly but there are no answering footsteps. Finally I ring her. She always leaves her phone on the
bedside table in case of emergencies.

Just before her voicemail would usually kick in, her sleepy
voices comes on the line.

'What?'

'Jeanine, it's me, Sabine. I'm at your front door. Will you open
it?'

'Sabine?'

'Yes, open the door, please.'

'What are you doing here?'

'I'll explain in a minute. Can you open up?'

I hide in the shadow of the doorway, keeping an eye on the
street, totally silent behind me.

The door opens and Jeanine's pale face, framed by spiky hair,
looks out at me. She's still half asleep. 'What's going on?'

I step inside. 'Can I sleep at yours?'

'What's happened? Can't you get into your house?'

'Olaf is busy trashing the place.'

Her eyes widen. 'Was the sex that bad?'

'It's no joke, Jeanine. He's not what he seems.'

'Tell me,' she says, leading me into her apartment.

After I've told her – I keep it brief – Jeanine shakes her head. 'Who'd have thought that of Olaf. Do you mind if we go to bed straight away? I'm passing out I'm so tired.' Jeanine yawns. 'Do you mind sharing my bed?'

I don't mind. I undress and crawl into the double bed next to Jeanine. She goes to sleep with the ease of someone who hadn't woken up properly but had just stumbled to the door on auto-pilot. As for myself, I remain lying on my side for a long time, staring at the outlines of furniture and other things, which the darkness relinquishes.

I expect to hear the phone ring at any moment, but it doesn't. Olaf hasn't noticed I've gone yet. Or is he on his way here? Will he be at the door soon? Or tomorrow morning, when I get up?

No, he doesn't know where Jeanine lives. He'll be able to find out, but not in the middle of the night. And he doesn't know I'm here and he has to go to work tomorrow.

Even so, unease drives away all sleep. I go to the living room where there's a rocking chair in the bay window. I sit down, open the curtain a little, and the window, and light up a ciga-rette. How would Olaf have reacted when he found out I'd gone? Perhaps he'll take a day off and spend the whole of Monday waiting in my apartment? I can't go back. There's no escaping it – one way or another we'll come across each other at work, but that's not so bad. As long as I don't have to be on my own with him. I should have made a complaint. How stupid of me. The police would have thrown him out and I'd have been able to go back home.

I blow the smoke out of the open window. I keep an eye on the road through the chink in the curtains and as the time passes I grow more and more uneasy. I smoke one cigarette after another, but there's still no sign of Olaf.

And then my phone rings. I shoot bolt upright, bang my elbow on the windowsill and bite back the pain as I rummage in my bag. My own home number appears on the screen. I answer.

'Sabine, it's Olaf.' His voice is calm. 'You'll have to come back at some point. I'll just wait here until you do.'

'If you're still there tomorrow, I'll call the police.'

'In that case I'll come and get you now. Where are you?'

I'm silent.

'Don't worry, I'll find you.'

I hang up. It takes me two cigarettes to calm down.

I stumble back to bed, slip under the cover and repress the urge to curl up against Jeanine.

'And now I want to know exactly what happened.' Jeanine sets a tray down on the bed. Delicious smells waft through the room. Coffee, a boiled egg, and toast with jam. She is dressed and made up.

'How sweet of you.' I sit up, prop the pillow against the wall and lean against it.

'You talked in your sleep. About Olaf, and "don't", and Isabel.' Jeanine sits on the edge of the bed. 'I left you to sleep it off.'

'What time is it then?'

'Eight o'clock. I have to leave for work soon.'

'Me too,' I say. 'But I don't think I'll go.'

I pick up my bag and check my phone. No new messages.

'How can all this have happened? It was going well between you, wasn't it?' Jeanine asks.

As I eat, I tell her everything. I tell her about my doubts over my relationship with Olaf, his pushiness, the emails, the stream of phone calls, the roses in my apartment, about Bart and how Olaf forced his way in with the spare key. I tell her about my visits to Den Helder, the meeting he'd planned with Isabel on the day she disappeared, about Eline's experiences with him, about his phone call last night.

'I'd have never thought it of Olaf.' Jeanine is visibly taken aback. 'Did he really hit you?'

'Yes, he can be very violent.'

'But to come to the conclusion that he murdered Isabel…' Jeanine eats the egg I've lost my appetite for.

'Isabel arranged to meet him at the Dark Dunes,' I say, my mouth full of toast. 'Let's presume they met each other in front of the snack bar. After that they walked a bit into the woods and Isabel told him she wanted to finish it. Olaf flipped, hit her and she ran further into the woods, but he caught up with her.'

'She could also have been attacked by a stranger after that. All kinds of weirdos hang out in the woods and the dunes.'

'But then why did he lie to me about his relationship with Isabel? Why didn't he admit to the police that he had arranged to meet her that day?'

'Haven't you asked him that?'

'I didn't dare. If he is so violent, and he is responsible for Isabel's disappearance…'

'Yes,' Jeanine says. 'Still, I can't imagine Olaf doing that.'

'He is strange, Jeanine. What kind of person leaves you messages the whole day when you're out?'

'Somebody who is really in love.'

'He was really in love with Isabel too.' I put the tray down on the floor. 'But there's one other suspect – Mr Groesbeek.'

Jeanine laughs at my account of the cat hairs in my tea and the chocolates. She is still laughing when I reel off the names of the cats, but falls quiet when I tell her that I went to the police. On the subject of the other possible suspects I can't get out of my head, I hold my tongue.

'You've been really wrapped up in this, haven't you?'

'If only I could remember what I saw in that clearing…Why didn't I call out for help? That's what's so strange, that I wanted

247

to forget it all. The only explanation that I can come up with is that I must have known the killer.'

'Are you sure they are memories, Sabine? I mean, it's all so vague. Perhaps you've dreamt it all. Why does the memory stop the moment you stand at the edge of the clearing? That's illogical, just like a dream.' Jeanine traces the floral pattern on her bedspread with a finger. 'When you try to retell a dream, it doesn't work, because large parts of it are made up of impressions and feelings. The images don't go together, everything is vague and misty. And often a dream repeats itself a few times, something is added, things join together until you begin to wonder whether it might have really happened.'

'I didn't dream it. Dreams usually veer off in strange directions, to something totally unrelated. When you're dreaming, the change of direction seems logical, but in the light of day you laugh about it. Or you've forgotten half of it. This is totally different, Jeanine.'

'Do you think you'll remember more?'

'I hope so, although I wonder how much it will help. The police didn't believe a single word of it. Even you don't believe me.'

'I do believe you, I'm just suggesting that you might not be drawing the right conclusion. But what you just said is true – dreams are very confusing and illogical. Your memories are chronological and sound real. Do you know what we have to do?'

'What?'

'We'll go together to that place in the woods. See if it matches your memories.'

'I did that already. It did match exactly: the woods, the clearing…'

'Then there's only one way of finding out whether you dreamt it or whether it's a real memory.'

'What's that then?'

'We'll go and dig ourselves.'

Just the idea of it sends shivers down my spine. I imagine us finding Isabel's bones, deep under the sand, and I begin to doubt myself. Is Jeanine right? Is my mind playing tricks with me? Have I assembled fears, suspicions and even past longings into images which have nothing to do with reality? My heart screams no, but reason says that I should face up to it.

As I'm sitting there, a new memory rises up.

It must have been right after Isabel went missing, because my father is still in hospital. It's late at night and I climb down the stairs, shaky with exhaustion.

My mother is watching TV, a glass of wine in her hand. Without saying anything I go into the hall and get my jacket.

'What are you doing, dear?' My mother comes over at once.

'I have to help Isabel,' I mumble.

My mother looks at me. 'Just go back to bed,' she says softly.

I burst into tears, my arm already in the sleeve of my jacket. 'But she needs me!'

My mother gently forces me back into my bed, and I go back to sleep at once. But each time this happens in the night, I wake up with traces of dried-up tears on my face and an unbearable guilt.

My memories are real.

The doorbell rings over and over again. I'm so alarmed I jump out of bed. Jeanine had gone to the kitchen and now returns.

'What should we do?' Jeanine whispers.

We peer into the hallway then creep to the front door. Through the spyhole we see Olaf.

'Quick, get dressed,' Jeanine says.

I fly back into the bedroom and am dressed within seconds.

The bell goes again.

This time Olaf keeps it pressed in so that the shrill noise cuts through the house like a warning.

'Yes, yes!' Jeanine shouts. 'Can't I just get dressed?'

She pushes me towards the open french windows in the bedroom. 'If you stand on the dustbin you'll be able to climb over the fence. Go!'

I'm already away. Jeanine throws my bag after me, closes the french windows and locks them. From the small back garden I hear Olaf banging on the door. I put one foot on the metal dustbin, pull myself up onto a strut and climb up. As if I hop over fences all the time, I sling my leg over the top and climb down the other side.

Jeanine's Turkish neighbour is hanging out the washing in her yard. She lets the sheet drop back into the basket and looks at me, speechless.

I run to the gate, slide the bolt and find myself in a damp alley. I run.

39

Where can you go when you're hiding from someone with the same circle of friends? Nowhere. I can't even go to work. There's only one thing I can do – make sure there are plenty of other people around me.

I leave my car outside Jeanine's, convinced that this will keep Olaf waiting there, and take the tram into the centre. On the way I call work and take the day off.

I get out at the Leidseplein and sit down at a spot on a terrace that's hidden behind plants. While I wait to be served, I get my mobile out of my bag and check my voicemail. Nothing from Bart. I tap my mobile on the tabletop. Why hasn't he called? If he hadn't left a message on my machine, I might have been suspicious. Should I call him? Never call a man, my mother used to say. Sensible advice but not very practical. If I keep playing hard to get I'll still be single on my thirtieth birthday.

With a few quick taps of my fingernail, I look up Bart's number and press call. The phone rings a few times and then I hear, 'This is Bart de Ruijter. I can't come to the phone right now but try later or leave a message and I'll call you back.'

I don't leave a message. A girl with dark hair in a pony tail, and a white apron comes to my table, gets a notepad out of her pocket and looks at me.

'A latte, please.'

The girl leaves. Through sunglasses I watch the people around me, glancing at my mobile every now and again, willing it to ring. My coffee arrives. A junkie goes from table to table, hand outstretched, and tram 5 goes by. My eyes check every window.

A little later, tram 2 goes past. A tall, blond man gets off and walks towards me. I retreat into the grand café, only to discover once I'm inside that it's a total stranger. I look a little sheepishly at the girl who served me. She gives me an inquisitive look, smiles and carries on.

I pay at the bar, get into the first tram that stops and sit down next to the driver, just out of earshot. We sway through the centre of Amsterdam and in the meantime I look up the number of Den Helder police station in my mobile and ask for DC Hartog.

'He won't be in until this afternoon,' the duty officer says.

'Could you give him a message? It's urgent,' I say. 'Can you tell him that Sabine Kroese called. He knows my name. Tell him that I'm being harassed by a certain Olaf van Oirschot.'

Although I try to keep calm, my voice is higher than usual. The policeman promises to pass on the message.

Hartog is probably sitting at home drinking coffee and reading the papers and he won't do anything with this information, but at least I've tried. From now on I'm going to keep him informed of everything that's happening in my life, until he starts to pay attention. Tonight I'll find a small hotel and I'll call him again. Tomorrow I'll have to go to work, but hopefully Olaf will have cooled down by then. And, among my colleagues, I'll be safe enough.

I don't want to think much further than that. Jeanine was right, the best thing would be to go to Den Helder and dig in the place I saw Isabel. I don't want to think about the possibility of her *not* being buried in that clearing. If that's the case, I'd better check myself into a psychiatric clinic.

I get out of the tram just as my mobile goes off. It makes me jump. I look at the display – caller unknown. I answer, suspicious. 'Yes?'

'Am I speaking to Sabine Kroese?' an unknown female voice says.

'Yes.'

'This is the Gemini Hospital in Den Helder. I wanted to tell you that Bart de Ruijter was admitted here yesterday afternoon.'

'What?' I say, uncomprehending. 'Bart, in hospital?'

'Bart de Ruijter, yes. He had a serious car crash.'

'How is he? What's wrong? He's going to be alright isn't he? And why have you only just called me now?'

'It goes without saying that we told his family immediately and they came at once, but he asked for you this morning. I think you'd better come quickly,' the nurse, doctor or whatever she is, says.

'I'll come at once,' I say in a daze. 'How bad is it?'

'He's got various broken bones and a serious concussion, Miss Kroese. His condition is stable at the moment, but there's one thing we're worried about.' She pauses for a moment. 'After he asked for you, he lost consciousness. He hasn't yet regained it.'

I run to the Central Station as fast as possible and sprint to catch the Den Helder train. In the train I realise that I've forgotten to buy a ticket. I sit for an hour biting my nails. Muffled music drones from headphones, newspapers rustle. I want to scream when the train stops in a meadow in the middle of nowhere. After ten exasperating minutes we move off without any explanation of the delay.

Finally the train comes to a grinding, creaking halt in Den

Helder. I'm the first to the door, and I run to the bus stop next to the station.

'Are you going to the Gemini Hospital?' I ask the bus driver.

'No,' the man says, and points to a bus which has just left. 'That's the one you wanted.'

I could scream. I find a taxi and have it take me to the hospital.

At the information desk I ask for Bart and am told how to get to his ward. It's quiet in the hospital, the visiting hour has not yet begun. I hurry to the lift and then along endless white corridors. Years ago, I must have taken the same route when my father was admitted here.

Room 205, room 205. My eyes flit along the name boards next to the rooms and I come to an abrupt stop when I see Bart's name.

I push open the door, prepare myself for tubes and monitors, but I'm completely unprepared for the empty bed in the single room. I look at the nameplate next to the door. I am in the right place.

I rush into the corridor and grab a nurse. 'I've come for Bart de Ruijter. His room's empty, where is he?'

'Who are you?' the nurse asks.

'Sabine Kroese. You called me this afternoon.'

The nurse checks her clipboard. 'Mr de Ruijter was run over by a car when he was crossing the road yesterday afternoon. Given the circumstances, he was doing reasonably well, he was even able to answer questions, but this afternoon he lost consciousness. They've taken him for an MRI scan. As soon as we know more, we'll tell you.'

She gives me a friendly nod and carries on. I stay behind, dismayed. Somewhere close I hear a muffled sob. In the waiting room, a blonde woman is sitting with her back to me, hunched over, her shoulders shaking. Next to her there's a portable cot with a small child in it.

Could that be Dagmar and Kim? But wasn't Dagmar ill? As if that would make a difference, I tell myself. Flu or not, I would have dashed from my bed at once.

On impulse, I go into the waiting room. 'Dagmar?'

She looks up quickly, expecting to see a doctor, her face tear-stained, her eyes swollen.

'Yes?' she says.

'I'm Sabine Kroese. I used to know Bart, and I met him again at the school reunion on Saturday night. What happened?' I ask in a gentle, sympathetic tone.

Dagmar shows no interest in who I am. She begins to talk at once. 'He was run over in my street. Practically in front of my door,' she says. 'The driver didn't even stop.'

'Did you see it happen?' I ask in shock.

'I heard a bang and then I saw a car taking off. I waited with Bart until the ambulance came. They're doing an MRI scan at the moment.' Dagmar looks at me more attentively. 'Who did you say you were again?'

'Sabine. Sabine Kroese. I know Bart from school.'

She nods, already back in her own dark thoughts.

What should I do now? Sit in the waiting room as well? I imagine us being called by a doctor who peers questioningly into the waiting room. 'Mr de Ruijter's ex-wife? Oh, and you're his current girlfriend? Well, unfortunately we can only admit one visitor into intensive care.' And then he'll study each of us in turn, with a look which indicates that we should fight out who sees Bart first between ourselves. How much right do I have to him after just one night?

I look at the baby. She's a pretty child. She looks like Bart. Suddenly I feel incredibly jealous of Dagmar. She and Bart might be divorced but she'll have a life-long bond with him through that sweet child. Of course she wants him back, I can see that, so we've got something in common. I'm prepared to fight for him, but not here, not in a hospital.

255

I mutter goodbye, but Dagmar has turned to the baby.

I leave the hospital and the warmth hits me in the face. I walk to the bus stop. I'm not in so much of a hurry that I need to take a taxi. Dagmar has given me something to think about and the fifteen minutes' wait at the bus stop is ideal for this. Is it possible that Olaf could have had something to do with Bart's accident? He saw us together and I know for sure that he followed us back to Bart's house.

I get out my mobile which I'd turned off when I was in the hospital and switch it on. Four missed calls.

'Sabine, I need to talk to you. Call me back.'

'Where are you? I need to talk to you. It's urgent.'

'You must be in Den Helder with that prick. He's not there, Sabine. He'll never be there for you.'

'Call me back, goddamn it!'

As I'm about to delete Olaf's messages, I change my mind. I realise what I have to do. The bus arrives and I get in. It's an endless sticky ride but finally the police station comes into view.

40

For some reason communication between DC Hartog and me just doesn't flow. He listens but I don't get any sense that he's taking me seriously. I sit opposite him in the same room as last time and repeat the story of my memory loss and how my memories are coming back bit by bit. Hartog stares at me as if I'm the product of an experiment. I tell him about my relationship with Olaf and that he also used to go out with Isabel. I recount what I heard from Eline and describe my own experiences with him.

'He can't deal with rejection, you see,' I say. 'He was violent with Eline Haverkamp when she wanted to end their relationship, and he came after me for the same reason. I think he murdered Isabel when she dumped him.'

Hartog taps his pen on the desk. 'During your last visit you voiced suspicions about Mr Groesbeek,' he reminds me.

'And now there's Olaf van Oirschot as well,' I say. 'It could have been either of them. It could also have been a total stranger who pulled Isabel off her bike in the woods. I'm not saying that I know who the killer is, Mr Hartog, I just wanted to tell you what I've found out. To be honest, it wouldn't surprise me if it was Olaf. I think he ran over Bart de Ruijter. You know, that hit-and-run yesterday.'

Hartog looks at me with a little more interest. 'There were no witnesses to that hit-and-run,' he says.

'No, but Olaf has a motive to deliberately run Bart down. Bart and I are seeing each other.' I lean forward to keep Hartog's attention, because he is leaning backwards as if he can do nothing with this information.

I take out my phone and play him Olaf's messages. He listens attentively, but I don't see his expression change.

'I'm sorry that you've got problems with your ex-boyfriend,' he says. 'But I don't hear anything here to suggest that he is responsible for Mr de Ruijter's accident.'

'He knows that Bart's not at home,' I cry. 'How could he know that? Because he put him in hospital!'

'Perhaps he was just saying anything?' Hartog suggests, still friendly. 'Listen, Miss Kroese, I do understand your anxieties and Mr van Oirschot's behaviour does seem curious. But it's not enough to arrest him, you understand. You've come along with a few vague suspicions and you expect me to act on them. But on the basis of this, I really can't do anything. I think you'd better sort out your problems with your ex-boyfriend.'

'I haven't finished yet,' I say.

Hartog rests his arms on the table. 'What else do you want to get off your chest?' His voice is resigned.

I tell him about my visit to Isabel's mother and the diary she showed me. His interest grows.

'Isabel was meeting someone on the day she disappeared,' I say. 'Did you know that?'

Hartog has a copy of the diary page in his file and takes it out.

'A *DD*,' he says.

'No, Olaf van Oirschot. DD stands for the Dark Dunes and that IO is not a ten; it's initials – Isabel Olaf. They were going out and Isabel wanted to meet Olaf that day to end it. I don't know if they did meet, but she did disappear right afterwards.'

Hartog pulls the diary towards him, looks at the page for 8 May and consults his file on Isabel.

'IO,' he says.

I lean backwards, not without some satisfaction. 'Olaf had a motive and the possibility to do something to Isabel. He came out of his maths exam about two-thirty. Isabel and I got out around ten past two and I followed Isabel on my bike out of the school grounds, on her way to the Dark Dunes.'

Hartog leafs through his file. 'According to Olaf's statement, he went straight home after the exam. His mother confirms that.'

I shrug. 'Isabel was murdered that day and according to Eline Haverkamp, Olaf could be violent when things didn't go his way.'

'How can you be sure Isabel was murdered?'

'Because I saw her body. For years I couldn't remember anything about it, but recently an image of her face came back. She was murdered, Mr Hartog.'

To my annoyance, Hartog doesn't seem that impressed.

'And you'd forgotten about it all this time.' He emphasises the word *forgotten*, making it sound ridiculous. 'And now you've suddenly remembered. Have you any idea why?'

I submit to his stare without blinking. 'Perhaps because I feel stronger now in myself and can better deal with the truth.'

'The truth,' Hartog says. 'And according to you, the truth is that Isabel Hartman was murdered.'

'Yes, I saw her lying there; I remembered it just recently. I saw her lying in front of me as if it had just happened. I saw her face, her staring eyes, the grains of sand in her hair...' I shudder. 'I don't understand how I could have forgotten it.'

'Me neither, Miss Kroese.' Hartog gives me a frank look.

'According to my psychologist, it's called repression,' I say. 'She already had the feeling I'd repressed something from my past.'

Hartog replaces the copy of Isabel's diary in his file. 'You're being treated by a psychologist?'

I look at him in bewilderment; I really don't want to go into this. 'I was treated in the past, yes. But not for long and now I'm better.' I cross one leg over the other and try to look calm, balanced. Hartog gives me a searching look.

'I don't know why that should matter,' I add. 'The existence of repression is well known in psychology. I don't understand why you're not happy that my memory has returned and that I'm helping you with your investigation.'

'But I am happy about that, Miss Kroese.' Hartog slams his file shut, leans back in his chair and places his fingertips together. 'Shall we just sum up — you witnessed Isabel Hartman's murder, you forgot about it for nine years and now everything is coming back to you. Do I understand correctly?'

'Yes.' My gaze doesn't leave his.

'You've put DDIO together to mean Isabel was meeting Olaf van Oirschot. That's tenuous at best. Did you also see who murdered Isabel Hartman?'

'No. All that I remember is that I saw her lying in that clearing in the woods. She was dead.' As I say it, I realise how this must come across to somebody else, particularly to a detective. Hartog sits looking at me, frowning.

'You didn't see the murderer?'

'No.' The little room feels stuffy.

'Can you remember if anybody else was present there, apart from yourself?'

I hesitate. In my dream I see a man going up to her, but how reliable is a dream? You can't really call it a memory and yet, it seems important to me. Perhaps Hartog will stop looking so distrustful if I tell him about that man.

'I saw a figure through the trees. A man.'

'What was he doing? Did he walk away, was he just standing there or did he go up to her?' Hartog asks. I'd hoped this news would represent a breakthrough in the investigation, but Hartog's questions are dutiful. He doesn't sound convinced.

'At first he was just standing there, but when she saw him, he went over to her.'

'Did she look frightened to you?' Hartog asks.

'No,' I say. 'She smiled at him.'

Hartog looks at the dossier and plays with his pen. 'Hmm,' he says and remains silent for a while. 'The question is, how reliable are your memories, Miss Kroese? Memories can become coloured by the intervening years.'

'You should excavate.'

'Excavate? Where?'

'In the Dark Dunes, of course. It's a bit complicated to explain where, but I could draw you a map.'

Hartog looks at me with renewed interest.

'Why don't you do that.' He pushes a piece of paper over to me. While he drinks his coffee, I sketch the footpaths in the Dark Dunes. I know them like the back of my hand, even the more remote paths which I wouldn't so easily have been able to draw if I hadn't been back recently. With a feeling of satisfaction, I push the paper back. I'm actually expecting Hartog to jump on the map and hand it over to an investigative team. Instead the look he gives my work is only cursory.

'Do you know, Miss Kroese, I've looked into you,' he says.

'Into me?'

'You weren't in the file.' He taps the folder in front of him. 'And I wondered why not. You were in Isabel's class at the time.'

'Yes,' I say.

'And you both went to primary school together.'

'Yes.'

'But you weren't questioned at the time of her disappearance.'

'No.'

'That was a big mistake on our part. I'm glad that you found it in yourself to come forward.'

I look at him.

'After making some enquiries I discovered that you didn't have a particularly relaxed relationship with Isabel Hartman. That's putting it mildly.' Hartog's manner is confiding, the tone of a detective posing as a friend. I don't fall for it.

'We were good friends at primary school,' I say.

'But after that you weren't. She made your life a misery.'

I remain silent.

'You were bullied regularly and attacked by the gang she was the leader of. It must have been a very difficult time for you.'

I go to speak but Hartog interrupts me.

'It was even so bad that you had nightmares and didn't dare go to school anymore, isn't that right?' he offers.

I straighten up in my chair. 'Isn't there such a thing as patient confidentiality for psychologists?'

'Not when it concerns a crime, Miss Kroese,' Hartog replies. 'Your psychologist told me that your brother often waited for you in the school grounds to make sure you got home safely. He wasn't very keen on Isabel Hartman either, was he?' Hartog's tone remains friendly, but I feel sweat prickling under my arms.

'Can we open the window?'

Hartog opens the window a little. A soft breeze comes inside. I long to be out in it. I shuffle around on my chair, lift my chin and say, 'Yes, Robin did wait for me after school sometimes. I don't see – '

'It must have been liberating when your tormentor disappeared from your life, wasn't that so, Miss Kroese?'

The tone in which Hartog says this drives me into a rage. It takes all my strength to contain myself.

'What do you mean by that?'

'I don't mean anything. I'm just stating a fact. For you it was a relief that she disappeared.' Hartog looks at me with an expression that suggests it goes without saying, but I don't intend to agree with him. I shrug.

Hartog removes a paper from the file. 'I've got your statement from your previous visit here. You said then that you remembered riding after Isabel from school. She was with a friend and when the friend turned off, she carried straight on. You followed at a short distance. At the crossroads of Jan Verfailleweg and Seringen Avenue you turned off in order to avoid being seen. Why didn't you want to be seen?'

'That seems obvious to me.'

'Were you so frightened of her? Even when she was alone, without her gang to back her up?'

'What would you have done? Ridden along next to her?'

'I ask myself why you followed her if you didn't want any contact with her?'

'I wasn't following her, I was just going the same way.'

'Did you often ride through the dunes to get home, Miss Kroese?'

I shrug. 'Not often. Only when it was really nice weather.'

There's a short silence.

'So when you turned off at Seringen Avenue, it was to avoid Isabel,' Hartog continues.

'Yes,' I say.

'You weren't following her.'

'No.'

'But still you claim that you know the place where she was attacked. More importantly, that you saw that she'd been murdered, and that it wasn't by the snack bar.'

'I rode past the snack bar and when I looked to the right I saw Isabel going into the woods with someone,' I say.

'And you decided to follow them. Why?'

'Because I wanted to know who she was meeting,' I say.

'Why?'

I shrug again. 'I suppose I was just curious.'

Hartog seems to accept that. 'And did you see who it was?'

'Yes, I must have done. Only I can't remember anymore.'

'Was it someone you knew?'

I reflect on this question. Was it someone I knew? Yes, one way or another I know it was. Otherwise I wouldn't have been so shocked. My mind registers the fact that I was shocked, something that had also slipped from my memory.

'Miss Kroese, I asked you a question,' Hartog says.

My hand jerks, an involuntary movement. 'It was someone I knew, but whether it was someone I knew well or just a bit, I don't know anymore.'

Hartog rubs his forehead. 'Do you know,' he says. 'After speaking to your psychologist on this matter, I've learned that memories can take on a whole new life of their own. It might well be the case that Isabel met somebody she knew, stood and talked to them for a while, then saw you coming and went into the woods with you.'

My answer is a scornful look. 'Then why do I remember that it was a man?'

'I don't know,' Hartog says. 'All things considered, you don't remember very much. You claim that you know it was a man, that you knew him, but you don't remember who he was. Your memory is rather selective, don't you think?'

I don't reply.

'Now try out the hypothesis that you were the one who went into the woods with Isabel. That you had arranged to meet her by the snack bar, because you had a few things to sort out. Doesn't that sound more realistic, Miss Kroese?'

My fingers are clasped together, white-knuckled, which can't be giving a good impression, yet I can't manage to free them and rest my hands on my lap.

I stare at a loose thread on the sleeve of my top and when I've drummed up enough courage, I look up.

'Now look here, Mr Hartog.' There's a slight tremor in my

voice. 'I don't know where you're going with this, but I didn't arrange to meet Isabel by the snack bar and I'm not the one who went into woods with her. It happened just as I told you. Why would I come here and tell you all of this, if what you are insinuating is true?'

I've got a point there, I see it in Hartog's face. I sit up straight. 'I suggest that you excavate that spot and if you find Isabel there, you can tell me about repression and how the memory works. And if you pick up Olaf van Oirschot at the same time, you'll have the likely killer too. It can't do any harm to have a chat with him and check if his car is damaged.'

'Perhaps not,' Hartog says.

He writes something down in the little notebook that, despite trying, I can't read upside down.

'Will you keep in touch with me?' I ask as I stand up.

Hartog puts his pen down. 'Believe me, Miss Kroese, if I have any questions, you'll be the first person I call.'

41

I'm so confused by the interview with Hartog that I can't decide what to do next. Should I go home or to the hospital or stay here? Where can I go? As long as the police don't do anything with my information, I don't have anywhere to go.

I let the bus take me to the centre and walk to my favourite pizzeria on Koningsstraat. It's busy and many of the tables are reserved. I'm pleased to get a small table in the corner where I can hide away. I order at random, am served up warm rolls with herb butter and as I spread the butter, I think over what to do next. I could get a hotel here, then I'd be near Bart. Would Olaf call the Den Helder hotels looking for me? I could give a false name but he would be able to describe me.

I tell myself not to exaggerate. A hotel in Den Helder is a good idea. Tomorrow afternoon I can go to Robin, perhaps I can stay the night at his.

I call Robin but it's a long time before he answers. 'Robin Kroese.'

'It's me. Is it alright if I stay at yours tomorrow night?'

'Hey, sis,' he says. 'Yes, of course you can stay at mine. Has something happened?'

'I'll tell you about it tomorrow,' I say.

'What is it then?' He sounds worried.

'It's a long story, I'd rather not tell you just now,' I say. 'Tell me, has Olaf been round to yours? Or has he called you?'

'Yes, he just came round. He's looking for you.'

'What did he say?'

'He asked if I knew where you were and if I'd call him as soon as I heard from you. Have you two had a row?'

'Yes. Will you please not call him and above all don't tell him that I'm coming to yours tomorrow.'

'Why not?'

'I'll explain everything tomorrow.'

'Alright sis, see you then.'

He hangs up. I look from my mobile to the tables around me. Can I trust Robin or will he let something slip if Olaf calls again? And Olaf is sure to call.

The lasagne al forno stands bubbling before my nose when I decide to give the hospital a quick call. I ask the receptionist to put me through to Bart's ward. Another receptionist comes on the line and then a doctor or nurse. Numbness creeps over me as they say that Bart has had an operation. The MRI scan showed a blood clot in his brain, which meant he had to go straight to the operating theatre. But the operation went well. He's still in the recovery room but he'll be able to receive visitors later in the evening. Am I close family? No? Then it would be better to come tomorrow morning. Mr de Ruijter's wife and parents are with him, so it might be a bit too much.

His ex-wife, I want to shout into the receiver. She's his ex-wife, so she has just as little or as much right as I do.

I don't want to visit when his family are sitting around his bed. Tomorrow morning will be fine, then I might have him to myself. I'll text him just in case he checks his phone tonight.

I burn my tongue on the lasagne, order ice cream and coffee and afterwards call a taxi to take me to Hotel Zeeduin on the Kijkduinlaan. I'm tired and I want only three things – a lie down in a hot bath, a bit of TV and an early night.

That's exactly what I get, but I don't sleep well in the unfamiliar hotel bed. The mattress is too soft, the bed covers are too thick and they smell strange. I don't like sleeping in strange beds. As a child I always had a problem with sleepovers. I loved it when my cousins came to stay at mine, but I never wanted to go to theirs.

I'm woken up at eight the following morning by the irritating high-pitched ringing of the alarm on my mobile phone. I sit up sleepily and turn it off. I call work, praying that Zinzy will pick up but it's Margot. I tell her that due to circumstances outside of my control, I'm going to have to take the day off.

'Another day off already? This really can't go on, Sabine,' she says.

'Why not?' I ask. 'I've got enough to take. Perhaps I'll take them all, it's not up to you.' I hang up without waiting for her response. Contrary to a few weeks ago, I've almost forgotten my work. It's another world that only vaguely exists at the back of my thoughts.

I crawl back into bed to doze a while but against my expectations, I fall back to sleep. It's almost nine-thirty when I look through my eyelashes at my watch. Light is streaming through the curtains. Visiting time has almost begun. To my delight there's a text on my phone from Bart but my joy turns to annoyance when I read the message: *Miss you. Can you come tonight? Dagmar's coming in the morning with Kim.*

'And what am I supposed to do in the meantime?'

Deep in thought, I look out of the window at the sheer blue sky. Will Olaf be at the office now? Probably. Unless he's still waiting for me in my flat.

I call my own number but no one answers. Then I dial the work number, ask for IT and get Olaf on the line. I hang up at once, relieved that he doesn't have number recognition. At least, I presume he doesn't. The phones in my office don't.

I have a quick shower, dress and am horribly conscious that

my jumper doesn't smell that fresh anymore. Well, I'll go home straight after breakfast. There's nothing else for me to do in Den Helder. Tonight I'll come back to the hospital.

In the dining room, I choose a table by the window. There's a view over the dunes and a radiant blue sky. In a different situation, I could have enjoyed it, and I might even have gone to the beach.

I choose from the buffet and am just breaking open a boiled egg when my phone rings. It's not busy in the dining room, most tables around me are empty.

'Sabine Kroese speaking.'

'This is Rolf Hartog, Den Helder police. I wanted to tell you that we checked out your story, Miss Kroese.'

'Oh?' I'm breathless.

'My team conducted a search of the Dark Dunes early this morning.'

My heart is pumping blood so fast that I become dizzy. I support my head with one hand and try to hold my mobile to my ear with the other.

'I'd like to talk to you some more, Miss Kroese.'

'What happened?'

'It's just as you claimed,' Hartog says in a low, serious voice. 'We dug at the spot you indicated.'

My heart begins to thump like crazy. 'And?'

'We did indeed find the physical remains of Isabel Hartman there. She wasn't buried very deeply. She'd been strangled.'

Hartog pushes a steaming cup of coffee towards me and watches as I add milk.

The door opens and a uniformed officer comes in. 'Detective Fabienne Luiting,' she says as she offers me a hand. She sits down on my left at the table.

My throat is dry and tight and I take small sips of coffee to soothe it.

'Was it a big shock?' Hartog's voice is unusually sympathetic.

I nod.

'There was always a chance that you'd remembered incorrectly, of course,' Hartog says.

'Poor Isabel,' I say. 'However much of a bitch she was, she didn't deserve this.'

'Was she a bitch?' Fabienne Luiting asks.

I don't feel like talking to her and turn to Hartog. 'Have you told her parents?'

'Not yet,' Hartog says. 'First we wanted to check the dental records and make sure it was really Isabel.'

'So she was strangled,' I say.

'Yes.'

'How could you tell?'

'There was a fracture to the hyoid bone consistent with strangulation.'

'Oh.'

'Did you know that Isabel had been strangled?' Hartog asks.

I look at him in incomprehension. 'No. How could I have known that?'

Both Hartog and Fabienne are staring at me. There's something threatening in the air between us.

'Because you knew where we could find her,' Fabienne says. 'It's clear that you were at the scene of the crime before Isabel was murdered because you saw her before she was buried. That suggests that you know who did it.'

'That might be the case. I mean, I should know. I think it was Olaf, but I can't remember seeing him. I've no idea who else might have been there.' I see the look they exchange, the pinched corners of Hartog's mouth, the detached expression on Fabienne's face.

'I wonder why not,' Hartog says, lighting up a cigarette. I feel

270

like a cigarette too, but I'm afraid he'll take it as a sign of nerves.

'I've forgotten, that's all,' I say. We're having the same conversation: memory and repression. I can't explain it any better than last time.

'Why do you think you've forgotten it?' Hartog blows the smoke behind him so that it won't bother me. I'd rather he blew it in my face and obscured his view of me. His keen blue eyes make me nervous. But I always feel like that with the police. If they drive behind me on the motorway, I always expect to be signalled to pull over, when they're just going the same way as me. It's that uniform and the searching, sceptical look they've all got. I have to pull myself together so as not to give the wrong impression.

'Are you going to arrest Olaf or not?' I ask.

'We'll need to have a few words with him. Could you give us his address?' Fabienne asks.

'With pleasure.' I write Olaf's address on the notepad they slide over to me. 'Please pick him up quickly, then I can go back to work tomorrow.'

'Where do you work?'

I write down the address of The Bank on the notepad as well.

'Olaf works there too,' I say. 'He's working today.'

Hartog removes a card from his inside pocket. 'This is my mobile number. Call me if anything occurs to you.'

I study the number on the card and memorise it on the spot.

'If I remember anything about the murderer,' I say, 'would that count as evidence?'

'After nine years? I'm afraid not,' Hartog says. 'But if we know that we've got the right man, we can go looking for evidence ourselves.'

'Or a confession,' Fabienne says. 'In any case, it must have been someone strong, Isabel was a big girl. Not someone you could strangle just like that.' She looks at my hands and I see the question in her eyes.

'We'll call you again,' Fabienne says.

It's a long train ride back to Amsterdam. For an hour I hang out of the window and watch the fields and cows, the platforms and railway bridges.

My flat is in a state. I gaze at the upside down drawers, the empty cupboards. In the kitchen all the storage jars have been emptied out onto the lino, knives and forks have been thrown on the counter, the shelf with the tins where I keep stamps and bits and pieces has been swiped empty. The kitchen stinks of beer, there's a pool of it on the floor. There are shards of glass and broken crockery.

It's going to take hours to tidy this up, but I don't mind, I'm too restless to sit still. I get to work with the radio blaring. Now that everything is in disarray I can at least tidy up properly. I take out a roll of bin-bags from the kitchen cupboard and throw away everything I can live without. Soon there are three full bags in the hall.

Every time the news comes on, I listen, but there's still nothing about the discovery of Isabel's body. However, Fabienne does call and when I recognise the number my heart begins to race.

'Fabienne Luiting here. We've taken Olaf van Oirschot in for questioning,' she says. 'I thought you'd like to know.'

I take a deep breath and exhale.

'Thanks,' I say. 'Thank you very much.'

When the phone rings again that evening, I rush to it.

'Sabine, are you still coming over tonight?' It's Robin and he sounds impatient.

'Robin, I completely forgot. Something came up.'

'Well that's nice.'

'They found Isabel.'

The silence that descends is complete. It lasts so long that I'm the first to speak.

'The police called me. They wanted to talk to me.'

'Where did they find her?' Robin's voice is strained.

'In the Dark Dunes.'

'At that place you remembered?'

'Yes.'

Again that silence.

'And now?' he asks.

'They've arrested Olaf.'

'Really? But that's ridiculous.'

'Not that ridiculous. He had a date with Isabel on the day she disappeared, in the Dark Dunes. I don't know whether he went, but I think so. And I think she dumped him.'

'That's true.' Robin's voice becomes alert. 'When we were walking out of the sports hall after the exam, he told me that he was meeting her. It seemed like he meant to go.'

A memory surfaces of Olaf telling me he'd left while Robin was still in the exam.

'And then he strangled her in the woods, took the key to her bike, buried her and took her bike with him to the snack bar,' Robin says.

'Yes.'

'I don't believe one shred of it. He murdered her because she broke up with him? That's not a strong motive.'

'Not for you perhaps. But what about for guys who can't deal with rejection?'

We both pause for a while.

'Well, we'll never find out what happened,' Robin says, finally. 'And why should we bother ourselves? Leave it to the police. I don't believe for one second that Olaf is the killer.'

'Why not?'

'I know him. He was my friend for years.'

'He was your friend years ago, you mean. And you were the one who told me about the fights he would get into.'

'A fight is different to murder. Listen Sabine, if Olaf has got something to do with Isabel's death, and I say emphatically *if*, then it's going to be difficult to prove it. I don't think the police will be able to hold him for long.'

'I think they'll hold him until he confesses,' I say, but my heart begins to skitter like a restless horse. What if Olaf doesn't confess?

'I have to hang up,' I say to my brother. 'I'll call you tomorrow.'

'So you're not coming anymore?' Robin asks.

'No, do you mind?'

'No.'

I dial Hartog's number right away. There's no answer. I tap my foot on the floor impatiently, until a dry voice tells me that this number is not being answered and that I should leave a message on the voicemail.

'Hello Mr Hartog, it's Sabine Kroese,' I say. 'I was wondering how the questioning was going. In fact, I was wondering whether I can sleep peacefully tonight or whether you've let Olaf go. Could you keep me informed?'

I hang up and feel exhaustion sweep over me. I had wanted to go to the hospital but I don't know whether I've got the energy to drive to Den Helder. And now I think of it, my car's still in front of Jeanine's house.

I take the phone to the sunny balcony and sit down in a wicker chair. I call Bart and he answers at once.

'Bart, it's Sabine.'

'When are you coming?' he asks.

'I wanted to come this evening but I'm afraid I won't be able to. I'm at home in Amsterdam and I'm so tired. I'm going to get an early night.'

'Oh.' He sounds so disappointed that I almost change my mind. Could I really not just race over to Den Helder? I rub my forehead. A serious headache is brewing.

'It really wouldn't be safe for me to get behind the wheel right now. It's been such an odd day.'

'Tell me about it.'

'I'm not going to bother you with it now. Just work on getting better so that we can spend some time together. How are you doing?'

'Fine,' he says, although he sounds tired and weak. 'I miss you.'

'And what about Dagmar?' I ask.

'What about Dagmar?'

'I saw her in the hospital waiting room. She was completely distraught. To be honest I got the impression that she wanted you back.' I stare at the ironwork of the balcony and hardly dare listen to Bart's response. Next thing he'll be saying that he regrets the divorce.

'I don't want to be with Dagmar. Especially not now I've met you again.'

I'm infinitely relieved.

'Are you sure you can't come?' he asks. 'No. You do sound tired. What have you been up to?'

'That's quite a story.' I'm absolutely not going to worry Bart by telling him that Olaf is after me.

'I've got all the time in the world,' Bart says, and I can tell he's upset by my caginess.

'They've found Isabel.'

My announcement has the expected effect.

'What?' Bart shouts.

'In the Dark Dunes, exactly as I'd always dreamt it,' I continue. 'I'd advised the police to go and dig there and this morning they called me. I've spent the whole day in the police station.' That's a bit of an exaggeration but it explains my exhaustion.

'Shit,' Bart says, impressed. 'Do they know how she died?'

'She was strangled.'

There's a deep silence.

'And now?' Bart asks.

'We have to wait. They're investigating.'

'Call me when you know more,' Bart says and I promise I will. After endless murmurs and I-love-you's we hang up. I let the phone drop into my lap and stare at the house opposite, lit up by the evening sun.

In the middle of the night the front doorbell sounds through the flat. I'm so alarmed I shoot bolt upright and look around in confusion. One hand on the clock, completely dazed, I try to work out whether I'm really awake or whether the sound has come from a dream.

It's 5 a.m.

In the sitting room I peek through the curtain. I can't see a black Peugeot. But I go to the door and undo the double-lock. I sneak onto the landing and take the dark stairs to the front door. Look through the spy-hole.

Olaf.

My heart beats wildly. I duck as if he can see through doors. He rings again, but then I hear the sound of a key in the lock. Shit, he's got a front door key! Why did he ring first then? To give me a fright? I run up the stairs, stumble into the corridor and to my own front door. Olaf doesn't make any sound at all. He doesn't speak, his feet don't make any noise on the stairs, I don't hear him breathing and yet he's suddenly behind me.

He grips me by the arm, puts his hand over my mouth before I can scream and pushes me inside.

Olaf closes the door softly behind him and swings me around. His face looming over mine is distorted with rage. I am making a muffled sound from under his hand. He takes his hand away and I go to scream, call for help, but all of the energy and courage drain from my body. Terrified, I take a step backwards, into the sitting room.

'So you think I did it?' Olaf says in a hoarse voice. 'You had them pick me up from work like a criminal. Do you know how long they kept me at the station? The whole night. The whole night! Do you know what that feels like? Do you know what it's like to be looked at as if you're not worth spitting on?'

I shuffle backwards towards the telephone, although I'm not sure I'll get to it. Olaf follows me step by step in the darkness.

'No, you don't know,' he continues. 'You didn't think for a second what it would be like to leave the office in handcuffs and be stared at by the whole department.'

A weapon, I need a weapon. My hand feels along the mantelpiece and finds a metal jewellery box with sharp corners.

'Why, Sabine? Why are you doing this to me?'

In two steps he's upon me and gripping my wrist tightly. I hold back a scream, more because the box falls to the ground than because of the strength of his grasp.

'Why?' Olaf screams in my face.

I rock backwards but he still holds me tightly and slams me against the mantelpiece. Anger mixes with fear. I shove him back and take a few steps away from him. 'Why not?' I scream back. 'You wanted to be forgiven, didn't you? You had something terrible on your conscience? Why tell me? What was I supposed to do with that information?'

There's an ominous silence. It's horrible not to be able to see his face in the dark. 'Renée,' he says, low and dark. 'I was talking about Renée.'

'Renée?' I repeat.

'I wanted to help you. That stupid bitch needed to be taught a lesson. And I did help you. Things are better now that she's out of the way, aren't they?'

The imploring sound in his voice is even more awful than his rage. I shuffle away, towards the front door.

'Did you do that for me?' My voice trembles.

'And Isabel? Did you do that for me too?' I angle, with a cautious sideways glance. If I sprint now, I can make it.

Olaf lets out a sound like a wounded animal and paces up and down the room. He passes right in front of the door each time.

'No, you slut! I told you I didn't have anything to do with that.' He is screaming. 'Why don't you trust me?'

The moment he turns away from me, I run to the front door, jerk it open, set one foot in the corridor. I am pulled back by my hair. I lose my balance and fall backwards on the floor. Before I can get up, Olaf has kicked the door shut and is sitting on me, his legs on either side of my body. His hands close around my throat but don't apply any pressure. I can only stare at him, unable to believe that he's actually going to do it. Olaf bends down over me.

'This is how it happened according to you,' he says. 'It's true that she ended it. Yes, we were in the woods. And I was angry and she ran away. But I didn't follow her. I didn't murder her.'

In the darkness, he's just a shape with a voice I no longer recognise. A shape with hands which are pressing down on my throat.

'It hurts when somebody you love doesn't want you anymore. I love you, you know that. Or loved, I should say. Why do you look so scared? Do you really think I'd be able to do something like that? Perhaps I could. Perhaps you're right and I'm lying through my teeth. Let's have a good look, Sabine. Let's see where my limits lie.'

His hoarse whispering sets off all the alarms in my body. I come out of the stupor I'd been in and try to wriggle free. My hands come free and I try to pull his off me. Olaf laughs quietly. He makes pressing movements on my larynx which cause immense pain. Goggle-eyed, I look at him, my hands still on his.

'Please,' I whisper.

'It's so simple,' he whispers back. 'So easy and so fast. A minute at the most. Would Isabel have struggled? I don't know. I wasn't there, so how could I know? But you were there, my dear Sabine. Tell me, how long did it last? You saw it. Why don't you tell the police what the real killer looked like? Why does your memory refuse to give up that information? Haven't you ever asked yourself that?'

His thumbs push my larynx inwards. It's not the lack of oxygen that makes strangulation such agony; it's the pain in my windpipe.

At the peak of the pain, something snaps in my head, bringing to the surface an image which had been hidden for a long time. Consciousness follows a fraction of a second after the event. From the tingling of my skin, the faster beating of my heart, I know I've understood. All the pieces of my bewildered mind fall into place.

But it takes a little longer for it really to sink in. Appalled, I open my eyes wide and stare at Olaf.

I spread out my fingernails and scratch his face. I kick, thump his back and when that doesn't help, I try to find his eyes with my fingers. He puts his knees on my arms and I become helpless.

But he's not pressing anymore. His hands hold my throat in a tight grip but allow in just enough air to keep me conscious. I hear his ragged breath, smell the dried-up sweat and cigarette smoke on him.

'It wasn't me,' he says. 'We both know that it wasn't me, isn't that right, Sabine?'

I manage to make a gargling sound. The pressure on my throat eases off.

'Haven't you known it all along?'

I manage to nod and there's suddenly room around my throat.

'They can't prove anything.' Olaf's face descends. First I smell his breath, then I feel his damp mouth on mine.

'There's no proof, not after nine years. It could have been anybody. All we have are your memories. Do you remember it, Sabine? Do you remember seeing me going into the wood with Isabel?'

'Yes,' I whisper, his lips still touching mine.

'I saw you too, although you didn't know it. Oh, not at first. Later, after the row, when I walked off in anger. I saw you were hiding behind a tree with your bike. And tell me, Sabine, was Isabel still alive then?'

'Yes,' I murmur.

'So you saw me murder Isabel? Well, say it?'

'No. It wasn't you,' I whisper.

'There was someone else there, isn't that true?'

'Yes,' I say with a sob.

He sits up a little and looks at me for a long time.

'So you know who did it?'

'Yes.'

He smiles and releases me. He removes his knees from my arms, takes my hand and pulls me upright. I lean against the doorpost like a drowsy puppet.

'It's still a mystery, how the mind works,' Olaf says. 'I thought I might be able to give you a helping hand.'

He turns around and goes out of the door. I know I won't see him again, as surely as if he'd said it. I stagger to my bed, sink onto the edge and cry like I've never cried before.

42

'I'm afraid we have no evidence against Mr van Oirschot,' Rolf Hartog says. 'On 8 May he came out of his maths exam at half past two. His mother claims that he arrived home shortly afterwards. This means that he could never have met Isabel around that time in the Dark Dunes.'

I sit on the sofa in my dressing gown, a cup of steaming tea in one hand and the telephone in the other. It's nine o'clock and the morning sun makes a mockery of the fear and confusion that had hovered between these walls earlier.

'That's why I'm calling you.' My voice is still hoarse. 'Olaf van Oirschot hasn't got anything to do with Isabel's death.'

A silence falls at the other end of the line.

'Oh?' Hartog says. 'Where do you get that from all of a sudden?'

'Early this morning the final pieces of the jigsaw puzzle came together. I remembered what happened – I know who murdered Isabel.'

Silence.

'It was a stranger. He was kneeling next to her, digging. Isabel was dead. I saw her with her head back, her eyes and mouth wide open. At one point the man looked up, as if he could feel that he was being watched, but he didn't see me. At that moment

281

I got a good look at his face. I was afraid he'd spot me and I ran away.'

More silence. I hear papers rustling and visualise Hartog, busy taking notes.

'Would you be able to recognise that face if we showed you some photographs?' he asks.

'Yes,' I say. 'I think so.'

I take an indefinite period of leave from work, explaining to Zinzy in as few words as possible what's going on, then I call Robin. He's at his office, but offers to come round straight away when I tell him why I'm calling. Within half an hour he's standing opposite me in my sitting room.

'Sabine!' He looks at the pressure marks on my throat in shock. 'Was that...'

'Olaf.' I nestle back into my corner of the sofa and pull up my dressing gown further so that Robin can fix his appalled gaze on something else.

'I'll kill him!' Robin says. 'You have reported him, haven't you?'

'No, and I'm not going to,' I say. 'Olaf didn't murder Isabel, Robin. I know it for sure.'

'He might not have killed Isabel but he almost killed you! Why aren't you going to report him?'

'He's not coming back.' I stare ahead. 'He wasn't planning to murder me. He was angry, incredibly angry. And so would you be if somebody had wrongly accused you of murder and you'd spent all night in a police station. In a way he helped me by doing this.' I rub my throat.

'How?' Robin snarls.

'The final piece of my memory came back. When I experienced the same thing as Isabel, it was if I could go back there...'

I sob and bite my lip to keep my emotions in check. 'It's a terrible way to die,' I whisper. 'Terrible!'

Robin sinks down next to me on the sofa and wraps his arms around me.

'I believe you,' he says. 'And that's why I find it hard to let that bastard get away with it. Shall we go to the police together?'

I shake my head.

'Just leave it,' I say. 'Let it go. It's infinitely more important that I know now who murdered Isabel.'

With shock in his eyes, he looks at me. 'Is that what you meant by the last piece of your memory?'

'Yes.'

He needs some time for the information to sink in, stares ahead and then gives me a questioning look.

'Who – '

'A stranger,' I interrupt. 'It wasn't a face I recognised at all. Well, that's not quite true. I do recognise the face a bit, but I don't know from where.' Robin looks at me in silence.

'It was quite a young man,' I say. 'He had blond hair, a narrow face, lines from his nose to his mouth…I've seen that face before but I don't know where. That's what I've been trying to work out all this time.'

Robin continues to stare at me. 'And now?' he asks.

'I'm going to the police station in Den Helder. Hartog wants to show me a few pictures to see if I recognise anyone.'

We both remain silent.

'Do you want some coffee?' I ask.

'Sure, go ahead.'

I go into the kitchen to make a pot of coffee. As the percolator comes bubbling to life, I return to the sofa and look at my brother. Robin has stood up and is in front of the window, his back to me.

'What are you thinking about?' I ask.

He doesn't turn around.

'About Isabel. About her murderer,' he says.

'Yes,' I say softly. 'I'm still thinking about that too. Her murderer. What pushes someone so far that they take another person's life? How do you carry on living after that? How can you keep silent about that kind of thing?'

Robin says nothing.

'You read the papers, watch the appeals for information, hear the pleas from the parents on the television. How is it possible to stay cool through that? Wouldn't you feel regret, or are you just afraid of being caught?'

Robin turns around and gives me a long, questioning look.

'You just told me that the last missing piece of your memory had come back.'

'Yes.' I study my nails so that I don't have to look at my brother.

'And this afternoon you're going to report the killer.'

'Yes.' I still avoid looking at Robin.

'Are you really going to do that?' There's something in his voice which compels me to run over to him and throw my arms around him. But I don't. I carry on sitting on the sofa with my knees pulled up and I can't even look at him, let alone touch him.

'I have to,' I say.

'Why? Are you so sure? I mean, your memory let you down all this time. You said yourself that you regularly dreamed about what might have happened to Isabel, so who says it's not a dream you're remembering?' Robin paces around the room, one hand in his pocket, the other waving about like he's a lawyer in court.

'I don't believe it's a dream,' I say. 'But the police said the same thing as you. I don't get the impression that they take what I say that seriously. It's up to them to decide, I'm just telling what I think I remember...'

I look cautiously in Robin's direction and see an expression of deep concern on his face. 'Do you want me to go with you?'

'No, that's not necessary.'

'Are you sure?'

'I'll manage.'

'Yes,' Robin says. 'Yes, in one way or another you always manage.'

He comes over to me unexpectedly and embraces me. This surprises me, we're close but we don't often hug.

'I love you, sis.' He kisses me on the cheek.

'I do know that.' I smile, although I feel far from happy.

It's the end of June but the summer seems like it's over already. As I walk to my car an hour later, my keys in my hand, the street is full of puddles. A sudden stormy wind has brought a premature cold. It gives me the opportunity to wear a jacket and a matching scarf, hiding the marks on my neck.

I drive back to Den Helder, and this time Rolf Hartog is already sitting waiting for me. He asks me how I'm doing and then gets to the point. In the same small room as before he sets a file of photographs down in front of me.

'Take your time to look at them,' he says. 'Go at your own pace.'

I open the file and look at the unfamiliar faces, all wearing the same expression. 'Have all these people been under arrest?' I ask as I leaf through.

'Yes,' Hartog says.

'Then he's not necessarily in here,' I say.

'If Isabel's murderer isn't someone she knew there's a large chance he's already been convicted of a similar offence.' Hartog puts down a mug of coffee in front of me. He stands with his back to me and smokes a cigarette in front of the window.

I carry on as though he's not there and study each page at my leisure. Dark men, blond men, women, old and young, ugly and handsome, nothing catches my attention. Just as I'm beginning to lose hope, I stop and inhale sharply.

Hartog turns around at once and fixes his gaze on me.

'This man,' I say, and indicate the picture in the right hand corner. 'This is the man. Blond, narrow face…'

Hartog extinguishes his cigarette in the ashtray and comes over to stand next to me. He looks at the photograph I'm pointing at. There's nothing written next to it.

'Are you sure?' he asks.

'That's the face I saw. Those deep lines from his nose to the corners of his mouth…It's him.'

Hartog looks at the photo for a while. 'Jack van Vliet,' he mutters.

'He probably saw Isabel and Olaf fighting and followed Isabel into the woods when she ran away.'

'Did Olaf van Oirschot follow her?' Hartog asks.

I shake my head. 'He took a few steps towards her, screamed after her, but then he turned around and walked away. I remember pulling my bike further into the bushes when he passed close by me.'

'And then you went after Isabel.'

'Yes, I threw my bike onto the ground and followed her.'

'Why?'

'I was worried about her, isn't that logical?'

Hartog pulls a face. 'I don't know,' he says. 'Was that logical? You weren't such good friends, were you?'

'But we had been once,' I say.

Hartog remains silent and looks at the photo of Jack van Vliet.

'He is known to the police, isn't he?' I ask.

'Not only to the police,' Hartog says. 'Also to the general public. You yourself mentioned him the first time we met. In relation to Rosalie Moosdijk's murder. His photo has been shown quite often. You must have seen it before.'

I can hardly deny that and nod.

'Sexual assault, GBH…Yes, we've got a nice list of offences he's committed. He was arrested a few years ago for the murder of Rosalie Moosdijk, two years after Isabel disappeared, but he always denied his involvement in Isabel's case.'

I nod again.

'What I don't understand is why you didn't recognise him when you saw his picture on television.' Hartog frowns.

'He did look familiar,' I say. 'But I thought it was because of all the media attention. I'd no idea that I'd actually seen him.'

Hartog lays the photo down on the desk and looks at me for a long time. I look back, refusing to be the first to break the silence. This is a fight that must be fought without words and I know I'm up to it, I know I can suppress my nerves and withstand Hartog's searching gaze.

Hartog gives in first. With a sigh he leans back and rubs his forehead wearily. 'We'll look into it,' he says. 'It's a pity that van Vliet isn't alive anymore. He died two years ago in Bijlmer prison but I'm sure you know that. Van Vliet is not the only suspect we've got our eye on. Olaf van Oirschot has an alibi, but there are others. Others who also knew Isabel well. The problem is that you can suspect everyone in this kind of case, you might even be sure, but at the end it revolves around the evidence.' He leans forward unexpectedly and I resist the urge to pull back. 'As far as I'm concerned this case is not one hundred per cent solved, not even if all the clues indicate van Vliet, Miss Kroese. I'm not going to drop it.'

I look back at him without blinking. 'As you say, Mr Hartog,' I say, 'it all depends on the evidence.'

The newspapers are full of it for days. All the dailies of any worth put out the same message:

Isabel Hartman murder case may be solved – van Vliet probable killer

Nine years later has murderer been found?

They leave aside how the murder case has been solved. Some papers say that an unexpected witness who remembered some important facts turned up, leading to the case being reopened. The outcome was that Jack van Vliet who frequently hung out in the Den Helder dunes was seen by a witness digging a hole in which to bury the body of fifteen-year-old Isabel Hartman. The witness was, for reasons the police did not want to reveal, previously unable to give a statement. Jack van Vliet committed suicide two years ago in prison where he was serving a life sentence for the murder of Rosalie Moosdijk.

I read all of the papers, cut out the articles and when I've read them so often I know them off by heart, I lay them on the barbecue on my balcony and put a match to them. In less than a minute there's nothing left but some curled, blackened scraps of paper which fall apart when I touch them.

It's over.

43

There are no banners but everyone kisses and greets Renée. I look on from behind my desk, my hands relaxed in my lap. The throng around Renée subsides, gaps appear as everyone returns to their workplaces and our eyes meet. I don't get up.

'Hello Renée,' I say. 'Great that you're better.'

'Thanks.' Her gaze glides from my face to the desk I'm sitting at.

'As you can see I've moved back into my old place,' I say. 'It wasn't that practical, having Walter's right hand sitting in the corner.'

'Walter's right hand?' she echoes.

I nod at her. 'In practice and on paper. We needed one, since you were away for so long. Naturally you'll stay head secretary.'

But under me. I don't need to say it aloud for the message to get across. It's a while before Renée regains her ability to speak.

'I thought you'd go to HR,' she said.

'Walter had a better suggestion,' I answer.

'Oh,' she says.

I give her another friendly nod and return to work.

She remains standing in the middle of the office, opens her

mouth to say something and shuts it again. Then she turns around and sits down at her desk. Far away from mine.

Zinzy sits opposite me and looks at me with sparkling eyes. 'You're enjoying this, aren't you?' she whispers.

'Not really,' I say. 'I know only too well how she feels.'

Zinzy raises her eyebrows and keeps looking at me. 'Well, okay, but perhaps I'm enjoying it a bit,' she says with a grin. 'I still can't understand why you're leaving. You've finally got things your way and you go and resign. And you don't even have another job.'

'I don't need another job,' I say. 'I like the idea of not doing anything for a while. I want to travel and live off my savings, just live for the day.'

'Have you sold your apartment already?'

'Yes, I'm moving out next week.'

'What are you going to do?'

'I'll drive to southern Spain first, to my parents. Do you know how hot it is there now? Over thirty degrees.'

'Wonderful.' Zinzy sighs.

'And after that I'll go to London for a while, to Robin. Then I'll see. I've always wanted to do a round-the-world trip.'

'Who hasn't,' Zinzy says. 'If I had the money…'

I laugh. 'As if I do. I'll earn it somehow. I'll wash plates in a restaurant if I have to. I don't care.'

'You're really going to do it. Everybody dreams about dropping everything and leaving, but you're actually doing it. Wonderful, Sabine. I'm going to organise a leaving party for you.'

'No, don't. I haven't told anybody I'm leaving.'

'Not anybody?'

'Only Walter, of course. And I'd rather keep it that way.' I glance over at Renée. 'I'd rather give some people the impression that I'm never leaving this office.'

Epilogue

I've written a letter to Bart explaining that I'm confused, that I can't see him for a while. Perhaps never again, but I'm not sure yet. I now know why I ended it before, why I refused the comfort of friendships and happiness.

If I could change the past, I would. Isabel died because of me. I turned on her when she needed me the most. How can I allow myself to be happy, to carry on living while shouldering the responsibility for her death? I need to say goodbye to her, to tell her how sorry I am. I can't do that in the churchyard where she's buried, I have to go to the place it happened.

A week before I leave for Spain I drive to Den Helder, to the Dark Dunes. I park my car at the snack bar on the edge of the woods and walk to where it happened. Under the barbed wire fence, through the undergrowth into the woods.

The girl walks behind me like a shadow. She's crying.

'Why are you doing this? What's the point? The case has been closed, hasn't it? What more do you want to remember?'

'Nothing,' I say as I push through the bushes. 'I know everything.'

'Forget it again!' the girl pleads. 'You did that before and was that such a bad decision?'

291

'I can't do that a second time,' I say.

'But why return then? What are you doing here?'

We arrive at the clearing and consider the cluster of black-berry bushes.

'Saying goodbye,' I say. 'Saying how sorry I am.'

The girl looks off in another direction. 'I'm not sorry.'

I turn around and look at her.

'I am,' I say gently. 'And you are too. You didn't mean it.'

She looks away.

'You don't have to try to be strong.'

She turns her face to me and I see tears in her eyes. 'I didn't mean it.' Her voice is hoarse. 'It just happened, I really didn't mean it.'

I watch as she goes to the place where Isabel had fled, alarmed by Olaf's anger. When she noticed that he wasn't following her, she felt a fit coming on and continued to the clearing sheltered by the trees, where she couldn't injure herself and where she'd be hidden from prying eyes. I followed her, lost sight of her and walked the wrong way a few times. Why did I follow her? I've no good explanation for it, apart from the hope that we'd be able to become friends again one day. That there'd be a moment when we were on our own together, with-out the pressure of the others, and that I'd get the old Isabel back. That was the reason I wormed my way through the undergrowth.

Then I stood on the edge of the clearing, saw her lying on the ground and understood at once what had happened – she'd had an epileptic fit. It can't have lasted for long but must have been quite a heavy one. Her face was pale, she rested her back against a tree trunk, exhausted.

I stood stock still between the trees with a vague hope that the shadows hid me. But as if she could feel my presence, Isabel looked over. Right into my face. I didn't move an inch and neither did she. We stared at each other in a vacuum of time and silence in which all of the years and everything that had happened between us fell away. There was only the rustling of the wind in the treetops and the warm sand.

One of us had to take the initiative and break the silence. We couldn't carry on staring at each other forever. I was on the point of saying something when Isabel's voice reached me, quiet and laborious.

'Haven't you ever had enough?'

I look at her without comprehending. 'Of what?'

'Of following me and saving me.'

I didn't know what to say. 'I saw you going into the woods,' I said at last.

She made a weak gesture with her hand, closed her eyes and let her head rest on the tree she was leaning against. It was obvious the fit had drained her strength, like sap from the trunk behind her.

'Are you alright?' I took a few steps towards her and entered the small sandy clearing which separated us.

Isabel opened her eyes and shook her head. 'You never change, do you?' she said wearily.

I looked around. I didn't have a clue what she meant. I just stood there, my arms by my side.

'Take a look at yourself,' Isabel said. 'How far can you be pushed, Sabine?'

'Why don't you just leave me alone?' I pleaded. 'We don't have to be friends like before, but you could still leave me alone, couldn't you?'

Isabel didn't react. Did my reference to our friendship remind her of the past? Of the sleepovers and shared holidays?

'How's your father?' she asked.

I looked at her. 'As if you care.'

She shrugged. 'Your father's alright. Your brother too by the way.' Something in the way she said it made my skin creep. I gave her a searching look.

'It's over with Olaf,' Isabel said. 'And with Bart. But I think Robin likes me.'

Deep within me something churned, something I could no longer repress, like an air bubble in boiling water rising up to the surface.

My eyes narrowed, anger rose up in me. It hurt. Perhaps Isabel was right. Robin was loyal and crazy about me, but he was also a boy. I'd seen him looking at Isabel when he thought no one could see. She wanted him and she'd get him.

A chill spread from my heart to the rest of my body. Isabel laughed at the sight of my face. She tried to stand up, but her muscles let her down and she fell back. I didn't rush to her assistance as I'd been planning to do a few minutes earlier.

'It will take a while to get used to him waiting for me at school instead of you,' she said.

I flew forwards. I was upon her so quickly that she didn't have a chance to fend me off.

With spots in front of my eyes, I grabbed her throat with both hands and pressed. There was no fear in her eyes, only surprise, but that quickly changed.

She couldn't offer any resistance as I pressed and pressed. I hardly needed any force. She struggled but I was stronger. She opened her eyes wide and the expression in them was imploring, as mine had been for all those years.

If her fit had been milder, she might not have been so weak and she might have been able to put up more of a fight. I continued to press.

After a while her body stopped convulsing and her eyes stared at me.

The spots disappeared. I let go of Isabel's throat and looked at her dead face, at my hands which had been capable of such a thing. I don't know how long I sat there, my hands raised. Then what I'd done dawned on me and I began to shake. It couldn't be real. I hadn't really done this. It was another Sabine, someone I didn't know at all, someone who'd possessed me and had squeezed Isabel's throat shut. Not me. It wasn't me.

The other personality deep within me took the lead. I saw her search the surroundings and return with a piece of hard plastic, a battered warning sign which had lain in the bushes. She used it as a shovel to dig as deep a hole as possible in the blackberry branches. I looked on as she took the bike key from Isabel's trouser pocket, dragged the body over to the hole and pushed it in. She threw in the bag and jacket which were still lying by the tree and covered everything with sand.

I stumbled back to my bike, numbed by what I'd left behind me, but Sabine Two was thinking practically and soberly. At the snack bar she unlocked Isabel's bike and pushing it with one hand, rode to the station with it. With the key in the lock it wouldn't stay there for long.

After that she dumped me and I had to ride home on my own. The Lange Vliet road was interminable. However fast I pedalled, Isabel's face followed me. Thoughts raced through my mind. My whole body shook in disbelief. That might be the heart of the matter – I refused to believe that I was capable of doing something so hideous.

It worked for a long time. How something like that is possible, I don't know, but after a few days I believed myself that I never ever could have been capable of doing such a thing.

I turn around slowly and walk back through the trees to the footpath. Alone.

The girl has disappeared, for good. I don't need her anymore. We've both faced up to what lay close to the surface but remained so well hidden. I don't think I can hide it away a second time, not in Spain, not in London, not even on the other side of the world.

But I'm going to try.

'This suspense is terrible. I hope it will last.'
OSCAR WILDE

A MODERN INTELLECT
....

A Word from the Author

OVER AND OVER AGAIN
....

Things to Think About

WELL OR BADLY WRITTEN
....

What the Critics Say

WHAT YOU READ
....

Books to Read Next

LITERARY CORNER

A MODERN INTELLECT

'To expect the unexpected shows a thoroughly modern intellect.'

OSCAR WILDE

Here the author Simone van der Vlugt talks about her experiences of making the transition from being a successful children's author to writing a thriller, and how she developed a taste for crafting the unexpected...

I always thought I had it in me to write a thriller. Ever since I was eighteen, I've been crazy about them. Back then, I devoured Agatha Christie novels. I tried to go in that direction, and offered a manuscript to a publisher, so the desire has always been there. When I realised that children's novels no longer gave me the satisfaction I wanted, I decided to try a different avenue.

I had to delete a lot from the first draft of *The Reunion* because I had written too much about Sabine's childhood. I was afraid people would know that originally I was a children's author, and consider the book too juvenile.

However, although this book is in a different genre, some similarities still remain. One thing all my writing has in common is that I write as if the events happened to me, expressing my feelings and thoughts through the main character. Some people might consider this limiting, but I think it's one of the best ways to keep characters whole and rounded: by using true-to-life experiences.

It's almost as if I'm the main character in my book. Not in every way of course, but there are resemblances to my life that can be glimpsed from the plot, both in my children's novels and *The Reunion*. I'm not Sabine, but we have similarities. The crime in this book is not even the central focus point; that was important to me because if the reader realises who did it, they still have to be captivated to read on by the pure strength of the story.

In fact, even though it is a thriller, I think character was still the most important element to me. As with the children's books I write, it's the journey the main character takes that I'm most interested in. You can see the development of Sabine from the beginning to the end. I want the reader to see how events can change and develop a person.

And for people to be fully rounded of course, they have to be flawed. There are no heroes in my book. The individuals have to smell of sweat.

In many ways, it feels like this is another debut. In Holland you're labelled very quickly. 'Once a children's writer always a children's writer.' People advise you against it; they say, 'The book will end up in the bin or only have a tiny print run.' But for me it was something I *needed* to do. I didn't want to be eighty and regret not trying. And I was prepared to lose face, which is an important quality in a writer. You have to be brave. You have to be able to take risks. But it didn't end up with a tiny print run and I'm delighted that I was so stubborn.

SIMONE VAN DER VLUGT

OVER AND OVER AGAIN

·····································

'If one cannot enjoy reading a book over and over again, there is
no use in reading it at all.'

OSCAR WILDE

From Socrates to the salons of pre-Revolutionary France, the great minds
of every age have debated the merits of literary offerings alongside questions of politics, social order and morality. Whether you love a book or
loathe it, one of the pleasures of reading is the discussion books regularly
inspire. Below are a few suggestions for topics of discussion about *The
Reunion*...

▶ How does the author use red herrings in the book to misdirect the
reader's attention? How successful is this device?

▶ On page 151 Sabine starts to read about the nature of memory:
'Memories are constructions; they grow and mature as our lives
progress. Be on your guard against the certitude of "I remember it
like it happened yesterday."' To what extent is this passage useful to
understanding the events in the book?

▶ A writer once said the only reliable narrator is the one who knows
he is unreliable. Do you agree with this statement? Do you find it
useful when looking at *The Reunion*?

▶ The majority of the book is written in the present tense. How does
this inform your experience, as a reader, of Sabine's actions? Why
might the author have decided to write it in this way, and how does
this illuminate the themes of memory and the past in the book?

▶ The book is entitled *The Reunion* and yet the event of the reunion
itself only occupies a tiny fraction of the book. How can this event
be seen as driving the action throughout? How effective is this
tactic as a device of suspense?

► One key theme in the book is that of friendship. To what extent can it be argued that Sabine's alienation at work is self-imposed? There is a passage at the end of the book that suggests she may bring her loneliness on herself, as a way of atonement. How convincing do you think this is?

► The theme of deception in the book is twinned with the idea of self-deception. Sabine has worked hard, and for a long time, to believe certain things about herself, but which other characters in the book might also be accused of self-deception?

► Who is responsible for the other missing girls? Is it Jack van Vliet or Mr Groesbeek, or neither? If Mr Groesbeek is not responsible, why do you think he named his cats as he did? And does it matter that these issues are not resolved conclusively, or does this add to the realism of the piece?

► *The Reunion* has two endings, a false one and a final one. How satisfying do you find this technique? Were you convinced by the ending?

WELL OR BADLY WRITTEN

••

'There is no such thing as a moral or an immoral book. Books are well written or badly written.'

OSCAR WILDE

'Thrilling...Hard to put down.' *Cosmopolitan*

'Like all good psychological thrillers, the entertainment lies not so much in the who-done-it factor but in the texture of the life of the protagonists and the undercurrent of anxieties that preoccupy them...Van der Vlugt creates a sense of immediacy that is sustained throughout the novel... Well known in Holland, van der Vlugt is a thriller writer worth pursuing.' *Age*

'The author builds a great atmosphere of tension as the truth slowly, horrifyingly, comes into focus.' *Sunday Telegraph*

'Good stuff, and van der Vlugt does the domestic murder mystery very well indeed.' *Weekend Herald*

'Sabine is a wonderfully sympathetic character. Her tribulations...keep you hooked. Dutch crime queen van der Vlugt's first English translation is a terrifying account of victimisation and its potential consequences.' *Adelaide Advertiser*

'A stunning psychological thriller to keep you wondering.' *Woman's Day*

'A riveting psychological thriller from this renowned Dutch author that builds to an unexpected climax.' *Cherrie Magazine*

WHAT YOU READ

....

'It is what you read when you don't have to that determines what you will be when you can't help it.'

OSCAR WILDE

If you enjoyed *The Reunion,* you might be interested in these other titles from Harper Press...

The Lace Reader by BRUNONIA BARRY

The Whitney women of Salem, Massachusetts, are renowned for reading the future in the patterns of lace. But the future doesn't always bring good news – as Towner Whitney knows all too well. When she was just fifteen her gift sent her whole world crashing to pieces. She predicted – and then witnessed – something so horrific that she vowed never to read lace again, and fled her home and family for good. Salem is a place of ghosts for Towner, and she swore she would never return. Yet family is a powerful tie and fifteen years later, Towner finds herself back in Salem. Her beloved Great Aunt Eva has suddenly disappeared – and when you've lived a life like Eva's, that could mean real trouble. But Salem is wreathed in sickly shadows and whispered half-memories. It's fast becoming clear that the ghosts of Towner's fractured past have not been brought fully into the light. And with them comes the threat of terrifying new disaster.

April 2009

The Book of Fires by JANE BORODALE

Brought up in rural Sussex, seventeen-year-old Agnes Trussel is carrying an unwanted child. Taking advantage of the death of her elderly neighbour, Agnes steals her savings and runs away to London. On her way she encounters the intriguing Lettice Talbot who promises to help. But Agnes soon becomes lost in the city, losing contact with Lettice. She ends up at the household of John Blacklock, laconic firework-maker, becoming his first female assistant. The months pass and it becomes increasingly difficult for Agnes to conceal her secret. She meets Cornelius Soul, seller of gunpowder, and hatches a plan which could save her from ruin. Yet why does John Blacklock so vehemently disapprove of Mr Soul? And what exactly is he keeping from her? Could the housekeeper, Mrs Blight, with her thirst for accounts of hangings, suspect her crime or condition?

May 2009

Visit www.harpercollins.co.uk for more information.